A DEADLY AFFAIR

A DETECTIVE JACK BRODY NOVEL

J.M. O'ROURKE

INKUBATOR
BOOKS

Published by Inkubator Books
www.inkubatorbooks.com

Copyright © 2023 by J.M. O'Rourke

J.M. O'Rourke has asserted his right to be identified as the author of this work.

ISBN (eBook): 978-1-83756-129-2
ISBN (Paperback): 978-1-83756-130-8
ISBN (Hardback): 978-1-83756-131-5

A DEADLY AFFAIR is a work of fiction. People, places, events, and situations are the product of the author's imagination. Any resemblance to actual persons, living or dead is entirely coincidental.

No part of this book may be reproduced, stored in any retrieval system, or transmitted by any means without the prior written permission of the publisher.

PROLOGUE

Marie Kennedy opened her eyes and looked around the darkened room, the paint peeling from its walls and smelling of mould. For a moment she forgot where she was, and then it all came back to her. This had all been a mistake, a BIG mistake. Please, she thought to herself, just let me get back to my warm bed in Dublin. Why the hell did I agree to come here?

Her heavy eyes slid to the edges of their sockets, taking in her watch and the torch, still switched on, lying atop the bedside locker where she'd left them.

She noted the time and blinked... what?

She reached for the timepiece and brought it close to her face, squinting.

And blinked again.

This couldn't be right... could it?

The watch told her it was one o'clock in the morning, which meant that three hours had passed.

Three hours!

Three hours since he'd said it'd take him only a few minutes to go and work out whether or not he could fix the bloody boiler... oh, and the fuse board too, because the electricity wasn't working either in this godforsaken place. What a shithole it had turned out to be. Nothing worked. Relax, he'd told her, there was no problem, he'd go and sort it out. Like Donagh Hughes was a plumber now too? As well as an electrician? But the man's unfathomable self-belief and boundless confidence was, she had to admit, a turn-on in a way. The man really believed he could do anything. It was why he was so successful, she supposed. It was why she had decided to start an affair with him. It was why she was lying here waiting for him.

She sat bolt upright and turned her head to take in the other half of the bed. He might have slipped in, and maybe she hadn't noticed. But no. His side of the bed was completely undisturbed. So where the hell was he? She felt a sensation like cold water trickling down the back of her neck.

The last time she remembered feeling that sensation was when she had gone to interview Walter Kelly as a cub reporter. The man who'd hacked his parents to death had been released on licence and was living quietly somewhere in the wilds of west county Galway. She had driven all the way from Dublin on spec, hoping to find him and get him to agree to an interview. She'd spent the entire day driving around as she chased up yet another lead, and as darkness began to fall, her car got a puncture. She'd ended up walking for an hour in the driving rain. By the time she'd finally arrived at the house where she thought he lived, a full-blown storm was raging. She banged on the door, soaked to the skin, forgetting who it was that might be living here, thinking only that she wanted to find somewhere dry and out of the storm. When the hall light flickered on, she remembered who it was... and stopped banging. But too late. She heard the door latch slide back, and with it the details of the case came flooding back. Of how Walter Kelly had stabbed his dear mummy and his dear daddy over eighty-six times – each. Of how he had then taken a chainsaw to their bodies and cut them up, again and again, until they were literally tiny pieces.

And there she was, knocking on this crazed killer's door. What if he wanted to do the same to her? Well, what then? He hadn't much to lose? Not now, now that he was an old man. And, she imagined, from first appearances of this place, prison would be considered the lap of luxury in comparison to this hovel. No, there'd be no loss on him if he were to go back inside. And arriving at his door the way she had, if this was indeed where he lived, maybe she'd given him the perfect opportunity.

Fast-forward to the present day, she thought of all this now, lying here in bed in this hovel, waiting for Donagh to come back. It was the same feeling.

As it turned out, the bearded and bespectacled Walter Kelly had been an absolute gentleman. He'd repeated what he'd said in court, that his actions were those of revenge, but for what he'd never mentioned. Also, he'd told her, there was the matter of an acid trip, a very bad acid trip. Walter had liked to dabble back then. He actually reminded her of her grandfather, and she'd felt right at home. He'd gotten her something to eat, given her an exclusive interview that had effectively launched her career. Afterwards, in the middle of the night, he'd insisted on returning with her to her car and helping her change the wheel.

The rest, as they say, was history.

She called out Donagh's name, 'Where the hell are you?' trying to imbue her voice with a bravado that wasn't there and failing miserably. She looked about, couldn't spot her mobile phone. She tried to remember where she'd left it, but didn't have a clue.

Okay. Okay. Hold it together. Don't panic. There's a reasonable explanation for all this, has to be. There always is. Just like that night back with Walter Kelly, there's nothing to worry about, *she told herself.*

Take a breath, that's it, in, out, in, out, much better now...

She pulled back the duvet, swung her legs onto the cold, wooden floor, shivering as she stood, feeling the frigid air wrap itself around her like a wet blanket. She'd forgotten that she was almost naked, with nothing on but a tiny nightdress, her clothes draped over the back of a chair just inside the door. A door that was still open, just as it had been when she'd nodded off. She went and quickly pulled them on, then stood looking out of the room, at the raised trapdoor in the middle of the hall, a faint, anaemic light seeping out from it.

She called out his name again, but got no reply.

'Come on, Donagh, where are you?'

But still, there was no reply.

She cast her eyes slowly along the hallway. There was one door on the left leading to a small living room, another next to it to a bathroom, and in the wall on her right there was the door to the kitchen. None of the rooms looked like anyone had used them in years. And at the end of the hallway was the front door. She stepped out.

'Come on,' she called, 'where are you?'

No reply.

This is ridiculous, *she thought.*

There was no use thinking about it or being scared. Like old Walter Kelly, it was all mere setting and atmosphere. Nothing to be scared of at all. Especially not out here in the middle of nowhere. The place to be scared was in the city, where you could pass any type of headcase on the street and not even know it. That was where the real danger lay, not here. No, definitely not here. Atmosphere and setting, nothing more...

Or was it?

Yes, yes, of course it was.

He'd fallen asleep or something, that's all, nothing more than that. Had to be. She stepped out into the hall and stood above the small open trapdoor in the floor. Looking down, she could see the light from his torch casting long shadows onto the floor and wall beneath. She called, 'Are you there, Donagh?'

No reply.

Despite everything she'd told herself, it returned, the coldness trickling through her. She tried to ignore it, but it was impossible.

And she became aware of something else too.

A silence. Deep and heavy, it seemed to have a sound all of its own, a crackling, fizzling white noise. As she listened, that silence seemed to grow louder, in equal proportion to her ratcheting fear. She stood looking down into the pool of weak light seeping up from the basement through the open trapdoor, could see the wooden steps descending, and felt the urge to clamp her hands over her ears and drown that sound out.

But she didn't need to. Because just as suddenly, it ended, the silence was gone, replaced by something more tangible, an actual, real sound – that of tinkling glass. She held her breath, straining to make sense of it, and blinked as a bead of sweat dripped into her eye. She was no longer cold. No. Instead, she felt like she had just stepped into a sauna.

The noise sounded again.

Oh Jesus.

'For fuck's sake, are you down there or not?' she shouted. 'Come on, stop messing around. Come up here, for God's sake. Come up now!'

She listened, could feel her heart beginning to jackhammer inside her chest, blood pumping through her ears, sounding like a waterfall.

But only for a moment, as the sound began to fade once more...

A realisation had begun to dawn on her, so obvious that she cursed herself for not having thought of it earlier. It jarred her back into a more rational – though still frightened, just not as much – state of mind. She thought: What if he's had a heart attack?

Like. For real?

Middle-aged men were always getting heart attacks, weren't they? It'd be just her luck, because all she could see in this were the ramifications for her. Selfish, yes, but how would she explain it? Shit.

Oh Christ, what to do if that was what happened? What if he was lying down there on the cold floor right now? W-what... w-what if he was dead? Shit. Shit. Shit. How was she going to explain it?

Like seriously. How?

She knew there was only one way to find out if he was down there. And that was to go down herself and have a look. Just don't think about it. Do it.

She turned, facing the bedroom she'd left a moment ago, her back to the trapdoor now, and stretched down one leg, feeling about for the first step, then finding it, following with the other. Slowly, leaning forward onto the old wooden floor, she began to descend. She went down, placing her hands onto the floor to support herself, looking along the hall ahead of her, unable to see where she was going, heading down, down, down... I won't think about it, I won't think about it, I won't...

There was a sick sensation in the pit of her stomach when she reached the bottom and straightened again, and with it a certainty that she would find him here. Because she had to find him here. Where else could he be? There was nowhere else for him to go... was there? No, there wasn't. It was impossible. He had to be here.

The sick feeling in her stomach was so bad she felt like retching. She thought again, What if he's dead? *And clamped a hand over her mouth. Like, what the fuck happens then? She retched, feeling the bile trickle up the back of her throat, and swallowed it back down. He could be, he might be dead, he HAD to be dead. Otherwise why hadn't he answered her calls earlier... well, why?*

Oh my God. Oh my God. I'm going to find his fucking body down here, aren't I?

She stood there completely motionless, listening, the silence becoming like a feral scream. On the floor against the wall a few feet away from her, she saw the torch he'd taken down with him, its aura of weak light scarcely enough to reach the steps or beyond to the oil boiler next to it. On top of the oil boiler sat a rusty spanner. All else was consumed by the pitch dark.

And once more she heard it, that tinkling glass sound, from somewhere behind her. She froze as the torchlight flickered and died, the basement falling into an inky blackness. And like a dam that had been breached, panic swept through her.

Then she screamed.

1

The crowd was gathered around the memorial stone, awaiting its unveiling to the memory of the Old Man. There was the Old Man's widow, Alice, their two children, and their children, also the brass, or the spaghetti hats, and the uniforms and plainclothes, the washed and unwashed, the great and the good. All here, together, in tribute to Chief Superintendent Tom Maguire, dead four months to this very day.

Voyle could not help but think just how unfair it was, to be cheated out of life as retirement beckoned on the horizon. The Old Man didn't deserve that.

The priest said some words, and a member of the colour party stepped forward, removed the flag of the Republic from the memorial stone, revealing the black granite slab beneath, on it the outline of a Celtic cross etched in gold leaf. A second member of the colour party stepped forward to join his comrade, and together they took a corner each, stepped to the side in opposite directions, extending the flag fully before swivelling about to face each other and moving in again. In a series of synchronised movements, they folded the flag until it was in a tight, neat square. One placed it onto the open, outstretched palms of the other, and he carried it to the tall, regal woman with the sad but proud – very proud – expression. Alice received the flag and held it close to her chest.

And so the curtain had come down on the final act in the Old Man's life. Who knew what lay beyond it. Maybe the Old Man did now. But all that was certain for Voyle was that he was gone from this God's green earth, and gone forever.

The priest bowed his head, and the congregation was silent. They did not make a sound. All that could be heard was the rustling of the branches of the trees in the park where the Old Man liked nothing better to do than walk his dog, and the chirping of a single bird. A robin maybe. Voyle'd heard the dead sometimes returned as a robin. Or was it the other way round, that the robin was a harbinger of death? Whatever.

The family, the priest announced, would like nothing better than for everyone to make their way to the Green Valley Hotel for a slap-up lunch. It was what the Old Man had wanted. He'd left specific instructions.

It was then a telephone rang. Voyle cursed. What was it with everyone? Was it too much to ask that they switch off their phones during a solemn, sacred occasion such as this, a memorial to the Old Man, for God's sake. Seemed that it was. If they couldn't turn it off for this, then for what would they turn it off? He shook his head in disgust.

The phone rang again.

Voyle felt something nudge him roughly in his side. He looked in the direction of that nudge and saw Marty Sheahan staring at him. The phone rang for a third time. Marty indicated with a sharp nod of his head, and Voyle realised, *Shit, that's my phone.* He was nothing if not cool under pressure and acted like nothing had happened. Quickly and discreetly he placed a hand into his pocket and knocked it off, brought the hand out clutching a tissue that he used to wipe his nose, like he wasn't the one who'd farted in the elevator. But then, he couldn't believe it...

The phone rang for a fourth time.

Shit and double shit, shit, shit.

He put his hand back into his pocket, ostensibly to return the tissue, stooping as he did so, looking at his shoe like he was inspecting it. He whipped out the phone, crouching to knock it off, but it didn't, it kept on ringing. He answered, snapped, 'What?' before raising his eyes again to see that it was no use: no one had been fooled, they were all watching him. With no choice now, guilty as charged, your honour, Voyle raised his free hand in a mortified gesture of apology, and stepped back into the crowd, gratefully swallowed up by it. He pushed through and emerged out the other side. It took a little while; the crowd was very big, this being the Old Man after all. Voyle was half listening to the voice on the other end of the phone, which sounded panicked, but then he stopped in his tracks when he realised who it was... *Her.* And as he listened, he felt only sad regret for what had once been and was lost, and for what might have been but never was.

When she fell silent, Voyle tried to unscramble what Marie Kennedy had said exactly, so lost was he in the sound of her voice that the words she'd said held no meaning. He asked her to repeat them. And she did. It was all very simple, really.

Voyle fell into step alongside Brody in the crowd shuffling to the car park.

'Your phone, Steve, couldn't you have turned it off? Awkward. Jesus.'

'I thought I had, boss. Awkward, yes. Sorry. It was... um,

Marie Kennedy.'

'Marie Kennedy?'

'Ring a bell?'

'Should it?'

'*Good evening, and welcome to the nine o'clock news.*'

'Oh, that Marie Kennedy. And she rang you?'

'Yes, she rang me...' They reached the tail end of the crowd forming a bottleneck at a gateway. Voyle didn't speak again until they'd filtered through into the car park on the other side. 'She rang me bec–' he started, but before he could finish, a voice boomed.

'Brody, is that yourself? You auld bastard.'

A man stepped forward from the crowd, a big man in an oversized, ill-fitting suit, with a red face, a thin moustache and a shaved head. Every inch of him screamed 'mule'. Another fella appeared, smaller and wider, his suit just as ill-fitting and unmistakably of the same species, mule. *Laurel and Hardy*, Brody thought.

The big man came over and extended his thick, chubby hand.

'Eddie,' Brody said, taking it. They shook hands like they were swinging a skipping rope. 'And Mickey.' Brody repeated the procedure with him. 'You fellas still in Mayorstone Park?'

'For our sins.' It was Eddie.

'The fucking place is worse than the Wild West.' It was Mickey. 'I mean, like literally.'

'Get this.' It was Eddie again. 'We arrested a gouger last week, you follow?'

Brody smiled. *You follow*, a catchphrase of his.

'Yeah, I follow.'

'We did more than that,' Mickey chipped in. 'Eddie here pulled him off a horse, didn't you, Eddie? Tell him.'

'Honest to God, I did, Jack. We gets this call of a raid on a betting shop right in the city centre. We gets there, and out the door comes Billy the fucking Kid on a piebald fucking pony, you follow? I ups and grabs him by the leg and pulls him off it. I says to him, if you want to be a cowboy on my patch, ye little bollocks, you gotta deal with Sheriff Eddie James Hanratty first, yes, sir, ya little prick. And I gave him one around the back of the head for his trouble.'

They both cracked up at that and high-fived each other, then fell silent, like they'd suddenly remembered where they were.

'You going back to the hotel?' Eddie said, all serious. 'For the slap-up, Jack? Alice wants us to. Can't let her down. What a lady.'

'Of course.'

'We'll talk then,' Eddie said. 'See ya.' As he and Mickey walked away, Brody heard him repeat to his sidekick, 'Sheriff Eddie James Hanratty, yes, sir, ya little prick,' and they both cracked up again.

Voyle grabbed Brody's arm.

'I need to talk, boss.'

'Yes, I know.'

'Marie Kennedy, boss, remember?'

'Marie Kennedy. Of course I remember. She rang you. You told me. What is it, Steve?'

'Yes, she rang me. Um, we both, one time, me and her, that is...'

'So? You get around, Steve. I know.'

'Well, yeah, but it wasn't like that... well, it was, but it wasn't. I liked her, boss. I did, I really liked her. She's, you know, smart... and everything.'

And everything. Yes, and everything. Not so long ago Marie Kennedy boasted the biggest fan mail of anyone at TV Global News Network. Recently she'd turned forty-three, which Brody only knew about because she'd coloured out her hair, and that had made it onto the front pages of the red tops. Everyone now knew her age: the newsreader herself had become the news. That was how big Marie Kennedy was. And washing the colour out of her hair had the benefit of adding more gravitas to her role as one of the nation's most trusted newsreaders. Little did they know.

'She's a bit older than you, isn't she?'

Voyle shrugged.

Brody worked it out, at least ten years.

'She and Gary...'

'Her husband?' Brody said.

'... yes, her husband, they've never been, I don't know, whatever word you want to use, close, but they're still together.'

'What's he do?'

'Member of the board of directors. Of TV Global News Network, other companies too. He's a, I believe the word is "shaker" in the business world. Anyway, they've been having problems, for years, that is. Anyone who knows them knows that. To use the term, they have an "open relationship".'

'So they both knock around with other people, do they?'

'They do, but like I say, they've stayed together, for the kids' sake, I suppose, I don't know. The *kids* are late teens now, early twenties maybe, two of them. Anyway, she was having an affair with this fella and...'

'Can I stop you right there.'

Voyle fell silent.

'Wasn't she married when you were with her too?'

'Of course. It's not that long ago. Yes, she was married. But it's an open relationship, I just told you; that doesn't count as having an affair?'

'Whatever. Who's she knocking off now?'

'I don't know. She wouldn't tell me.'

'So what's the problem?'

'If you'd just let me, boss, that's what I'm trying to tell

you.'

'Go on.'

'She and this man booked a night away at a holiday rental cottage, somewhere down country. They drove there yesterday to spend the night together, were due back today. She's reading the news tonight. They squeezed each other in, you might say.'

'I bet they did. Get to the point.'

'Well, he's disappeared. That's the point.'

'Disappeared?'

'Yes, disappeared.'

'What do you mean disappeared? As in vanished? That disappeared?'

'Exactly. Gone. Vamoose. Into thin air. She rang me, said that when they got there, to this location, the cottage, well, there was no electricity, no heating, a shithole is what she called it. He went down to the basement to see if he could fix things, get them working. He never came back up... Well, she thinks he never came back up, because she didn't see him again after that. She went down, heard what she thinks were rats, and then the light went out. She almost had a canary.'

'And where was she when he went down first?'

'Asleep.'

'Asleep? Hm. And absolutely no sign of him since?'

'None.'

'Of course, that's what she's telling you.'

'Yes, that *is* what she's telling me. But she's not one for bullshitting.'

'Maybe she killed him and fed him to the pigs. Did you ever think of that?'

'No, I didn't.'

'Does she seem the type?'

'What's the type?'

'Good question. But if he's missing, let her report it to her local station. That's what she should do. Why's she telling you? And why are you telling me?'

'Because she hasn't reported it. She's telling me because she doesn't know what to do.'

'She reports it, that's what she does, officially that is; what else is there to do?'

Voyle stroked his chin like he had a beard there, which sometimes he had. 'She *can't* report it, boss.'

'Why?'

'Because it would destroy her; if this gets out, her career that is, it would be over. No doubt.'

'I don't see how. She's in an open relationship, you just said so. Her choice.'

'But the public don't know that, now do they? They trust her. They wouldn't trust her if this got out.'

'Maybe she should have thought of that beforehand.'

'It doesn't suit you to be self-righteous, boss.'

Brody laughed. 'No, Steve, it doesn't. How did they get down there, anyway?'

'He drove. She took his car back.'

'Odd one alright. What does she want *you* to do about it?'

'Wants me to find him, that's what. Simple. He's not returned home either, if that's what you're thinking. She knows this because she got someone to ring his house. Seems he just, well...' Voyle put his hands together and parted them again in a gesture of a miniature explosion. '*Poof*, disappeared, just like that.'

The car park was almost empty now. Brody checked the time; it was coming up on half twelve.

'We need to get to the hotel. Alice won't like it if we're late.'

'What do I do, boss?'

'You have lunch. That's what you do. We'll talk again after.'

THE BANQUETING HALL of the Green Valley Hotel was packed. At Brody's table they talked of the Old Man in the way the Irish always talk of the dead, with all that was good elevated to near sainthood, and all that was bad not mentioned at all. Dying the way he had, of a heart attack, might be viewed as an anticlimax after thirty plus years of service, might not be the heroic death to ensure someone's name would be etched onto a memorial, to live on forever, not only on this memorial, but on every other memorial to the fallen throughout the land. If anyone had thought this, they were wrong. While yes, the Old Man had died at home, and while yes, he had been officially off duty at the time (but is there any such thing? Especially for senior officers?), the fatal heart attack that had done him in might as well have been a fatal shot from a blagger's shotgun, or a hundred other perils related to the job. Because in the Old Man's house at the time of his heart attack had been an intruder. His name was Daniel Willow. The Old Man had arrested him many years before, and subsequently the judge had thrown away the proverbial key. Willow spent practically all of his life in prison. When he was eventually released, he was a pensioner, a harmless old man, or so people thought, especially the parole board who'd given the green light to his release. But he wasn't. On the contrary. Daniel Willow had immediately set about exacting the revenge he'd been meticulously planning for years.

There was no doubt the Old Man could have dealt with him had he not had that heart attack. But as it happened, and as the Old Man lay dying, it was his wife, now widow, polite, softly spoken Alice, who had rammed her pointed, best heavy antique brass poker into the back of Daniel Willow's neck, severing the artery. That was the end of Daniel Willow, but so too was it the end of the Old Man.

In a way, it was almost as if Daniel Willow had won. But just as much as people wanted to keep the name of the Old Man alive, they wanted the name of Daniel Willow erased from history, to make sure that he did not win. And it was, more or less.

Today, at his memorial dinner at the Green Valley Hotel, everyone had a story to tell, with each story more fantastic than the last, so that by the time the coffees arrived, the Old Man had already become an urban myth, a modern-day, swashbuckling Cú Chulainn.

Death for the Irish is never morbid; rather it is often a celebration.

And with the arrival of coffees – mostly coffees anyway, it was still the middle of the day after all – his widow, Alice, tall and regal, stood, tapped a spoon against the side of her cup, and the room fell silent. She cleared her throat and looked out at the faces of those gathered in memory of her husband.

'Friends and colleagues, thank you for coming here today. Tom would have loved to know that so many of you had taken the time to turn out and say your last goodbyes. I didn't think he even knew so many people.' She smiled. 'It must be the free meal.'

A ripple of laughter went through the room.

'Tom's life is a life to be celebrated, and so is its passing. Because it was a life that was lived. The only sadness is he never got to see out those retirement years he was so looking forward to. That *we* never got to live them out, I should say. But nothing ever works the way we plan. As he often liked to say, whether he'd forgotten the litre of milk I'd told him to get, or the lawnmower had spluttered out of petrol halfway through mowing the lawn because he'd forgotten to get petrol, which was often, "Well, feck that, Ted."'

The room laughed, a loud, genuine, belly rumble this time round. When it settled down, she continued.

'I'm not going to go on, you'll be glad to hear. Tom wouldn't have wanted that...'

And she didn't, her eulogy was succinct and infused with just the right amount of humour to keep everyone entertained. Brody was impressed.

'To Tom,' she said, lifting her cup, even if it seemed a little odd to use a cup in a toast. The room lifted their cups and glasses in return.

'To Tom,' everyone chorused.

'Talk to Marie Kennedy,' Brody said, leaning into Voyle, returning his cup to its saucer. 'Tell her she must report this matter.'

Voyle looked at him and said nothing.

'And tell her that if she doesn't tell you who this person is, and tell you immediately, then she herself will end up announcing this little story on the evening news; she'll become the headline herself.'

'That's what she's afraid of.'

'But this isn't about her, that's what she's forgetting, and you can tell her that too. This is about him, whoever he is.' Brody was liking Marie Kennedy less and less. 'I'll give you the rest of the day. I want that name; otherwise she *will* be the story. But you've got to go back to the ranch first, we all do; someone wants to meet us, introduce herself.'

'*Herself*. A woman? The new CO, you mean?'

'You're smart, Steve. Yes, that's who I mean.'

'That was quick.'

'Seemingly she'd been selected a long time ago. The Old Man planned on early retirement.'

'I see. She's not here, is she?'

'I don't know. I've never met the woman.'

'Anyway, that doesn't give me a lot of time, to talk to Marie Kennedy, that is.'

'It gives you enough.'

2

She was waiting when they got back to the Phoenix Park, their bellies full and feeling a little sleepy. It was late afternoon. She was sitting in a chair at the top of the unit room, arms folded, like a portrait titled *Patience*. Brody was first in, followed by Nicola Considine, then Steve Voyle and Martin Sheahan. They sat at their desks, but Brody merely leaned against the wall by the door. His office was upstairs, and he didn't have a desk in the unit room. No one spoke as the portrait silently observed them before getting to her feet and beginning, 'My name's Superintendent Fiona Ryan, your new unit commander. Hello.'

'Hello,' they answered, and the unit room suddenly felt like a classroom.

She was five eight, Brody guessed, with dark hair tied back in a ponytail, athletic – at one time, that is, his second guess. Now she was turning stodgy, too much time spent behind a desk, Brody's third guess. She wore no make-up, her skin fresh and pink, a face that was neither pretty nor plain, but features in perfect proportion – except for the eyes, that is, which seemed too close, lending her a hard and dark, almost reptilian expression. A good face for interviewing gougers, Brody thought, and one that would rarely, if ever, see her stopped and asked for directions by strangers.

'Introduce yourselves, please?'

They did. And so ensued ten minutes or so of banter. All that was missing were the beers and the barbeque. Then she got down to business.

'I intend to be a fair CO,' she said, draping one leg over the other and beginning to swing the foot lazily through the air, 'just to put that out there... Now, this might sound like a cliché, yes, I know, but I want you all to be aware my office door is always open. Anyone who wants to come see me, they can. About anything. Please understand that.' Her voice stiffened like it had just caught a gust of wind as she added, 'Because my job is to run this unit efficiently, and I won't be able to do that if people think they can't come and see me whenever they want, about whatever they want. I need you to know you can trust me, that I'm on your side. Do you understand?'

The classroom nodded.

'Because I *am* on your side.'

They nodded again.

Brody was suspicious. Why voice something that didn't need to be voiced in the first place? What she said should be a given. It had always been a given with the Old Man.

'Good... but that works both ways. If you show me respect, I'll show you respect. And fundamental to this is transparency.'

Now Brody wanted to smile, but he didn't. Instead he looked down at the floor. *Fundamental* and *transparency*, two words in the ammo belt of those gardai who carry cans of blowback repellent on their hips like gunslingers. He'd heard the words a thousand times, along with others, like *impartiality*, *respect*, and *effective administration*... See how far those words got you when faced with a gouger wielding a machete he was hell-bent on burying into the top of your head.

When he looked up from the floor, he saw those eyes – those snake eyes – waiting for him.

'Sergeant, I don't want any secrets in this unit. Clear?'

Before he could say anything, she flicked them about the room.

'Now, has anyone got anything that I should know about?'

Her eyes drifted and settled on Voyle.

Brody wondered, *Does she know something?* About Marie Kennedy? Or anything else? Or was she simply fishing?

'I'd like a word,' she said to Voyle. 'Okay with you? In my office?'

Voyle nodded, said, 'Okay,' like he had a choice in this, which he didn't.

'I KNOW ABOUT YOU,' she told Voyle.

She was sitting behind the Old Man's desk. In the Old Man's chair. Everything was the Old Man's except that he wasn't here. He was dead. A point she had yet to comment on. 'Your appraisal says "a good officer but one who can be a bit reckless at times, who is prone to sexist and inappropriate remarks, who does not work well with female colleagues". Anything else you want to add to that?'

Voyle looked like he'd been slapped across the face.

'Really? It says that? No one ever told me.'

'You're being told now.'

'Yes, I suppose I am.'

'And the look I caught between you and Sergeant Brody. I don't like it. A look like that hides secrets. I don't like secrets.'

Voyle was coming to a conclusion. Superintendent Ryan here, she who wanted to run this unit efficiently, who didn't want secrets, whose door was always open, blah, blah, blah, was turning out to be a royal pain in the hole.

'No, there's nothing.'

'Nothing?'

'No. Nothing.' Voyle was beginning to believe the lie himself. 'And all because of what? Seriously. All because of a look?'

'The eyes are the windows to the soul. Don't you know that?'

'I know that. So?'

'I don't like your tone.'

'And I don't like yours.'

Above the windows to her soul, the eyebrows peaked in surprise. She fell silent. Then: 'I'd watch my mouth if I were you.'

'Oh, so we *can't* talk about anything. You want to run this unit efficiently?'

'I do.'

'It already runs efficiently. Chief Superintendent Tom Maguire made sure it ran efficiently. You've inherited his good work and a good team.'

The eyes zeroed in on his. God, they were mean. They never left his, not once, never blinked, a death-ray stare.

'I was with the Special Detective Unit before I came here...' Like he should be impressed, that she was a superior life form.

Which made sense to Voyle. The domestic security agency was a unit within a unit, like the KGB, legends in their own minds.

She sat back and curled her fingers against her palm, studying them. Then she looked up. 'How good are you?' she asked.

'Excuse me?'

'Because I have a little loose thread I want you to tie up for me.'

'You do? What, like a test? I don't think you can...'

'I can do what I want. Listen up.'

Voyle said nothing, listening up.

'Some months ago, actually, twenty-eighth of January, that's when it was, a Tuesday to be precise, the body of a Mr Robert Gilsenan was found in a locked room at his home just outside of Arklow. You ever hear about it?'

'I heard about it. Of course. Everyone heard about it, the bigwig chairman of something or other, ATW packaging company, yes?'

'Yes.'

'And wasn't there something about him, that he was meant to collect the keys to a Maserati sports car he'd waited a year to take delivery of on the day he died?'

'Yes. He'd also run an ironman triathlon the month before he died as well. Not the actions of someone about to kill themselves. I want you to look at it again for me.'

'You do? Why? Despite everything, it's a suicide.'

'The Coroners' Court is this day week, next Wednesday. Have a last look at it for me by then, yes? No reason. Just do it.'

'No reason, you say? Don't you believe it's a suicide?'

'How do I know? I wasn't there. Yes, believed to be a suicide. Probably is a suicide. Probably a waste of time. Just have a look at it, like I ask.'

'The Coroners' Court is this day week?'

'You're not deaf, are you, Voyle? That's what I just said.'

'But... how am I supposed...? There's not much I can do, is what I'm saying.'

She shook her head. 'Tut-tut. Not the can-do attitude I expect from the members of my team. I need people I can rely on, twenty-four seven, 365 days a year.'

'Not a lot of time. That's all I'm saying. And for what? Is this a test? Come on, what's this really all about?'

Something passed behind those snake-like eyes. Voyle knew then what this was really about.

'I never said it was a test,' she said. 'They're your words, not mine.'

It wasn't about the suicide, no, that was for sure. A very fishy suicide, yes, because you'd think a man who'd waited an entire year for a Maserati would have driven it at least once before doing himself in. But then again, there were no rules to suicides; they didn't have to make sense and often didn't. No, what Voyle considered this was really about was the first pull on an elastic that Superintendent Ryan would keep on pulling until it eventually snapped. That was what this was really about. A purge, a clean-out, call it what you will. Of him.

'Why me?' he asked, but he already knew the answer. 'I had nothing to do with this. I wasn't part of the original investigation.'

'Considine will be with you,' she replied, ignoring the question. 'What? You don't look too happy. Is there a problem?'

Voyle didn't move. The mention of Considine's name stuck like a piece of gristle at the back of his throat. He wanted to spit it out. Instead he coughed.

'C-Considine?'

'Yes. You heard me. Look, I know you two don't get along.'

Which is exactly why you're putting us together, isn't it? Bitch!

The elastic stretched just that bit tighter.

'Yes,' she said, 'I know. You both can't stand the sight of each other, actually. And that's not good for team cohesion. It's a situation I can't allow to continue.'

Voyle said nothing.

'Don't you agree? Speak.'

'Whatever.'

'Detective Voyle, you're doing nothing to improve my impression of you. Explain to me why you and Considine don't get on.'

'I can't explain it.'

'Or won't explain it.'

He shook his head.

'No. I would if I could. But we just… sometimes you don't need a reason. She's chalk; I'm cheese. Or the other way round, it doesn't matter.' He shrugged. 'That's what people say about us.'

'Yes, that I know too. And it's why I'm putting you two together.'

Superintendent Fiona Ryan smiled. Voyle was surprised. She had a lovely smile, and he hadn't expected it, her teeth even and white, her face changing from a winter's day into one of a warm, glorious summer. When she smiled, it was like she was a different person.

He realised how tense he was. Voyle relaxed his jaw and dropped his shoulders.

'Because if you two can't get along,' she said, sounding like she loved the idea, 'then one of you will be saying goodbye to this unit.'

'You don't say?'

'No, doing nothing to improve my impression of you at all.'

3

There was a smell in the air, of something rotten, how he imagined meat and vegetables would smell if left to putrefy, though he no longer noticed it so much. For the first couple of hours he had, and he'd had to breathe through his mouth to stop himself gagging. He was in a shed, a dark shed. He knew it was a shed, the ceiling of rippled corrugated iron, the light seeping in from outside giving it the appearance of a blackened Swiss cheese, the walls of drystone, the ground damp and stodgy. He lay hogtied in a corner, completely still, trying not to move a muscle. He had no choice; it was the only way to stop the pain from exploding in his head again. The least movement set it off, stirred it up like a swarm of angry wasps, the worst pain he'd ever experienced, along with a tightness, a heavy weight, like a brass hat had been clamped to his head. At its epicentre was what felt like a swollen mass of skin and hair where he remembered being struck by something cold and blunt. When he came round, he was here, hogtied like a beast in a pen at the market.

From outside he heard a sound, like a rustling of paper, followed by a silence, and then another sound, the unmistakeable sliding of a bolt on the other side of the door. But he didn't react, his sole focus, everything, was centred on stopping that excruciating pain from igniting in his cranium again.

He watched the door slowly begin to open. A shape materialised, the shadowed outline of a giant standing before him. A giant that made a strange grunting sound, half animal, half human.

The man forgot about the pain in his head; he forgot about everything, everything, that is, but the palpable sense of violent evil emanating from this creature. The giant took a long, slow step towards him. Still, the man did not move a muscle.

4

'I'm fucked,' Voyle said.

Brody closed the filing cabinet drawer and returned to his desk, a bunch of files clutched beneath his arm. He sat down and set them on the desk before him.

'That's a bit harsh.'

'It's true, boss. She wants me to look under the bonnet of this Robert Gilsenan suicide. The Coroners' Court is next Wednesday.'

'Nothing suspicious was found on that, isn't that right?'

'Right. Nothing suspicious.'

'Hm...'

'Exactly... A poisoned chalice, that's what it is. And when I can't find anything either, because there's nothing to find, what happens then? And...'

'And...?'

'She's put Considine on it with me.'

'Considine. Torture... for both of you. Probably breaches some UN charter or other.'

'What?'

'I'm joking, Steve.'

'Well, she's not. She wants me gone. Simple as. I know it.'

Brody said nothing. He thought it sounded like maybe she did.

'Did she mention any of this to you, boss?'

Brody said nothing for a moment. He was about to speak when a knock sounded on the door.

'Come in.'

And speak of the devil. The door opened to reveal Nicola Considine standing there. She looked at Brody, but completely ignored Voyle, just stood there, saying nothing.

'You're making me nervous, Nicola. God, come in, will you? What is it?'

She finally did.

'Now. Take a seat.' He pointed to a chair.

She went and sat down, crossed her legs and folded her arms. She still hadn't said a word.

'Yes,' Brody said, 'to answer your question, Steve. Superintendent Ryan did tell me about it. But what I want to know, did you tell her, about Marie Kennedy, that is?'

Voyle shifted in his seat.

'Thought so. No, you didn't, Steve, did you?'

Considine finally found her voice. 'Tell who what?'

'It's none of your business,' Voyle said.

'You're wrong. It is her business. You've just made it her business.'

'I have?'

'You have.'

'Will someone please tell me what the hell's going on? And, boss, why'd you call me in here?'

'Tell her, Steve. And don't forget Marie Kennedy.'

'She doesn't need to know.'

'She does now. Tell her.'

And Voyle did, but he was talking to the desk, not to Considine, telling the desk about the phone call received from Marie Kennedy, and finishing with the Coroners' Court next week.

When he fell silent, Considine unfolded her arms and joined her hands together like she was praying. 'Aw, boss. Please get me off this. Throw me a life raft, will you? I'm begging. Let this man go down on his own sword; it's only a matter of time before he does anyway, you know it. I know it; everybody knows it. Don't bring me in. And why am I being brought in anyway?'

'He's just told you. Superintendent Fiona Ryan wants you in, that's why.'

'Yes, but for what purpose?'

'To slow torture me,' Voyle muttered, 'because she wants me gone, that's why. God.'

'What's he muttering about?' Considine pointed at Voyle.

Brody didn't answer. Instead, he did something he'd never done before, didn't even realise he was doing it. It was something the Old Man used to do. He only became aware of it when he saw Considine and Voyle staring, and following their gaze, discovered his fingers tapping on the desktop.

'Christ, Steve, you've dug a hole and kept on digging, haven't you?' He stopped tapping on the desk and pulled his hand back.

Voyle seemed confused. 'I'm disappearing down the hole I'm digging, and' – nodding towards Considine – 'she needs a life raft?'

'Don't get smart, Steve.'

'Sorry, boss.'

'I don't feel so good.' It was Considine. 'I think I'll go home and call in sick.'

'You're not sick, Nicola.'

'Okay. I'm not sick. Why doesn't someone let *her* know what's going on?' She pointed vaguely in the direction of the new super's office.

'I'm thinking about it,' Brody said, 'believe me.'

'Please' – an uncharacteristic pleading to Voyle's voice – 'you can't, boss. I can't; we can't. *Pleease.*'

'Ah, Jesus, boss,' Considine said. 'I really don't feel well at all. Can't I just go home? This isn't going to end well, it's just not. Maybe you should do the same. And' – she jerked a thumb toward Voyle, but still didn't look at him – 'who's this character she told him about, the one she went on a dirty night away with? Voyle's not saying, is he now?'

'Because I don't know, that's why. And if this gets out, her career, her marriage, everything will be on the line... I don't want that on my conscience.'

'As if you give a shite about any of that,' Considine said to the desk.

Brody ran a hand over his face and sighed loudly.

'Why did you come to me in the first place with this, Steve? Christ. Why didn't you just look into it on the quiet yourself and say nothing?'

'Because that's Voyle all over,' Considine muttered.

'You've got me wrong.' Voyle sounded hurt. 'I'm not the heartless bastard you all have me pegged out to be.'

'Oh, really?' Considine muttered again. 'God, you had me well fooled, then.'

Brody sliced a hand through the air. 'That's enough. Both of you. I don't want anyone to speak for a minute. Let me think about it. Jeez. Not a word.'

They all stared at the desk.

'Okay,' Brody said when the minute was up, 'this rented house that Marie Kennedy and her lover were renting, you at least know where it is, don't you? Somewhere in Wicklow, you said. That right?'

'Tinnock. Yes. A few miles outside of it. The arse end of nowhere is how she put it. But I have the postcode.'

'And the suicide was in Arklow?'

'Yes,' Voyle said, 'and?'

'And, geographically speaking, you could do both, couldn't you?'

Voyle looked away, then nodded. 'I could.'

'Only if...'

'Only if?'

'You're quick about it, Steve. And...'

'And?'

'You find out who this man is, lover boy, and where he's at. Assuming all's well, we say nothing, everyone's happy, no one's any the wiser.'

'Fine, boss, that's a plan.'

'But...'

'Yes.'

'Not fine, Steve. Because if something is wrong, then you're on your own; you go straight to Ryan's office and you tell her. Myself and Considine know nothing about any of this. Understand? That's the best I can do.'

Voyle nodded. 'Yes, yes, boss, of course. I understand.'

'Get this fella's name, like I said, okay? If she doesn't give it, then you tell her you make everything you know official. I mean it, Steve. I told you.'

'Yes, boss, I know. I've arranged to meet her after I leave here, in fact. I'll get it.'

'Where is she now, by the way?'

'With a friend. She told people she was visiting the Aran Islands for work purposes and wouldn't be back until a little later today, so she has to lie low for a while, can't show her face until later.'

'Heeeello...' Considine raised a hand. 'I just tag along, is that it? Don't I have a say in any of this?'

'You have any better suggestions?' Brody asked.

'I don't owe him anything, boss...'

That statement hung in the air.

'You're right, Nicola, you don't. What'd you want to do? Your choice.'

'Well...' She looked to the door. Brody and Voyle looked to her.

The seconds dripped by.

'Well...' she began again before jumping to her feet. 'Oh, Jesus, we haven't got all day if we're going to get this done.' She looked at Voyle for the first time and then to Brody. 'This is for you, boss, not him, just so we're clear.'

'Clear,' he answered. 'Go on, Steve, before she changes her mind.'

Voyle stood, and Brody watched them file out of the office.

5

Considine reversed the grey unmarked Hyundai from its parking space, spun the steering wheel with one hand until the SUV was pointing toward the exit barrier. A uniformed guard in the security office peered out as they approached, nodded his head in recognition, and the boom barrier began to rise. They passed through, pausing for a break in traffic before emerging from Garda HQ onto the North Road, turning left for the city.

'Address?'

'Number 269 Normandy Road.'

'Off Landsdowne Road, correct?'

'Correct,' Voyle said.

He looked out the window, at the clear, unusually balmy, late February day.

Neither spoke again until Considine pulled into the kerb outside a sumptuous period house a half hour or so later. It stood on its own grounds behind a high brick wall overshadowed by towering trees. They were about to get out of the car when Voyle paused.

'I need to do this on my own,' he said. 'She's not expecting you, only me.'

'Oh, now you tell me.'

'I thought you knew.'

'I only know what you told me. And you didn't tell me that.'

Voyle got out, then stooped and put his head in the open doorway.

'I thought it was ob–'

'What? Obvious? Shit, I can feel it already; I'm beginning to get tangled up in your web. She thinks no one else knows, doesn't she? You promised her you wouldn't tell anyone, didn't you? Yes, you did. Well, you've already broken that promise. I don't know who's worse, you or her. You'd better set her straight, Voyle. I'm telling you–'

Voyle slammed the door shut, turned and walked away. Only because he knew she was right.

He went through the open gates and along a short driveway, up the steps to the front door and pressed the button in the centre of a gleaming brass surround. It opened almost immediately. Standing there was the woman who'd once opened a trapdoor beneath his world and sent him tumbling through it. A woman who'd occupied his every waking thought, and many sleeping ones too, a woman he'd lusted after and loved in equal measure, a woman who'd been like a drug he had to be high on all the time. And looking at her now, for the first time in a long time, he knew she still had the power to do it all again. Marie Kennedy wore a white silk blouse and short black skirt, on her feet pink slippers at the end of long, bare, slender legs. She'd been crying.

'Oh, thank God, thank God you've come. Steve, come in, come in.' She opened the door, and Voyle stepped into the opulent hall. She closed it again and took him by surprise by flinging her arms around him. 'Hold me, Steve. Hold me. Just hold me.'

He did, breathing in her aroma, a hint of perfume long since applied and mixed with that of old and new sweat. He didn't care how she smelt. As long as the smell was hers, that was all that mattered. They stood, holding each other, and Voyle's thoughts turned to Considine sitting in the car outside. Very gently, he took her shoulders and nudged her back from him. 'Can we go and talk about this somewhere, Marie?'

She placed an index finger against her mouth and began nibbling on the nail, her other hand going to the top of her head and starting to churn through her hair like a food mixer set on slow. Finally, she leaned forward and held him again, whispered into his ear, 'Oh, Steve, you have no idea what an absolute nightmare this is. Really. It is. An absolutely terrible, terrible nightmare. I just want to wake up from it, that's all, go back to my normal life. That's all I want. Just want to wake up from all this.' She pulled back again and looked into his eyes. 'But I can't, Steve.' Her voice rose. 'I can't because it's real. It's real. It's actually happening. Oh God.' She began to sob.

'Let's go someplace and talk, Marie. Come on. Where can we go and talk?'

She sniffled a couple of times and ran the back of a hand across her eyes.

'Okay, Steve. Yes, okay. You're right. We need to talk.' She reached for his hand, and the unexpected touch of it sent a shot through him like a low, warm, sensual charge. Immediately he felt embarrassed. This wasn't the time. Then again, it was never a right time when it came to this woman.

She brought him into a room, a big, beautiful, bright room furnished as a room in a house like this should be furnished, period style, of exquisite taste and extravagance. She sat them down in the centre of a chesterfield facing a huge, green-tile-inlay cast-iron fireplace. She started to sob again.

'You got a tissue, Steve? I've used all mine up.'

'Um.' He began going through his pockets, found an open travel pack, and handed this to her.

'Thanks, Steve.' She fished one out and blew her nose.

A voice from behind Voyle startled him.

'Yo, babes, everything alright? I just heard the doorbell.'

He turned to see an older version of Jack Sparrow – or maybe Jack Sparrow's grandfather – standing there.

'It's my friend, babes, the one I told you about.'

'The cop?'

'Yes, a detective garda.'

Voyle recognised Tommy Flynn immediately, lead guitarist with CreteZ, a seventies heavy metal band who still played the festival circuit and other venues in far-flung places like Albania. He flashed two fingers to Voyle in a peace sign.

'Hey, man.'

Voyle wanted to tell him he looked ridiculous. Instead he nodded and thought again of Considine sitting outside, looked at his watch. Ten minutes had passed already.

'Cool,' Jack Sparrow said, 'catch you later, babes.'

Voyle heard his footsteps retreat down the hall and the front door open and then close.

'He's such a sweetie, lives in this big old house all on his ownsome. You wouldn't think it's his kind of place, would you? But it is. He loves all this old stuff. When I asked if I could hang out, he didn't even hesitate. CreteZ were bigger than Slade in seventy-eight, you know.'

A memory came to Voyle. Of that time he and Marie had gone to Corfu for five days. On the return they'd been stuck at the airport. A general strike, something. No food or water, sitting on the floor for twelve hours waiting for their flight. On his way back from yet another fruitless search to find someplace where he could get water, he rounded a corner to see her putting the top back on a bottle and shoving it into her bag, then wiping a hand quickly across her mouth. She didn't see him, or at least he thought she didn't, and he'd never let on. But it was a lesson, if he'd needed one, that the number one priority for Marie Kennedy was always going to be Marie Kennedy. He was glad in a way, because from then on he knew exactly where he stood with her. And afterwards, the relationship became much more about lust than love, yet no less intense. Now, unlike back then, he was no longer obsessed with this woman, and it was a timely reminder to keep it that way.

'Don't take me for a fool, Marie.'

She gave him a slow, uncertain smile, like an actress, or a seasoned TV news anchor, because both, after all, were much the same.

'What do you mean, Steve?'

He thought again of Considine sitting in the car outside.

'I don't have time. The one you were with. In that cottage. The one you say is missing.'

'He *is* missing, Steve. He is. I woke up, and he was gone. It's terrible, I told you. And that basement...'

'Yes, yes, your worst nightmare. You told me.'

'Steve, you sound cross with me. You're not cross with me, are you?'

'Who is it, Marie? The last time. I'm walking out of here if you don't tell me. And...'

'And...?'

'And then *I'm* going to have to report this...'

'No, Steve, you can't do that.' She clamped a hand onto his wrist. 'No, Steve, you can't.'

'Marie, don't you see, you'll have left me no choice.'

'Steve, I asked you to help. I didn't ask you to ruin my life.'

'Then why don't you tell me his name? I can't help you otherwise.'

'You're the detective, Steve, you work it out.'

'Oh, I see. Is that the way it is? You sound...'

'Yes, I sound what?'

'The way you used to sound. Back then.'

'The way I used to sound. Back then? Back when? What's that mean?' She leaned into him, her face close to his, her hot breath like a sweet, sensuous breeze, mere centimetres away. 'You never complained about the way I sounded before... back then, Steve, did you? In fact, you never complained about anything.'

He didn't answer.

'Why's that, Steve, I wonder.' Her hand was still on his wrist. She slid her fingers between his and lifted his hand up, held it to her, against the edge of her breast. He could feel the fullness of it through her silk blouse. She wasn't wearing a bra. *Jesus.* 'No, Steve, you didn't complain about anything back then, did you? You didn't. I wonder why.' A surge of lust swept through him. He suddenly hated himself for how little it took, the feel of a breast, to bring him right back there again. If she were to lead him to a bedroom right now, he'd follow.

He jumped to his feet and peered down at her.

'Steve, what is it?' Her voice was low, sweet.

'Marie, I'm walking.'

She silently observed him.

'No' – with a shake of her head – 'you're not.'

'You know, Marie, all you've talked about since I got here is yourself. So. Last time. Who is this person?'

She dropped her head.

'That's not fair, Steve.'

He'd had enough. He turned, walked towards the door

and had almost reached it when she said: 'Okay, Steve, okay, you win. I'll tell you.'

'Then tell me.'

She said it.

'What?'

'You heard me.'

'*Him.*'

'Yes, *him.*'

'Oh, Christ,' he muttered.

Y*es*, Voyle thought, walking back down the driveway from the house, *I have dug a hole for myself, and yes, I've kept on digging. But have I gone so far that I can't climb back out again?*

He knew the answer to that. Yes, he had.

He could see Considine watching him in the driver's door mirror as he approached. He got into the car, expected her to say something, to complain about him having been gone so long. But she didn't. He told her the name he'd just been given.

Her head swung towards him.

'Yes,' he said, 'you heard me right, *him.*'

6

It was getting late, their normal shift should be wrapping up soon, but Voyle and Considine kept on the treadmill. The name he'd been given ensured that. And with anything to do with police work, most activity, the important stuff, happened in the first twenty-four, forty-eight hours. They crossed the border from Dublin into County Wicklow on the N11 dual carriageway. Considine was following the blinking red dot on the GPS screen on the centre console, it in turn following the postal code coordinates she had inputted that would take them to the arse end of nowhere, as Marie Kennedy had put it herself. Brody's voice boomed through the speaker on the state mobile. Voyle had just told him the news.

'*Him.* Donagh Hughes.'

'Yes, boss.'

'The Minister for Foreign Affairs no less...'

'Yes, yes.' It was Considine. 'The Minister for Foreign Affairs.'

So, no doubt.

'Jesus Christ,' Brody said, and, as if that religious superlative weren't enough, added, 'My God.'

There was nothing but road noise and the white noise from the speaker of the Tetra phone.

'Right,' he said at last, 'where are you?'

'On our way to the location.'

'Which location?'

'The one Hughes went missing from.'

'You are?' Surprised.

'We are.'

'Why?'

'We might find him, boss; it's worth a try.'

'I don't think you'll find him. I'd bet my wages on it.'

Out of the corner of his eye, Voyle saw Considine nodding her head. She didn't agree to this either.

'How far away are you?' Brody asked.

'We're coming up on a turn-off now, half hour, give or take.'

Silence, Brody was working it out. 'Okay, swing by it, then, have a look, but I'm notifying Ryan as soon as I put this phone down.'

'Boss...' It was Voyle, before his voice trailed off and was lost to the white noise of the network again. 'Nothing, boss,' he said, 'nothing.'

Voyle knew.

They all knew.

This case was now bigger than any of them.

Brody didn't know whether to thank or curse Voyle. Thank him for discovering – in a roundabout way – that one of the nation's most senior members of government might be missing, or curse him for the very same reason at the same time too. He did neither. He finished the call, got up, and went to Ryan's office.

She was hanging a photo on the wall when he went in. He

got a glimpse of a faded rectangle of paint where the previous photo had hung. He tried to remember what had been there, and was disappointed when he couldn't. After all, he'd stood exactly where he was standing now often enough, so he should be able to. It was like the Old Man's memory itself was literally fading before his very eyes, while his body was still warm in its grave.

'Yes?'

He snapped out of his reverie. Fiona Ryan had moved behind her desk and was looking at him. The new photo was in place on the wall. *What the hell had been there?*

'I have something to tell you,' he said, getting straight to it.

'Then tell me.'

'Right. It's this. An old girlfriend of Steve Voyle rang, rang him, that is… though girlfriend might be too strong a word. They were actually in an affair; she was married at the time, still is, by the way, and to the same man.'

'But that's not really an affair, then, is it, from his perspective? He wasn't the one cheating, she was.'

'Donagh Hughes,' he said, not getting into it, 'the name of the man she's having an affair with now.'

Her mouth had formed a perfect O shape in preparation for whatever word she'd been about to say. But she didn't say it. Instead her lips collapsed into a pinched scowl. Brody took the opportunity to quickly run through the details. When he finished, her eyes became like tiny battlements behind which two sentries peered out at him. She was breathing through her nose; he could see them flare on each intake of breath.

'*You…*' she said at last, 'never told me? *He* never told me. But *you*. I would have expected more from you.' She moved to her seat and sat down like a dead weight. He remained standing. She pointed to the empty chair. He took it as an invitation to sit down, and was about to go and do so when she added, '*He* sat right there, in that chair, and looked me straight in the eye, never said a word.' It wasn't an invitation. Brody remained standing. 'The absolute bollocks. And how long' – the finger shifting to take in Brody – 'have you known about this? Huh?'

'Not long, we did the best we could, under the circumstances, until we found out who it was. Steve got a phone–'

'Don't try to fucking defend him. Boys sticking together gets right up my nose. I won't have it. Clear?'

'Clear. But if you could let me finish...'

She said nothing.

'What I was going to say is that we did the best we could...'

She made to speak again.

Brody cut her off, 'Let me finish...'

Superintendent Ryan closed her mouth.

'Thank you. Because Steve was asked specifically to keep this matter private, and he was approached in a personal capacity. He came to me with it, while he didn't have to. He didn't have to go to anybody with it; he could have said nothing.'

Brody didn't mention that he had told Voyle that keeping his mouth shut might have been the best option.

'But he *did* come to me. So I told him to try to kill two birds with one stone, excuse the pun, and look into it while he was looking into the suicide you detailed him to look into. Remember, he didn't know what we know now, no one did except for that woman, that is. And when you think about it...'

'Don't tell me what to think about.'

'... nothing would really have been done any differently, not until we found out who it was, which we just have done. I came to you immediately with it.'

'And who is this woman?'

'Marie Kennedy.'

'Rings a bell.'

'Presenter of the main evening news on TV Global News Network.'

Brody could almost hear the cogs beginning to turn in Fiona Ryan's brain. Glamorous media personality, darling of the afternoon talk show circuit, regular contributor to a number of respected Sunday broadsheets. A high-profile case, one that could make a career... or break it.

He watched a shadow pass behind the battlements, almost as quickly gone again, her expression like five balls out of the lotto drum had her numbers on them; she was now waiting for the sixth to come up.

Unlike the Old Man, he'd never liked high-profile cases.

'Yes,' she said, her voice notably softer, 'I can see how difficult a quandary this might have put you all in.' She sat back, and her gaze seemed to settle somewhere beyond him, perhaps the imaginary career totem pole, where she could see herself scampering over the bodies above her as she made her way up, up, up, all the way to the top maybe.

Or maybe Brody was being too cynical.

But he doubted it.

7

Tinnock consisted of nothing more than one long street, a church at one end, a garage at the other, in the middle a Centra supermarket. And that was it, with side streets running off on either side but going nowhere, petering out into the hinterland beyond. But the village seemed to make the most of itself, the one long street was tidy, and the buildings, in that quaint Irish tradition, were painted in a variety of Mediterranean colours. The GPS brought them through it and out the other end. The early darkness of winter had fallen, and quickly too, the clear, cold, blue sky replaced by a star-sprinkled canopy, a scimitar of white in one corner that was a half moon, bathing the landscape with a dull, washed glow. A half mile or so farther on, it pinged a left turn, and Considine turned onto a narrow back road. As they progressed, the road steadily deteriorated until it became nothing more than a rutted track, a little later rising sharply, levelling out again for a time before dipping, and they were driving along by a shingled beach next to the Irish Sea. The tide was out, and a long way off the shingles gave way to a mixture of sand and rock formations, reflecting the light like a still pencil drawing. Beside the track was a large metal sign with a warning:

Dangerous Currents and Underfoot Conditions. Strictly No Swimming.

So this place would never be a popular spot on any tourist itinerary, but as a place to hide and engage in an illicit relationship, it seemed perfect. Considine leaned forward, peering through the windscreen. The track ended at what appeared to be a bank of heather and a copse of trees, the trees permanently bent by the harsh easterly winds. The GPS still blinked, and now a postcode appeared at the top of the screen, blinking too, telling them they'd almost arrived. Neither spoke. In fact, they'd hardly said more than two words to each other the entire journey.

Considine stopped the car where the track petered out.

'There's nothing here.' It was Voyle, stating the obvious.

Considine didn't answer. She cut the engine and opened the door, got out. Voyle followed. The sound of the sea in the distance lapping to shore had a rhythm and sound to it like that of someone gently breathing. Voyle turned his face into the bracing wind, scanning the water's edge in the grey light, moving across the rocky, dangerous foreshore, over the shingles, back into the heather and copse of trees they were standing before. Nothing. Nothing whatsoever. Marie Kennedy was right. The arse end of nowhere. Or perhaps the GPS was playing hide-and-go-seek with them? It happened. Voyle was becoming convinced the second option was the correct one.

Considine stepped ahead to the edge of the copse. She didn't look too happy. He wanted to ask her what she was up to, but didn't, convinced she would tell him to fuck off. Which she probably would. He stood there watching her instead as she pushed apart branches, wondering again what the hell she was up to, and where the hell they were right now... and, more importantly, where the hell they should be.

He looked briefly away, and when he looked back, Considine was gone. 'Considine, where are you?' he called out, but there was no reply. What the...? It was if she had been swallowed up by the trees.

She heard him. 'Considine, where are you?'

Pathetic. Voyle had really started to irritate her, just by breathing, usually, but now by standing out there, his mouth open, catching flies and looking gormless. But it did seem the location was wrong: this place couldn't have a postcode, could it? If it did, then God's answer to all women had taken it down wrong. One or the other, had to be. *Gobshite.* The man couldn't do the small detail. Probably thought it was beneath him. It followed, if you couldn't get the small detail right, then you couldn't get the big detail right either. Or something like that.

She didn't want to give up just yet though.

Shit.

A thorn caught the sleeve of her soft-shell jacket, tore a strip open just above the cuff.

How the feck did I get landed with this? With him? Jesus. What did I do to deserve it, oh Lord?

She lowered her head and pushed through the copse. A bloody jungle, that was what it was. She came out on the other side, stood in a narrow clearing. Ahead she could make out a wall of bramble.

Well, yes, this was a waste of time. A complete waste of time. The wall of bramble seemed impenetrable.

I give up.

But then she noticed something. Not bramble. No, ivy. Through it she caught glimpses of something... a grey wall reflecting the light? She looked up, saw a corrugated asbestos roof, and above that, a chimney stack, and above that again, two chimney pots silhouetted against the sky.

'Voyle, get in here.' When she got no answer, she shouted, even louder, 'Voyle, I said get in here. Now.'

'Hello.'

She jumped. And spun around.

There he was, behind her, or, as he actually was now, in front of her.

'How the...?'

'Did I get in here?'

'Yes.'

He gave her a self-satisfied grin. She hated that about him, so up his own arse. Really. But Considine failed to realise that men like him usually weren't really – up their own arse, that is. They were compensating. For whatever.

'I came round, of course.' He pointed as she heard a clicking sound, a funnel of light following that cut through the air. Voyle had brought his flashlight. 'See there, that gable' – he swung the light in its direction – 'and that one' – swinging it to the other – 'both clear. And see' – to the trees now – 'a convex shape. Meaning the roots are concentrated, this ground is the only fertile patch around, so they cluster here. Downy birches, they favour the wet and the sun.' He swung onto a bank of heather. 'They need sunshine too and acidic soil, and right here they are getting both. So I knew there had to be open ground where the–'

'Spare me the nature class, Voyle. I get it.'

She realised she'd made the mistake of underestimating the man. Voyle might be a lot of things, and he was, but to not give him credit for some of the very good things he was, too, was a failure on her part. Because Voyle was a consummate outdoorsman. It might not be immediately obvious by looking at him: medium build, fair hair, piercing blue eyes, smooth skin, a similarity to a certain American A-lister movie star with the first name of Brad. Voyle might appear as a cosseted urbanite, someone who'd be completely lost if he strayed too far from his nearest Starbucks or gym. Which was Voyle too, but he also was a sublime rock climber, never more at home than when out in the wilderness. His holidays were spent travelling the world in search of such places, his body the closest to teak hard you could get without it being the actual wood itself. And he'd had the foresight to bring his torch.

He beckoned her with an index finger and turned, walking away. She followed. He led her round to the other side of the house. A cottage, she could see that now, facing the sea, standing on a narrow wedge of headland. A pristine wilderness landscape, silent but for the sound of the wind and the distant lapping of the water. Somewhere, a curlew made its distinctive call, beautiful and increasingly rare.

But there was something else. This side of the cottage was devoid of ivy or anything else, its walls, instead, bare and grey. She stared at the boarded-up windows and the front door, thick planks of wood that looked like they'd been there a long time. And by the front door Voyle's torch picked up a set of fresh tyre tracks.

She and Voyle stared at one another and didn't speak. This, they hadn't expected. Not at all.

Voyle took out his phone and rang Marie Kennedy, the only person who might provide an answer.

'This place doesn't look like it's been lived in for years,' he said to her. 'Are we in the right place?'

'Well, I'm not there, Steve, so how would I know?'

That was something else that Steve Voyle had started noticing about Marie Kennedy the second time round. The first time round, like the incident at the airport, his need to satisfy his lust for this woman ensured that he was prepared to accept everything and anything and any excuse. His priorities back then were sex, sex, and more sex. But not now. This time round he could be more objective.

This time round he could see it. She was beginning to play him for a fool. And, as he thought about it, he asked himself, had she always taken him for a fool? Probably. But this time round was *he* beginning to fool himself too, because deep down did he still think he might have a chance with her?

'The postcode, Marie. You sure it's correct is what I mean? We're here; the place is boarded up. No one has been here in years. You couldn't possibly have stayed in this place.'

'It's the right postcode... tell you what, Steve?'

'Tell me what? Go on.'

'You take a photo and send it to me. Okay, sweetie?'

Sweetie. She hadn't called him that since, well, since last time, the very last time they'd been together, that is. When he'd booked into a swanky hotel that had cost him an entire week's wages for just that one night. In the morning she'd turned onto her belly when he'd tried to get frisky. Because she was angry, although Marie would never admit it. She'd always smile even if there was smoke billowing from her ears. She was angry because she'd wanted to go visit someplace or other and he'd had to return to the city. So she'd turned onto her belly to punish him for not putting her first, even before his job. He'd wanted her even more because of it. But in that moment he'd known he couldn't go on, not like this, with her subtle mind games, her, essentially, control of the bedroom and so too her control of him: the woman was driving him crazy – literally. That was the last time they'd been together. *Sweetie.*

Still, maybe there was a chance...

'Will do,' he said, 'and you have a number for the owner of this property? We need to contact them.'

'No. Donagh looked after that. I know nothing about it.'

'Stand by for the photograph,' he said and hung up.

He took a shot, handing the torch to Considine, who shone it on the building for extra light, and sent it, then rang her back.

'It's boarded up,' she said.

'Yes, I know, I just told you.'

'Okay, Steve, I know you just told me.'

'Is it the place, Marie?'

'Yes, it's the place, Steve.'

'You sure? How can you be? Wasn't it dark when you got here too?'

'Yes, it was dark. But you ever hear of headlights, Steve? It's the place.'

Voyle was silent; this was messed up.

'Right then,' he said.

'Right then? What's that mean, right then? What happens now, Steve?'

'That's a very good question, Marie.'

'Can you answer it?'

'To tell the truth, Marie, I've never come across anything like this before, so I don't rightly know.'

'Oh God,' she moaned, and hung up.

8

One hour. That was all it took. For Voyle to ring Brody. Who in turn rang Superintendent Ryan. Who in turn rang the commander of her old unit, Superintendent Tony Harper, of the KGB... oops, SDU. And Ryan then rang the Department of Foreign Affairs, where an official gave her the home telephone number for the department's most senior civil servant, Secretary General Oisin Naylor. He didn't sound so much perturbed as relieved to speak with her when she rang him at home, reason being that while he might be responsible for one of the most important branches of government, when his minister Donagh Hughes had failed to show up to the department that afternoon as scheduled, he hadn't known what to do, so he'd done nothing. Reason being, if it wasn't included in a directive or strategy report, that's what civil servants did. Since then he'd been waiting in a state of suspended animation, a rabbit caught in a headlamp, for something, anything, to show or tell him what to do.

It came with the phone call from Superintendent Ryan.

'Did you know he was having an affair?' She got straight to the point.

'I certainly did not.' Oisin Naylor was nothing if not a consummate fabricator of information, or liar, but no one at the department used that word, oh no.

'And that he'd been staying down country with his lover last night?'

'I certainly did not. I told you.'

She didn't believe him. Not a word. Not for a minute. She even felt sure the man knew what the Minister had for breakfast each morning.

'Okay then, where's his security detail?'

'I don't know.'

That, she could believe.

'Mr. Naylor?'

'Yes.'

'This isn't over, not by a long chalk. I'll be speaking with you again about this, and next time I won't be so polite. Next time I'll want answers.'

She hung up.

When the headlights came down the track and across the wedge of headland to the front of the house, Voyle wondered how the driver of what turned out to be an unmarked Ford Ranger 4x4 knew to come that way. The access route to the house wasn't visible from that direction. You had to know it was there.

There were four of them, two males and two females. All in plainclothes, faded blue jeans and windbreakers. So they might as well have been in uniform because they'd all dressed the same. Just as Considine herself always dressed, except her windbreaker had GARDA emblazoned across the back. Theirs had SDU. The SDU's remit was domestic security, and a government minister going AWOL topped that list.

Which suited Voyle just fine.

The one who started walking towards them looked like a larger version of an out-of-shape Conor McGregor, with a strut to match. His windbreaker was pulled back on one side, revealing a pistol in its holster attached to his belt.

'Voyle,' he said, a statement rather than a question, 'and Considine.'

To which they both nodded.

He pointed to Voyle. 'You. Come with me,' and, looking to one of his colleagues, 'Jen, can you go and talk to the female, please?'

Voyle followed him to the vehicle. 'In the back,' he said.

Voyle got in and sat on one of three parallel bench seats. 'I didn't get your name,' he said.

The man sat next to him; his breathing heavy, he smelled of stale tobacco. He reached up and turned on the roof light.

'That's because I didn't give it. You don't need to know my name. Now, I'll ask the questions.'

'Fuck off, then.'

The out-of-shape Conor McGregor leaned forward and for a moment showed no reaction. Then he said, 'What did you say?'

'You heard me.'

Voyle tensed. He was ready for an open hand or a fist. But none came.

'Okay. I heard you. Now, you hear me. You do as I say. You answer the questions I ask. Do you understand?'

'No. I'm not answering anything until you tell me who you are. Got that?'

McGregor seemed at a loss for what to do. He sat back again, rested his head against the headrest.

'Listen, Voyle, are you stupid?' His voice was calm, not a trace of anger, nothing, merely resigned. And Voyle came to a conclusion, McGregor here was burnt out like a campfire in the morning, reduced to nothing but a pile of ash. 'Well, are you? Have you got some kind of, I don't know, mental impediment? Well?'

'No. I'm all there, me.'

'Good to hear it. So just co-operate. If you do, I'll forget about how much of a bollocks you're being right now.'

'You tell me who you are, and then I might think about it.'

McGregor shifted about like he had an itchy arse before he settled again.

'Cheeky bastard,' he said, but he seemed to be thinking about it. 'Duffy, okay, Seamus, that's my name. I was going to tell you anyway.'

Voyle didn't believe him.

'Now you happy? And now I'm going to ask some questions, and you're going to answer them, yes? So we can move this thing along. Otherwise...'

'Yeah, otherwise what?' Voyle said.

'There you go again, asking the questions. I told you. I ask the questions. You didn't mention what she told you to anyone, now did you? I can't help but wonder why exactly that is.'

'Marie Kennedy?'

'No, the tooth fairy. Yes, of course. You know well what I mean. Marie Kennedy. Don't take me for an eejit, Voyle. What's going on?'

'Nothing's going on.'

'My patience is wearing thin, me lad. And just a reminder of who we're talking about here. We're talking about none other than Donagh fucking Hughes, only the Minister for Foreign Affairs. Well?'

'Because she told me not to tell anyone, that's why.'

'Oh, of course, she told you not to tell anyone. A big man like you. Yes, that would do it alright. She told you. And why? Why would she tell you not to mention it to anybody? He's missing. How's not telling anyone going to help? If you don't have something to do with this yourself, that is.'

'Hey. No. Don't go there, sunshine...'

Duffy smiled. 'Okay, but you'd think the same if you were sitting where I am.'

'I told her I'd have a look into it, that's all. She didn't want it getting out. She thought he might have run home or something, I don't know. I was just looking into it, that's all, which is why I'm here. I wasn't even certain he was missing.'

'Maybe you told your sergeant, Brody, about it a lot earlier than you're letting on too? Maybe you were both keeping it in your bellies.'

Voyle opened his mouth and held it that way for a moment. Then he closed it again. He knew how it must look. What was he to do now? Tell them he'd told Brody and so implicate his boss. No, he couldn't and wouldn't do that.

'I told no one.'

'Of course you didn't.' Duffy looked like a fox circling a rabbits' burrow. 'No, of course you didn't. You told no one. You're on thin ice, me lad. This was all your little secret, was it?'

'It wasn't a secret. Once I found out who this person was, then I went straight to my boss, Detective Sergeant Jack Brody, with it. I just told you. And he in turn went to his boss, Superintendent Ryan.'

'Oh, suddenly found your tongue, have you, Voyle? I know all that anyway. That's old news, Voyle, Jesus. But in the beginning, when God made man, that's what I'm interested in. When Marie Kennedy *first* told you, there was a delay, a time lag, that's the bit I want to know about. Why did you delay, Voyle, why? Tell me.'

'I didn't,' he lied again. 'I just told you, when I found out, I went straight to Brody with the information. Aren't you listening? It was only a couple of hours.'

Duffy gave a smile, a self-satisfied, lopsided smile.

'Nah, nah, Voyle, you lying little toerag, you didn't. That's where you're wrong. Come on now, the hole is big enough to swallow you and all your bullshite whole without digging any deeper.'

Voyle laughed.

'What's so funny?' Duffy snapped.

'You wouldn't get it. I didn't delay, that's all. I told you.'

'But you just admitted that you did until you confirmed the person's identity.'

'Well, yeah... but I mean... then I went straight to Jack. Like I just said, I told you.'

'Yeah, yeah, you told me; you're twisting your shite, aren't you?'

'I'm not.'

'It doesn't matter, Voyle, because a little birdie told me. Told me everything.'

'A little birdie? What'd you mean, a little birdie?'

But Voyle already knew. And Duffy knew he knew. Because it couldn't be anyone else.

'A very pretty little birdie, in fact. You'd agree with me there, wouldn't you? Marie Kennedy, she is very pretty, isn't she? We've brought her in for questioning, you know.'

'She's lying,' Voyle said, because he could think of nothing else, knowing he was so far down in the hole he'd almost disappeared.

Now it was Duffy's turn to laugh.

'Textbook, Voyle. You, of all people, should know better. Come on. That's exactly what I'd expect some gouger to say. I'm getting fed up with this, I really am. If it walks like a duck and quacks like a duck, then it can only be a...'

He let that hang in the air, and stared at Voyle, who stared back, and finally threw away the shovel and stopped digging.

9

Jack Brody had managed to push everything from his mind. And in this job that was important. Otherwise, the pressure cooker would be forever sitting on a naked flame, the steam inexorably building. And there could only ever be one outcome to that. Tonight he had a date with Ashling, an evening they'd arranged weeks before. He couldn't let her down. In any case, Harper was making it known he was taking charge, the MCIU being consigned to the back seat.

In any case, now Brody's mind was empty, and he didn't have to punch the heavy to get it that way.

She sat across from him, looking beautiful and also something else... This evening she exuded a raw sexuality that literally caused his pulse to quicken, sending blood rushing to his head, making him feel fuzzy. Her breasts were on display, full and firm, cupped inside a tight, low-cut dress hung from her shoulders on spaghetti straps, her hair gathered in a bun, sitting above her long, slender neck, two wisps curling down on either side about her ears. Brody felt awestruck, not just because of how she looked, but because of how she looked for him.

Wow.

'You're very quiet.' She picked up her wine glass in one slender hand, the nails perfectly manicured and painted crimson.

Brody felt like a shipwreck survivor who had come ashore on a beautiful, bountiful, sun-drenched island. Here he had found everything he had ever wanted. A paradise. But he couldn't help but think, even the most beautiful of tropical islands experienced the most devastating of storms.

A phone rang, interrupting his thoughts.

In the near silence of the bar of the Oliver Theatre, where everyone spoke in hushed tones, it was an unwritten rule that mobile phones were always to be turned off, even in the bar, even, like now, during an intermission of the performance. Ashling Nolan was a regular and had hers off. Brody wasn't and had forgotten. Now it was his turn to feel as Voyle had felt earlier that day at the Old Man's memorial service. Had it really been only this morning? It seemed such a long time ago already.

From the softly lit booths and tables, patrons turned and frowned at Brody's faux pas. And Brody, used to dealing with the unexpected, quickly reached into his pocket and turned the phone off, just as Voyle had done at the funeral, acting as if nothing had happened.

But Ashling Nolan looked at him, a look he'd never seen before, both angry and sultry at the same time.

'I'm really sorry,' he said. 'I'd forgotten.'

'I noticed.'

She sat back and folded her arms.

'It's only a phone call. I'm sorry.'

'It's art, Jack. Don't you get it?'

'I do. The expression of love against the backdrop of the

brutality of war, the eternal search for meaning and the ultimate triumph... I get it.'

'It sounds like a synopsis.'

'It is the synopsis.'

'You read that in the programme?'

'Of course...'

She laughed, unfolding her arms.

'I'm sorry,' he said, 'but I need to ring back whoever just called. I won't be a minute.'

Her head nodded on its long, slender neck, but her arms crossed themselves again.

'Take as long as you need, Jack.' As if to say, *Don't bother coming back.*

He was tempted not to return the call until later, but he knew he couldn't do that. He wondered how long her patience would last with him. For someone like Ashling, he thought, not very long. She might be the best thing to have happened in his life since falling in love with Caoimhe. He didn't know what the future held, but he wanted to find out. He wanted to give this relationship at least the chance to breathe. He didn't want it to shrivel and die before it even had a chance to live. So no, he couldn't leave.

Still, he got up and walked out into the foyer, pressed redial, and put the phone to his ear.

A voice he didn't recognise said, 'Jack Brody?'

'Yes, that's me, Jack Brody.'

'We've been trying to contact you. Where've you been?'

'Where've I been?'

'I just asked you that.'

'What business is it of yours? And who is this, please?'

'SDU, Seamus Duffy, Special Detective Unit. Everything's our business.'

Brody wanted to laugh. The man sounded like a detective in a 1950s B movie.

'And…?'

'We have your man Steven Voyle here with us.'

'And?'

'Nicola Considine. Her too. I need your co-operation. Listen up.'

10

Secrecy is the same as lying, or little different to it. By its essence, it is something that can't be mentioned. Because that's what makes it a secret in the first place. So, also by its essence, in a way it is something that doesn't exist, yet does at the same time too. And in order to cover it up, the secret, or to make certain – or at least as certain as can be – that it remains just that, a secret, it is often necessary to lie. And in order to lie, or to successfully lie, that is, you must first make sure to have a good memory. But even then, if you have a good memory, even a great memory, the greater the secret, or the longer it must be maintained, whichever, then the greater the lies and the memory required to sustain it. Lies and secrets go together, like a hand in a glove, yet neither can last forever. Because a lie always breeds another lie, and another, and another, and so on in a self-perpetuating cycle until eventually the reason for the lie is either forgotten about or obscured, or both. Either way, it never ends well and is only a matter of time before the whole sordid edifice comes tumbling down. Secrets and lies, Brody thought, always ended in a mess.

Which was how he felt sure this would all end up too. The co-operation that Duffy demanded was an agreement to keep the matter a secret, as initially Voyle had done, to maintain the silence, to become the keeper of secrets. And this secret could not be, must not be revealed. At least, he assured Brody, for forty-eight hours, that is. That would buy enough time. Duffy said he did not trust Voyle and wanted him kept at an arm's distance from the investigation, but not so far that he couldn't keep an eye on him either. Which was why Voyle and Considine were sitting in their car out front of the cottage where Donagh Hughes had gone missing, as Duffy had requested them to. Had Brody any suggestions? He had.

He rang Voyle as soon as he'd finished talking with Duffy, who answered before the first ringtone had completely sounded out.

'Listen up, Steve, the Robert Gilsenan suicide.'

'What about it?'

'It's why you're down there, after all. Get to it.'

'Boss, they're not letting us out of their sight down here. It's like they think we'd something to do with it.'

Considine piped up in the background, 'Less of the *we*, Voyle. This has nothing to do with me, remember.'

'I spoke with Duffy just now,' Brody said. 'It's cleared.'

'It is? But I don't think I can. To tell the truth, boss, I don't feel very motivated.'

'Go home and get some rest,' Brody said, 'and get motivated.'

Voyle pulled the phone from his ear, glanced over at Considine, who was staring ahead into the gathering darkness, arms folded. Not happy. He shrugged. She turned the key in the ignition, fired the engine to life. Just as she was about to move off, there was a tap on the front passenger window. He turned, saw Duffy standing outside.

'No goodbyes?' Duffy smirked as Voyle lowered the window.

'We're already way behind on another case; do you mind?'

'Robert Gilsenan, right? I know that, and I'm way ahead of you.' He nodded to Considine. 'Of both of you. A waste of time, by the way. Ryan just wants to get rid of you, you know that, don't you? Well, off you go. Drive safely.'

'Bastard,' Voyle muttered as Considine spun the wheels, and the car lurched forward. She said nothing. He could almost taste the thick stew she was wallowing in. 'Christ, are you going to stay like this forever? Nicola, come on.'

She took a breath, glanced over to him, then back to the track ahead.

'I really should have fucking called in sick.'

ASHLING NOLAN LINKED BRODY'S arm as they left the auditorium. He liked that and liked the way she leaned in close so he could bathe in her aroma. They walked along the corridor towards the foyer, but just before they reached it, she pulled him into a darkened alcove, leaned in close, pushing him into a corner. Her lips found his and pressed in. He responded, looking over her shoulder at the patrons passing by outside.

He felt her hand move down his chest and hover just above his crotch.

He froze.

'What's the matter, Jack?'

'Nothing.'

Her hand moved lower.

'Well,' he said, '... um...' but his voice trailed off.

An elderly couple stopped outside, the gentleman beginning to search his pockets for something, then moved off again. Jack released his breath with a low *pufft* sound.

Ashling threw her head back and laughed, reached for his hand, and pulled him out of the alcove.

'It's all about freedom,' she said, leading the way as they walked towards the foyer, 'the freedom that comes from knowing somebody, from trusting them, you know what I mean?' She stopped and looked at him, her beautiful green eyes with their flecks of yellow catching the light as they searched his. 'I love that idea. It's not easy to find, you know. So forgive my silliness, Jack, but I trust you, that's all, and I was enjoying a bit of that freedom just now...'

They passed out of the foyer and stood on the pavement in the cold, clear night air.

'Now...?' he asked.

Ashling wasn't wearing a coat. He thought she looked like an exotic bird that had just landed amongst an overwintering, heavily fleeced, dowdy-looking flock.

'Now. Can we get a taxi and go home to my place?'

She walked to the kerb and raised her arm, signalling to an approaching cab. Jack hurried to catch up, his mind starting to summersault with a thousand thoughts – and loving every one of them. He felt like a giddy teenager all over again.

Voyle got home just before midnight. He didn't drink alcohol much; his lifestyle didn't allow it. But he felt he needed something now to soften the edges of his pissed-offness. He'd rummaged in the bottom of the fridge and found two 330 ml bottles of Carlsberg, polished the first one off in two swallows, was now sipping the second, feeling the beginnings of a warm, soothing glow start to go through him.

He lived in Dun Laoghaire, in a quaint Victorian terraced house that faced the sea. It had belonged to a bachelor uncle of his whom Voyle had no idea held any particular fondness for him until he'd died and left him everything, this house and a tidy sum of cash. At the time he'd been renting an apartment in a grotty section of the East Wall. That was eight years ago now, and not a day went by that he didn't thank his lucky stars and dear old uncle Rory.

He stood in the darkened living room, looking out the window across the road to the Irish Sea beyond, pinpricks of light on it from passing ships. He'd rather climb K9 in his bare feet than feel the shitty way he did right now. He was the outcast. He thought of Paul Quinn, the officer recently on secondment from the fraud squad who'd fucked up an arrest and nearly gotten both himself and Considine killed. The unit had turned against him because of it, ostracised him, as had Voyle himself. Now he knew what that was like. No, not a nice feeling, not a nice feeling at all. And for what? What had he done wrong? Nothing, that's what, except to be disliked by the new skipper – a bloody woman, for God's sake. Any troubles Voyle had had in this life were all caused by women.

Shite.

Who gave a fuck anyway? He turned and walked over to the dining room table, placed the half-empty bottle of beer down onto it. *I'm Steve Voyle. I can climb a sheer rock face without a safety harness, have a black belt in karate,* and *a heartbeat resting rate of a mere twenty beats a minute. Beat that!*

So the new boss has it in for me?

Fine.

Because she's a woman, isn't she?

That explained everything.

He climbed the stairs to bed. Superintendent Ryan had sent him on a fool's errand with this Robert Gilsenan suicide thing. That was fine too.

Yea, though I walk through the valley of the shadow of death, I will fear no evil.

I'll survive, Voyle thought. *Yes, I'll survive. I always do.*

Tonight, every Garda squad car in the entire country was prowling the streets, the alleyways, the back roads. Everywhere. Those quiet, dark nooks where the officers often pulled into for some shut-eye, all off-limits now. Everyone was out, on the streets, whatever. The word was that the local supers were about, a rumour often spread by night sergeants anyway – especially on major sporting weekends, to keep everyone on their toes. But no one paid any attention. It's impossible, after all, to lie to a room full of mules.

Except for tonight, that is.

Tonight was different.

Tonight it was possible. Because it wasn't a lie.

11

The morning light smudged through the curtains. Brody was dreaming, snoring gently. Dreaming of a woman with shoulder-length auburn hair and big, beautiful eyes, that he was lying next to her, that they were both naked, covered by nothing more than a thin, pink sheet. He was dreaming they'd fallen asleep having made love, where she'd dominated, orchestrating each movement, the tempo rising and falling, building from a pianissimo to an allegro and back again, sweeping him along, lost to everything but the sheer, exhilarating passionate intensity of it all.

Then he opened his eyes and realised he had not been dreaming. No. That everything was real. She was real: Ashling Nolan was sleeping next to him, her chest rising and falling with a gentle rhythm, her auburn hair splashed against the white pillowcase.

Opposite the bed was a bay window filled by grey, rippled clouds. The window seemed out of proportion to the small apartment. It was Jack's second time here. Ashling never bothered with pulling the blinds. She said she liked to wake up to the sight of the sky filling the window like a huge painting. The apartment was on the second floor, a typical example of overpriced, open-plan Dublin living. Yet Ashling had made the most of it, making the small space cosy and her own. He liked that. Next to the door rested her blue mountain bike, the helmet hanging from a loop on the handlebar.

He sat up onto his elbow, peering down on her. He thought her face seemed fresher, younger than he'd noticed before. He realised again he still didn't know very much about this woman... like, what age was she? He'd assumed mid-thirties. But now, looking at her as she slept, he wasn't so sure; she seemed younger.

She opened her eyes and smiled, reached out and cupped her hand onto the back of his neck, pulling him down to her, kissing his lips softly.

'What?' she whispered. 'You were looking at me oddly.'

'Was I?'

She kissed him again. 'Hm... Yes, you were. What were you thinking?'

'What was I thinking? That I want to know everything about you.'

'That's nice.'

'That you seemed so young lying there, with your eyes closed.'

She laughed.

'Really. Young? Is that important to you?'

'It's not. You just looked so... well, young, that's all.'

'I am young, Jack. But everything is relative. As my mother used to say, "Beware the young doctor and the old barber." I'm forty-one. There. I don't make any secret of it. Why would I? You want some breakfast?'

'Don't you want to know my age?'

'I couldn't care less.'

She jumped out of bed and pulled on a robe.

'Breakfast? Scrambled eggs? That alright by you?'

'Of course.'

'Right then.'

She walked from the bedroom area, across the wooden floor with its big rug in the centre, a sunburst of colours, over to the kitchen area. Had he detected… something in her tone?

'Ashling.'

She stopped and turned.

'Really, I was just curious, that's all. I don't care either way. It's nothing.'

She shrugged. 'Why mention it, then?'

'But…'

He closed his mouth.

Shit, he thought.

He heard a telephone ring, the sound coming from his trousers draped over the back of a chair near the bed. He stretched and grabbed them, took the phone from a pocket, pressed it to his ear. Before he could speak, Superintendent Ryan's voice sounded at the other end. 'Sergeant Brody, my office, half an hour.'

She hung up, and Jack dropped the phone onto the bed, looked across the room, and was silent for a moment. 'Ashling,' he said then, 'I'm really…'

'Let me guess. You've got to go.'

'I'm sorry.'

'Don't be. It's fine. I understand.' She replaced the two eggs she'd just removed back into the carton.

Jack jumped out of bed. 'Listen, I need to get back to my house to shower and change.' He pulled his trousers on and crossed to her, held her lightly by the shoulders as she scrambled eggs in a saucepan. He kissed the back of her neck. 'I'll call you later.'

'Whatever,' she said, not turning.

12

Superintendent Tony Harper, commander of the Special Detective Unit, was sitting at one end of the Old Man's old desk, now Superintendent Ryan's desk, when Brody went in. At least he wasn't sitting behind it – yet, that is. Ryan still occupied that position, a position that might depend on how she handled proceedings, he supposed. They both silently looked at Brody as he came through the office door. Harper was slight of build with a naturally sallow complexion, wearing a perfectly laundered shirt, with crisp lines along the sleeves and down the front, cutting through the very centre of the pockets as per the strictest interpretation of the dress code. But he didn't look like a police officer, he looked more like a holiday rep, which might give rise to the impression that he was more fluff than earnestness. A grave error to make, Brody knew.

Right now, his naturally smiling face – like a holiday rep's – wasn't smiling. Neither was Ryan's. But Harper's definitely had the edge on hers. Brody probably didn't look too happy either. He concentrated on Harper, who rubbed an index finger against the corner of his eye and looked at it, then looked at Brody.

'What's this Voyle fella like?'

'What, is that why you brought me in here?'

'I didn't bring you in here.'

'No.'

'*I* brought you in here.' It was Ryan.

Brody glanced to her, wondering what this was about. Even in the middle of an important investigation, it seemed like these two were playing games. Ryan held his eyes for barely a second before looking away.

'You know him better than I do,' she said. 'The personnel file doesn't give any light and shade.'

Light and shade? What was she, a police officer or an artist? Of course, she could be both.

'He can be a pain in the arse at times, if I'm honest, but he's, as they say, diligent and hardworking.'

'Is he indeed?' Harper said, and repeated it, 'Is he indeed?' like he needed convincing.

'Yes,' Brody said, 'overall he is.'

'Overall, hm... So you trust him?'

'Yes, I trust him.'

'Fiona's not so sure. She doesn't trust him. Do you, Fiona?'

Fiona looked like she suddenly had a nail in her shoe.

Brody glanced at her again.

'Well... I don't know him very well, do I?'

Nice one, Brody thought, *return serve.*

'It's more an instinct,' she muttered, applying a dab of blowback repellent.

'You're wasting your time,' Brody said. 'Voyle has nothing to do with any of this.'

'How so certain? You might be wrong. Everyone can be wrong.'

'Well, you'll only waste time in trying to prove it.'

'No,' Harper said, 'not me.' He uncapped his blowback repellent too, nodded to Brody. 'You,' and began to spray it all over. 'I want Nicola Considine to keep an eye on him, to report back anything; if he acts in any way suspicious, I want to know about it. Tell her that. Do you understand?'

'That's ridiculous,' Brody said. It might be how the KGB operated, but not him.

'I beg your pardon?'

'I said that's ridiculous. And I won't do it.'

Harper looked from Brody to Ryan – to *Fiona* – and back again.

'I want it done,' Harper said. 'Tell him, Fiona.'

'He has no jurisdiction,' Brody said to Ryan, 'tell *him*.'

But he knew immediately by her expression that she wouldn't be telling him anything. And he knew the reasons why.

'I do have jurisdiction,' Harper said, 'bestowed on me by none other than the commissioner himself. This is of national importance, Brody. Officially, it is now a joint operation between both our units. Soon, however, the commissioner himself could be in charge, depending on progress made, that is. This has gone all the way to the top.'

Brody was silent. It was no use. He nodded.

'But I want it noted. I'm not happy with it.'

'Duly noted, if that keeps you happy.'

'It does.'

Brody, however, had no intention of going along with any of it. Bollocks to the KGB.

'By the way,' Brody said, 'who the hell is running this investigation?' He nodded to Ryan. 'Is it you,' and nodding to Harper, 'or him?'

'You're pushing it, my lad,' Harper said.

Ryan stood.

'We're going to Dublin Castle,' she said to Brody. 'That's why I rang.'

He saw a look pass between her and Harper. And he felt he had his answer. Harper was the show master, Superintendent Ryan merely the puppet.

Jack got to his feet. The quicker he got out of this office, the better.

13

The scream of sirens stabbed across the cobbled stone courtyard of Dublin Castle, where member of parliament Kevin Mahon stood waiting to greet the visiting European foreign ministers. They were gathering for a foreign ministers' conference on climate change. Donagh Hughes's deputy worried what the dignitaries would make of his boss's absence. But then again, as Chuck Spalding, the US Foreign Secretary, liked to say, "Shite happens, dude." Mahon smiled. Yes, even foreign ministers suffered bad doses of food poisoning from time to time; they got the heebie-jeebies too, in this case scallops the night before that were way past their sell-by date. That was the official line. An official line he hoped would be believed. Of course, he told himself, it would be believed if he acted like he himself believed it: *Yes, I believe it, I believe it, a bad dose indeed, but he didn't need the hospital, thank God. He'll be right as rain in the morning; yes, he will. I believe it, I do, I do, I do...*

Oh God.

As the approaching cacophony grew louder, so did his anxiety levels. He turned to the senior departmental officials gathered round him, all briefed on the crisis, and said in a grave tone, 'Don't get into any personal stuff about the Minister, keep it strictly business, that way we're all singing from the same hymn sheet, and there'll be no miscommunication. Got it?'

They nodded. They got it. But he noted that they looked just like how he felt.

'And for God's sake, try not to make it seem like the plane you're on is about to go down in a ball of flames.' A remark aimed at himself as much as anybody else.

He was pleased it drew a nervous chuckle from the civil servants.

Two Garda motorcycle outriders sped through the gates, leaning low as they turned into the courtyard. Behind them, the tyres of an unmarked BMW X5, its blue grille lights flashing, made a fast drumbeat sound on the cobblestones. The Mercedes 500 with the German delegation followed. Fifteen minutes later the entire caravan had arrived and parked up, making Dublin Castle's courtyard appear like an exhibition centre for the German luxury car industry.

Mahon was an old hand politician, a quarter of a century of experience under his belt. He knew once he pressed the flesh of the first hand, he was off to the races. And he was. He fell into his role, moving easily among the foreign ministers, the civil servants and the entourages of journalists. He was relieved no one seemed to make a fuss of the fact that Hughes was missing. Shite happened, dude. It wasn't that unusual.

Then he spotted her, the one person here who made him feel like a randy schoolboy. Isabella Hernadez, the Spanish Foreign Secretary, oozed everything in a woman that Mahon craved. She was the kind of woman who came top of his checklist of the perfect female, and it took all of his tact not to let her know it. The waft of her perfume stirred something in him, and he lingered a fraction longer than he should have after he'd kissed her on both cheeks, his hand gently resting on an elbow.

As his eyes followed her as she passed into the castle at the head of her delegation, he heard someone call his name.

He turned; a man and woman were standing there; he could tell by their appearance and demeanour that they didn't belong to any governmental party or press crew that was here tonight. And behind them he spotted Max Slitz, the Austrian Foreign Minister, getting out of his car and starting to walk towards him in that distinctive gait of his, like a slow march.

One of them spoke; it was the woman. She had hard – very hard – close-set eyes and seemed uneasy.

'I'm Superintendent Fiona Ryan, Mr Mahon, and this is Detective Sergeant Jack Brody. We need to have a word, sir. I've been trying to get a hold of someone who can answer some questions. It's proving very difficult. We were left with no choice but to come down here.'

'W-what? A word? Now?' He was perplexed. 'You mean here? Do you know where you are exactly? This is a gathering of the Council of European Foreign Ministers. Are you aware of that? You can't just waltz in here and...'

'Yes, sir, I'm aware of all that. But I don't have time for formalities. And we didn't have a choice. This is an emergency, of national importance. Now, where can we talk? This won't take long.'

He was about to insist that they leave, and who did they think they were? Because such an approach usually worked. But it wouldn't work now; he knew that too. Max Slitz was drawing close. Shit.

'Please, please.' He nodded towards the colonnade that surrounded the yard, scrambling to move them quickly out of the way before the Austrians reached them. In the background, he heard the Department Secretary start to speak to

Max Slitz. 'Your Excellency, how lovely to see you again...' as if taking the place of the deputy foreign minister, and so, by definition, the Minister himself, was the most natural thing in the world for him. *Your Excellency* indeed. He'd have to watch that bastard.

In the shadows of the colonnade, Mahon returned to his street politician roots. He jabbed a finger towards Brody and Ryan. 'What the fuck are you playing at here? I can't believe this. Coming here, two big-foot plodders. I'll be speaking with the justice minister, don't you worry...'

Brody raised his hand and made a sweeping gesture with it through the air, almost, but not quite, touching the politician's finger. It had the desired effect. The finger fell away. Ryan took a half step back. Brody knew why. Now that she'd stated the reason for their visit and had made the introduction, she was reverting to type. Because the default setting among senior officers was to treat politicians with reverence. They wanted to be their friends, not their adversaries. Brody wondered why the hell she had bothered to come along. However, he felt he knew the answer to that. She was trying to play both sides of the fence, that was why. She was always thinking one step ahead to the next promotional board interview. He felt himself bristle.

'Speak to who you want, Mr Mahon,' Brody said, angry at Ryan, and angry at how things had gone earlier with Ashling, a little steam building in the pressure cooker. He knew that wasn't good. No. He thought of the heavy bag, clenched his fists and released them again, wanting nothing more than to send in a flurry. 'Look,' he said, 'the quicker you talk to us, the quicker we'll be out of the way. Now listen up.'

He saw out of the corner of his eye Superintendent Ryan shift from one foot to the other.

'Did you know that Donagh Hughes was having an

affair?' It was Ryan, stirring in a little authority, her tone flat, almost apologetic.

Mahon's brow furrowed the way Brody had seen it do countless times before on numerous TV political and current affairs shows as he looked at Ryan.

'Straight answer will do,' Brody said, keeping a reasonably hard edge to the proceedings. 'You shouldn't need to think about it.'

'You.' Mahon pointed a finger at him again suddenly. 'I don't like your tone, sonny Jim. Who are you, anyway? Brody, is it? A *sergeant*? And you' – turning the finger to Ryan – 'are a superintendent. Are you going to let him speak to me in this way, well?'

'If you could answer the questions, please, sir, we'll be on our way.'

Christ, Brody thought, *why don't you just ask him to drop his pants and bend over so you can properly lick his arse?*

Mahon looked ahead. The Polish Foreign Minister, Jodki Kokzow, was climbing out of his car.

'I really need to get a move on. Look, it's not against the law' – his tone somewhat contrite now – 'to your question about him having an affair, that is. Yes is the answer. Yes, I did know. So?'

'Fine. Next question. His security detail. Where are they? I presume they're here.'

'His security detail?'

'Yes. Security detail. Again, you shouldn't have to think about it.'

'Well, how the hell should I know? I don't deal with any of that. Now, I really need to get back. There are protocols to be observed. There is no circumstance under which you can just barge in here the way you have.'

'The security detail,' Brody pressed, 'we're not leaving until we speak to them. We'll stay right here.'

'Christ, didn't you hear me? I told you, it's nothing to do with me. You need to speak with the department responsible. I can't help you, especially not now.'

'Fine, Mr Mahon. But can you imagine how it'll look if we don't find Minister Hughes? And it subsequently transpires we spoke with you, and you were as much help as tits on a bull.'

'W-what did you just say? How dare you. I want to help; you've just caught me at a very inopportune time…' He was facing the courtyard, and he craned his neck, swung his head from side to side, muttering, 'Let me see, let me see. No, I don't see anyone,' then louder, 'Oh, yes I do. Garda Niall Moore' – he raised a hand and pointed – 'right there, see. I think he's one of them, the security detail, but I'm not sure.'

Ryan's and Brody's gazes followed his outstretched arm. The man being pointed to had a radio piece in one ear, and he spotted them immediately. A moment later he was standing before them. He was short and stocky, wearing a smart, navy-blue suit.

'A word,' Ryan said. 'Are you Garda Niall Moore, Minister Hughes's security detail?'

The man nodded. 'One of them.'

'Then I can go?' Mahon said. 'That alright by you?'

'Yes, of course.' It was Ryan. 'That's fine by me. Thank you for your co-operation.'

Yeah, right, Brody thought.

'Where is Donagh Hughes?' Ryan asked the officer, her tone lacking the sweet syrup she'd used on Mahon.

'I don't know.'

'You're the one looking after him.'

'No, I'm not. I'm just his glorified driver. He told me he didn't need me when I last saw him. It happens all the time. What was I to do? He's done this before, plenty of times. Goes off whenever he feels like it. But he always comes back.'

'Except he didn't come back this time.'

'I know.'

'Doesn't that worry you? Did you tell anyone?'

Ryan was on a roll.

'I was waiting for his phone call. I'm still waiting. I think I'll get it. I always got it in the past. You don't know what he's like. One time he disappeared for three whole days. I'm only doing my job. If I don't do it his way, it's the highway. That's just how Hughes works; he's his own man... By the way, I'm not saying anything else.'

'Fine, you can discuss it at the inquiry, then.'

'The inquiry?'

'Of course. That's what they do in cases like this. They hold an inquiry. How was it possible the Minister for Foreign Affairs went missing the way he has? Heads will roll.'

'They will.'

'Everything will come out. It'll be all over the news. If you don't want to find yourself down in Kerry checking tax discs for the rest of your career, you'd better tell me everything you know. And tell me now.'

'But that's all I do know. Anyway, I don't owe him anything. He was a bit of a bollocks, to tell the truth, but it was a cushy gig, so I just kept my head down and did what I was told. Look, if there was something else to tell you, I would tell you. But there's not. And that's the truth.'

'Did you know he was having an affair?'

'An affair? So? Most of them are having affairs. Did you think it was some kind of big secret?'

'Well, did you know?'

'Yes, of course. But only like I know there's a train to Galway. I just don't know the times, that's all. Same here, with his shenanigans. I don't know the details, and I don't want to know. He's been known to go on the odd bender. That's my bet. He's holed up somewhere, sleeping it off... you don't look like you believe me, but that's true. Like, remember years ago, on a stopover at Shannon, Boris Yeltsin, you remember, the Russian fella? Never made it out of his plane; all the VIPs were lined up on the tarmac, waiting for him. I was there. This is the same thing, in a roundabout way. Although Hughes has always been careful to pick a time and a place. There's nothing else I can tell you.' He indicated with a nod of his head. 'I'm driving the deputy. There's a bit of a backlog building up. I need to move along. Can I go? There's nothing else, and that's the truth.'

Brody considered that indeed it probably was the truth. He could imagine the relationship between Moore and his boss. Fundamentally, he had to go along to get along: chauffeur, gofer, security man, and whatever else his boss needed.

Ryan seemed to be of the same mind.

'You can go. We know where to find you if we need you.'

Moore walked away quickly without another word.

Brody watched him go. He had a bad feeling about this.

14

Voyle didn't know how to approach this Robert Gilsenan suicide thing. Get motivated, Brody had said, and he was trying to, he really was. As he'd already decided, this wasn't an investigation, it was a fool's errand. And it wasn't easy to feel motivated when you no longer felt like you belonged.

To tell the truth, Voyle had always felt like he didn't belong. Anywhere. It was why he felt most comfortable when out in the wilds, or climbing a rock face, or camping out on a desolate mountainside. With just himself for company. It was at those times that he felt happiest. But since joining the MCIU, he'd always felt at home, even if Considine was like a sister from hell. At least he used to feel that way. Before the new super came along. Ryan had it in for him. Damn, could things not go back to the way they were? When the Old Man was here. At that moment Voyle felt an almost overwhelming sense of love for his old commander. He wanted to cry. At least he still had Brody, who was like an older brother, although he'd never tell him that. And Marty Sheahan, who was like a younger brother. He wouldn't tell him that either.

Voyle didn't do emotions too well: rephrase, he didn't do emotions at all, full stop.

So why couldn't he feel the same about Considine? He just couldn't. That was mostly down to him. He knew that.

They had both spent the morning in the unit room at the Phoenix Park, feeling like strangers in their own home, because the SDU had taken over, even pulling in some spare desks, and ignoring everybody who wasn't a member of their own team. He realised this was not a joint operation like it was supposed to be. This was strictly SDU. Voyle began to think it was probably for the best that he had been banished to the wastelands. But what of Considine? Why had she been banished to the wastelands along with him too?

He had no answer for that.

He decided to forget it all by reading up on Gilsenan, a man who'd had the world in the palms of his hands before he'd chosen to crush it.

Or had he, chosen to crush it, that is.

It didn't make sense to Voyle.

At half eleven, Considine walked across the unit room to him and said, 'Can we get out of here, please?'

He smiled, and she looked back at him in bewilderment.

'What? Why you smiling at me like that?'

'Can't a fella smile at you if he wants to?'

'Most men who smile at me are pervs, Voyle.'

'Well, I'm not a perv. Perfect timing, that's all.'

'It is?'

'I just realised what I need to do with this Robert Gilsenan thing.'

'And...?'

'I need to start at the beginning, that's what. The very beginning.'

He got to his feet and began pulling on his jacket. 'You coming?'

Now it was Considine's turn to smile. 'I never thought I'd say this, to you, that is, Voyle, but yes, I'm coming. Even to the gates of hell, I'm coming. If it gets me out of here, that is.'

As they left the unit room, no one noticed. It was as if they were leaving the waiting room at a bus station.

It was almost two o'clock by the time they pulled up outside the high gates of Ash Hall, where Gilsenan had lived and had died, it being both the beginning and the end.

'What do you want to get out of it? It's not a crime scene. What do you hope to a*chieve*, Voyle?'

'Achieve, how very corporate PowerPoint of you. I don't know.'

'Right, so you don't know.'

'No, I don't. This house is one of four Robert Gilsenan owned. He lived alone. The others are in Monaco, New York and Dubai. He spent a total of three months of the year here, not all together now, but interspersed over the twelve months, for tax purposes. He employed a household staff who travelled with him, usually, that is. But here it was slightly different. Here there was a caretaker couple. So...'

'Yes, you've been doing your homework.' Her voice just that little bit lighter, telling him that she was beginning to suffer him after all.

'Yes,' Voyle said, smiling, 'of course. Just like when you free dive off a cliff face, or parachute out of an aircraft, whatever. You have to do your homework first. I learnt that the hard way.'

'You did?'

'Yes, when I–'

'That's okay, Voyle. I don't really care. Continue with the story.'

He shrugged. 'Fine. But there isn't a story.' He opened the door. 'Someone might be home is what I'm saying. I checked. The caretaker couple should still be here. I don't think they will have had time to go anywhere else. I'm going to go and ring that bell in the gate pillar there and see what the craic is. That's what I'm saying; that's what I'm going to do.'

'Did you call ahead?'

'No.'

'Okay.'

Voyle sat there.

'Then just do it. Such a palaver. It's not like you're jumping out of a bloody airplane door now, is it? God.'

He got out of the car and strode over and pressed the bell, kept his finger on it way longer than was necessary, stopped, and was about to press it a second time when a voice came through a speaker somewhere in the top of the pillar.

'Please, there's no need to ring the bell like that. Who is this, and what do you want?'

'Sorry to disturb you, sir. I'm Detective Garda Steven Voyle; could I have a word?'

'You both gardai?'

'Yes.' Voyle knew that whoever this was was observing them. He looked about, trying to spot a camera, but couldn't. 'And that's Detective Garda Nicola Considine in the car,' he said.

'Sorry, but this is not a good time. Could you make an appointment for tomorrow, perhaps?'

'Can I have your name? I didn't catch it.'

'I beg your pardon.'

'Your name,' Voyle said, 'what is it?'

'Patrick O'Connor.'

'And you are? I mean, what's your role here?'

'I'm the...' he paused, 'caretaker.' A drop in octave with

that word, like he was uncomfortable using it, didn't like using it.

'I hope you won't make me insist,' Voyle said. 'I could, but on the other hand, you could just allow me in without having to do that. I mean, it would be much easier that way, wouldn't it?'

'What do you mean?'

'Just that it would be easier, that's all, Mr O'Connor. Without making phone calls, you know.'

'Oh... And you insist, do you?'

'I insist.'

There was silence for a moment.

'Fine then,' the caretaker said. 'I'll open the gates. Drive through. I'll meet you at the main door.'

'Thank you.'

As Voyle returned to the car, the gates began to silently glide open.

15

The driveway twisted its way across fields towards Ash Hall, grazing animals in them – horses mostly, seemed like – standing like cardboard cut-outs. The Hall itself was a vast, rambling, limestone affair, multitudes of chimney stacks and three rows of windows. What is referred to in Ireland as a *Big House*.

They parked on the gravel forecourt by the front door and got out, went up the stone steps, the door opening ahead of them before Voyle had a chance to press the bell or bang on the knocker. Standing there was a man, Voyle guessed mid-fifties, straight of stature, square chin jutting forward like a soldier on parade, dressed in black slacks, white shirt and grey tie and waistcoat. His shoes, Voyle noticed, polished like gleaming black snow. He gave off a sense of rigid formality, a strict observance to rules. In fact, a perfect butler. Voyle had never met a butler before.

'We just spoke on the entryphone,' he said. 'Patrick O'Connor. That right?'

'Mr O'Connor. Yes, that's right. Come in, please.'

Whatever, Voyle thought and stepped into the large hall

with its chequered black-and-white marble floor and huge chandelier hanging from a ceiling somewhere far above them. Considine followed. Opposite, a majestic staircase wound its way to the upper floors. Voyle could smell cigar smoke and wondered where it came from. Jeeves here? There was also the ever so slight sweet tang of liquor – whiskey if he was to make a guess.

Jeeves brought them into a living room, deep pile carpets, antique furniture, dark wood panelling, a giant stag's head, complete with enormous antlers hanging above a massive stone fireplace.

'A previous owner shot it up in the Scottish Highlands,' he said, noting Voyle's interest. 'Lord Alderbrook. This used to be his family's estate.' He used both hands in an expansive gesture. 'This amazing house was built in 1757. That's older than America.'

Voyle thought he sounded like a pompous tour guide.

'Patrick,' he said, 'that's your name, isn't it?'

The butler blinked.

'Well... you can call me Mr O'Connor.' A loftiness to his voice, like he was Lord Alderbrook himself. 'That's what Sir used to call me, and visitors too.'

'You live here with your wife, is that right?'

'Yes.'

'What does she call you? Mr O'Connor too?'

He blinked again.

'No. She calls me Patrick of course.'

Considine hadn't spoken yet. She was too busy looking about the room, taking it all in, because the size of this one room alone was at least three times that of her entire house on the north side of Dublin.

Voyle had found the source of the cigar smoke, a stogie in an ashtray on a side table next to a brown leather button-back armchair.

'Is that your cigar?' he asked, pointing to it.

Patrick O'Connor blinked once more.

'Um, yes.' Not sounding so lofty now.

Considine saw that next to the ashtray was a cut-glass tumbler with amber liquid in it.

'Are you the caretaker, Patrick?' she asked.

Yet another blink.

'Actually, my wife and I are the caretaker couple, but I prefer to call myself, personally, a butler. It is a profession I have been in for over twenty years, after all, a very proud profession too.'

'And your wife,' Voyle said, 'what would you call her?'

Blink. 'I would… well, she is responsible for house affairs. So, the house manager I would call her, yes, and myself, the butler, together we make up the caretaker couple.'

'Caretaker couple?'

'Yes.'

'Are there any other employees?'

'Well, yes, but they're not staff. Maintenance and gardening people, contractors.'

'Where is your wife?'

'Judith's away at the moment, visiting her sister in Galway. She'll be back next week.'

'So just yourself, on your lonesome, in this big old house? And you and your wife? I mean, Mr Gilsenan has been dead a while now. You're still here. Why?'

'We continue, of course, in a caretaking capacity. A house like this needs constant maintenance. Also, there's the security aspect. The executors, a legal firm, don't ask me, I don't know who they are, want the lights to be kept on; they want someone living here.'

Voyle nodded. 'Makes sense. However, do you often make a habit of sitting in here, drinking whiskey and smoking cigars... in the early afternoon? Whose whiskey and cigars are they, by the way?'

'Um, I have to say, I don't like your line of questioning. Or your tone. No, I don't.'

'You don't have to like it. Just answer anyway?'

'Mr Gilsenan wouldn't object to me relaxing a little. In fact, he'd encourage it.'

'Really? How do you know? He's not around to ask now, is he?'

'I worked hard for Mr Gilsenan. It's the least I could... he wouldn't object is what I'm saying.'

'So it's his whiskey and cigars, is it...? Look, Patrick O'Connor, I don't have a problem with you smoking his cigars or drinking his whiskey, sitting in here, in his living room, playing lord of the manor... you have separate quarters, I presume?'

'What?'

'You don't live in this house, do you?'

'What's that got to do with anything?'

'Do you?'

'Of course I live in this house. I had to be available twenty-four hours a day for Mr Gilsenan.'

'Where exactly?'

The butler shuffled his feet. 'Well... downstairs, if you must know.'

'Like I say, I don't have a problem with you doing whatever you're doing. In fact, I'd encourage it too...'

'You would?'

'Of course. We're all the same at the end of the day. We all put our trousers on one leg at a time, don't we? When you think about it, it's just not fair, is it? How one person can have all this' – it was Voyle's turn to gesture with his arms now – 'while another, me, you, for instance, Considine here too, can have, well, relatively speaking, fuck all, and that's a fact, well, nothing worth talking about, that is. Look at it this way–'

'Can you show us where he was found?' Considine asked, cutting Voyle off. 'We'd like to get something done today if we could.'

She shot Voyle a look.

'The conservatory.'

'The conservatory?'

'It's this way.'

He led them along a series of hallways. It was to the rear of the property, at the back of an annex. The door to it was ajar. O'Connor pushed it open, and they went in. Dark clouds had gathered outside, blocking out the sun, and he turned on the lights, their reflections staring back at them in the glass panels. It was nothing fancy either and surprisingly small, simply furnished too, just a wicker settee and a couple of wicker armchairs, with a plaid rug neatly folded across one cushion of the settee.

'He could spend hours in here,' Patrick O'Connor said.

'Is that a new door?'

'Yes. The old one had to be replaced.'

'Okay,' Voyle said, 'what would he do in here?'

'Nothing. Absolutely nothing at all. Just sit.'

'Read?' Considine asked.

'Listen to music?' It was Voyle.

'No, absolutely nothing at all. Sitting. Just, sitting.'

'He wasn't depressed, was he?' Voyle asked, turning in a full circle, looking about the room.

'I would prefer to call it melancholy rather than depressed.'

'So he was.'

'I didn't say that.'

'Who found the body?' Considine asked. 'You?'

'Yes.'

'Where, exactly?'

'Sitting there, on the settee, on that exact spot where the rug is folded now. He had it across his knees. An empty whiskey bottle was on the ground, and four empty blister packs of sleeping pills.'

'Four?'

'Yes, four, you don't forget a thing like that, now do you?'

'No, I suppose not... what type of whiskey? I mean, the brand. Do you know?'

O'Connor said nothing for a moment, then shrugged.

'No, actually, I don't remember.'

'But you remember four empty blister packs... and what's it you said, oh, yes, "You don't forget a thing like that," that's what you said. I'd have thought you'd have remembered the brand of whiskey too.'

'Well, I don't. He drank all sorts, but strictly single malts; nothing else would do.'

'What happened to the bottle?'

'The bottle?'

'Yes, the bottle of single malt he'd been drinking. Where'd that go?'

'Well, I disposed of it, of course.'

'And the blister packs?'

'The same.'

'When? That night? The next day? When?'

'I don't know... that night, maybe the next day. I'm not certain.'

'Hm...' Voyle said, and looked at him.

'What?'

'Didn't anyone ask you about them?'

'About what?'

'The bottle and the blister packs.'

'No, actually, they didn't.'

Typical, Voyle thought.

'Did he have a problem?' It was Considine.

'A problem?'

'Yes, with alcohol.'

The butler shook his head. 'Certainly not. He was a connoisseur.'

'And the bottle was empty too, was it?'

'Y-yes, it was.'

'Are you certain? You don't sound it.'

'I am. Yes. The bottle was empty. I'm certain.'

'Tell me exactly what happened,' Voyle said.

'It's very straightforward. It was evening time. He was late for supper... beans on rye bread with avocado.'

'Really?' Considine said.

'Yes, really. He wanted it for seven o'clock.'

'And you left it until half past before you went to get him.'

'If you could let me finish. It wasn't unusual for Mr G to be late. He could be late, twenty minutes late, so I'd have to pop the food in the microwave for a few minutes. He didn't mind. But at half past, I went to get him. I knocked on the door, but he didn't answer... I could see, through the glass, that is, that he was, well, I thought he was sleeping. Then I tried the door. It was locked. So I knocked again... actually I banged on it, and when I got no response, I immediately rang the emergency services. I knew something was wrong, I could see he was pale, very pale, and his glass had fallen onto the floor. There was a puddle, of whiskey, and those four blister packs were lying there. When the guards came, they had to break down the door. He was gone too far to do anything, and was pronounced dead right here.' O'Connor shook his head. 'One of the finest people I've ever had the privilege to work for. Gone. So very sad.' He blinked his eyes and rubbed his hands across them, like he was fighting back tears.

Tears, Voyle noticed, that never came.

16

Brody pummelled the punch bag in a flurry of fists, crouched to the left, sent in a sneaky jab, straightened, placed his weight onto his right foot, swivelled with a slight bend of the knee, funnelling all his power up and through his hip, into his arm, into his fist, the knee snapping taut as all his weight was placed behind that one pound of flesh and bone, ramming it forward, like a charge in the chamber of a gun, the velocity transforming it into two hundred pounds of forward motion before crashing into the punch bag, which shuddered, slipping on the hook attaching it to the floor stand, almost knocking it off before it jolted back into place.

That was the main benefit of having an office of his own. He could keep a punch bag in the corner, just for times like this.

He took off the gloves and hung them from the hook on the side, feeling a little better. Ryan had disappeared into her office, closing the door for a powwow with Harper. Everything she'd said when she'd introduced herself was not only turning out to be untrue, but the exact opposite of all the hot air about openness and transparency.

It was no way to run the unit, and he would have to tell her.

But right now, that wasn't what bothered him the most.

No.

What bothered him the most was that Ashling Nolan was not returning his phone calls.

17

There was a chip shop next to the supermarket in the middle of Tinnock. They hadn't noticed it the first time, but they did now, lit up as it was like a Christmas tree. Voyle went and ordered the fish and chip special for both of them, and they ate the food in the car. They ate everything, even the small grizzly bits of chips that'd gone through numerous frying cycles before finally being scooped into a bag. A group of smokers stood outside one of the handful of pubs in the village, all formally dressed. Voyle guessed they'd been at a funeral or a christening; it could be either. By their expressions and subdued demeanours, he guessed funeral.

For a long time neither of them spoke, but it wasn't an uncomfortable or angry silence, just a quiet one... or so he thought.

'Did you notice?' Voyle said eventually.

'What?' A sharpness to Considine's voice that he thought had been fading a little over the last couple of hours. 'Spit it out, come on.'

'Wow, normal service resumed, has it?'

'Voyle? What the fuck is it? You know you have this ability, this unique, unenviable…'

'Unenviable?'

'… ability to piss people off.'

'You mean you.'

'No, I mean everybody.'

'Marty Sheahan?'

'What about him?'

'Jack Brody? I don't piss them off.'

'I mean, Voyle, name one woman who doesn't hate you?'

'Aha, there we have it. It's not everyone I piss off, it's every woman I piss off is what you mean? So that's it, *women* hate me.'

'I didn't say hate you.'

'I think you did. But if women, some women, that is, seem to hate me, that doesn't mean they can't at the same time *like* me. Oh yes, there's a difference. They do like me, they like me a lot.'

Considine shook her head and squashed flat the cardboard box her meal had come in. She folded it in two on her knees and squashed it down again.

'Turn the key. I want to lower the window. This car stinks of fish.'

He did. They fell silent again. Stalemate.

'Here, let me.' He held out his hand for her squashed and folded takeaway cardboard box. He got out and deposited it into a bin along with his own.

'What do we know about Gilsenan?' Considine asked when he got back in. 'Is he married? Was he married? What?'

'Both,' Voyle answered, watching someone stumble out of the pub, stop and hold on to the wall, then stumble over to the group of smokers. One of them put their arm around his shoulder and steadied him. 'Ex-wife lives in Argentina with their two kids. She's American, by the way, was a professional cheerleader before she met him.'

'Really, you can be a professional cheerleader?'

'Of course.'

'Step up in the world for her, then, marrying him.'

'She lives on a three-thousand-acre estancia now.'

'A what?'

'Pronounced s-tan-cia, it's what they call a ranch down there. There were attempts to oust him from the board of ATW. A hostile takeover, ongoing at the time of death, by a director, his name...' Voyle clicked his fingers a couple of times, trying to think. 'Bart Ingram, yes, that's it. Gilsenan had mentored him, brought him up through the ranks.'

'Some thanks he got. Did he get the company?'

'Yes, as a matter of fact, he's now CEO of ATW International.'

'How convenient. Could there be a link, you think?'

The drunk pushed the arm away from around his shoulder, gestured to the others, turned and stumbled back into the pub.

'I don't see how. He was in America at the time, Columbus, Ohio, to be precise. It's easy to track people like that. They leave a trail.'

'Maybe he wanted to, leave a trail, that is.'

'I know they say business is ruthless,' Voyle said, 'but they don't usually kill each other like that. Why would they? They don't need to. They're already very rich people. Not like the street gangbangers. By the way, you didn't notice anything back there, did you, at the house?'

Considine said nothing. Voyle knew she was thinking, that she wouldn't like him noticing something if she hadn't.

'Apart from the butler with a case of Dunning-Kruger effect, that is?'

'I don't mind telling you I haven't a clue what that is.'

She smiled, looked at him. 'The opposite to imposter syndrome. A butler, for example, who believes he *is* the lord of the manor.'

'I get it. Yes, apart from that.'

She looked ahead. 'No.'

'The door, to the conservatory, it was open, and he made no attempt to close it as we were leaving.'

'So?'

'So. Probably nothing. But I thought it a little odd.'

'You did? Why?'

'I don't know. Just did.'

And Voyle still did.

He watched a taxi pull up outside the pub with the smokers gathered by its door.

'By the way,' Considine said, 'when you were getting the takeaways, I got a phone call.'

'You did? What about it?'

'They want me back at the Phoenix Park.'

'They do? But not me?'

'Not you.'

'Charming. Oh, I get the message alright, Superintendent Ryan, loud and bloody clear.'

He watched someone get out of the front passenger seat and approach the door, pause to speak to one of the group.

Voyle did a double take, forgetting about what Considine had just said, and leaned forward, pressing his face almost to the windscreen, as the person disappeared into the pub.

The person was Patrick O'Connor.

18

It had started to rain as Brody drove out the gates of Dublin Castle. By morning, if Hughes had still not returned, or not been found, whichever, then the big red button would be pressed, and this incident would be international news. Ryan had told him that much. Yet here, in the eye of the storm, all was deceptively calm.

He was heading to the news centre. But there was no point getting there before 10 p.m. because Marie Kennedy would not be available. She was recording her popular political analysis show, *Perspective*. So he went home, threw a spaghetti bolognaise ready meal into the microwave, and ate less than half of it. It was no use. He rang Ashling Nolan again, and again got no answer. Christ, he hated this. All that was missing from his teenage years was the acne.

He went into the back garden and lit up a cigarette. He rarely smoked, and it made him feel dizzy. But he was glad to feel something other than the way he'd been feeling all day.

Enough, he told himself.

He closed his eyes. He thought of the old saying, 'If you

chase the butterfly, it flies away. If you stand still, it comes to you'.

Fine, I'm going to stand still.

He forced Ashling Nolan from his mind. Back to business. Instead, he thought of Marie Kennedy. She'd been interviewed by the SDU, but, typical of them, they'd placed everything under protected status on Pulse, to which he had no access.

If the KGB wanted to freeze him out, or use him as a fig leaf to give the impression this was a joint operation, they were in for a surprise. Two could play at that game.

At 9:15 p.m. Brody left home, giving himself what he thought was plenty of time to cross the city and get to the news centre on time. But traffic was heavy. He hadn't expected it to be heavy, not at this time of evening. But it was, *and* it was raining. The wipers sliced back and forth as he drew up at a line of traffic waiting on a red light. At this rate, he might not make it in time. He flicked on the blue flashing grille lights, and the traffic began to part before him. He drove through the junction, cleared the city centre in a matter of minutes, and a little later was turning into the Media Hub campus on the south docks in Ringsend. The *All Ireland News* studios occupied a striking, modern, circular glass building set in its own landscaped grounds.

The security man at the boom barrier had spaghetti on his shoulders, more spaghetti on the shiny peak of his hat, and a bright red strip down each side of his trousers. His hat was pulled so low it obscured his vision, forcing him to tilt his head backwards as he looked at Brody. The uniform appeared like it had come straight from a rack in central comedy casting. But there the joke ended, because the fella peering at Brody's ID was making it look like Brody was seeking entry to the vault at the Central Bank.

'You want to see Marie Kennedy, is it?'

'If she's still here. Is she?'

'Maybe. Just so you understand, but this card here, with your picture on it...'

'My ID, you mean? What about it?'

'Yes, yes, well, that's what *you're* calling it.'

'Because that's what it is.' He looked closer at the fella. A kid really, no more than nineteen years old tops, if even that. The ridiculous uniform had maybe gone to the lad's head.

'What do *you* think it is?' the young fella asked, angling that head with the hat pulled low. He was probably trying for an intimidating sergeant major look, but instead he came across like an inquisitive puppy. 'I'm not saying it's not genuine, oh no, I'm not saying that, but I have to be sure, you understand? I have a boss to answer to, who's looking at us right now through that camera up on the pole there.' He nodded discreetly but didn't look up.

Brody took a breath.

'He is?'

'He is.'

'Bring him out here, then; I'm beginning to lose patience. Come on, I'm in a hurry.'

The lad was unfazed though. 'I get that a lot, people in a hurry. They just want to breeze right through. But I'm only doing my job here. Get all sorts trying to bluff their way in here, you know, lots of famous people inside that building, so there is.'

When it came to famous people, Brody knew, everything was relative.

'Seriously, I don't have time for this. What's the problem with the ID? Well?'

The fella looked at his watch. 'You're right. You don't have time for this. Those IDs are so easy to fake, you know that too? I only had one last week. I might just have to make a phone call, just to be certain, you understand... no, what was that?' He looked to the side, like there was a person there, but there wasn't.

'Tell you what,' Brody said, and revved the engine. 'I'll just drive through. What about fucking that? And we can sort it all out later. Then you can explain yourself when you're under arrest for impeding the progress of an investigation.'

If such a charge existed, Brody wasn't certain, but it sounded good. He inched the car forward.

'Fine. Fine. I was going to let you through anyway.' He pointed to his ear. Brody noted an earpiece there, which explained his odd behaviour a moment ago when it looked like he was speaking to the invisible man. 'Boss says you can go through; he recognises you. Punch in four zero two one on the security pad by the door; there's no one at reception at this hour. You're looking for studio three.'

The fella disappeared into his hut and put his head out the sliding glass hatch. 'Seriously, you can arrest me for that, for impeding the progress of an investigation?'

'Yes,' Brody said.

The boom barrier went up, and he drove through.

19

Meanwhile, Marty Sheahan was back at the ranch. The unit room at the MCIU had more bodies in it than it ever had: fifteen officers, though it felt like a lot more because the unit room was so small. Marty was the sole member of Major Crimes. He'd come in four hours earlier from his regular night class on Family Law and Property Rights, as he always did on a Thursday evening. Now, sitting at his desk, he was wondering why he had even bothered. Because he was being ignored. And this was his unit room, after all, now full of strangers, yet it was he who was made to feel like the stranger.

The desk phones started to ring like a small flock of chickens. An ongoing glitch meant that if one phone rang, they all did. Of course, no one bothered to pick up... except Sheahan, of course.

'Detective gar–'

The voice on the other end cut him off. 'George Johnson. I need to speak to him. Just shout out Johnsie.'

A good legal eagle never responded in the face of provo-

cation. Sheahan bit his lower lip, then: 'Johnsie,' he called.
'Who's Johnsie?'

'Me.' It was a young fella sitting behind a desk at the end of the room.

'Pick up; you've got a call.'

Sheahan watched Johnson pick up, and replaced the receiver. Most of the people in the room were from the Special Detective Unit, along with two or three more from the Crime and Security Agency. But where was Brody? And where was the rest of his team?

Although it was only yesterday morning since he'd attended the Old Man's memorial service, in that time it seemed to Sheahan that the world had been turned upside down.

A half hour later he was still sitting there, literally twiddling his thumbs, a law book open before him, because he might as well use this time to study. Not that he could concentrate much, he couldn't.

It was then she came in, made a beeline for his desk. She had long, luscious red hair and was dressed like she was about to go out on the town, in a black, belted, sparkly-edged jumpsuit that complemented her hair perfectly.

IN FACT, Sergeant Denise O'Brien had been about to go out on the town, but not to let her long hair that was already down, down. No, it was not for any enjoyment – except for the enjoyment of a job well done, that is. It was, in fact, an undercover operation, at an airport hotel, the finer details of which she would not be privy to until she arrived. Which was never going to happen, not now.

Harper had given her some details of why she was here, something to do with a missing government official. An emergency, he'd said. Too right. And she wondered what it had to do with the MCIU, because from what Harper had said, this had SDU written all over it. Harper had told her that Marie Kennedy had contacted a Detective Garda Steve Voyle, because this Voyle and Marie Kennedy *knew* each other. Sergeant O'Brien had almost laughed out loud at that, but had somehow managed not to. Because *she* and Voyle *knew* each other too, or had known each other, a long way back. Voyle got around; a lot of women *knew* him. Although, to be fair, it was easy to see why. You just had to take one look at that face, and body, let's not forget that body, oh no. Also, let's just say he knew what to do and how to do it too. Most men, O'Brien knew, didn't, couldn't, wouldn't, nor were they interested in learning how to either. But she wasn't going to tell Harper any of this, of course, no way.

She crossed the unit room, her high heels clicking on the vinyl floor tiles, exchanging banter with the others, and stood next to the desk. She placed her hands onto her slim hips and looked down. The man sitting there looked up from inside the raised hood of his hoodie, a grey hoodie, the letters NYC across the front. His jeans were ripped strategically as was the fashion – among young people, that is, but she thought this fella looked just that little bit too old for that. She caught sight of a page of the book he was reading, the heading *Civil Law and Criminal Law Act 2020*. On the floor next to him was a rucksack, and she could see more books inside it, law books.

'Who're you?' he asked, looking her up and down.

Normally that might piss her off, his looking her up and down like that, but under the circumstances, she could understand it. She glanced at the clock on the wall, a couple of minutes before ten o'clock.

'Sergeant Denise O'Brien. You Brody?'

'No. I'm not.' The man got to his feet. 'I'm Martin Sheahan.'

In her heels, O'Brien had a height advantage on him.

'The books? You training to be a lawyer?'

'I'm studying law... well, returning to studying law, and...?' His eyes looked her up and down again.

She laughed. 'Oh, don't mind me. I'm supposed to be undercover tonight.' She held on to a corner of the desk, pulled off one shoe, dropped it to the floor, did the same with the other, exhaled loudly. 'Oh, thank God.'

Sheahan adjusted his gaze downward to take account of the height adjustment, but not by much.

Superintendent Ryan's head appeared in the open doorway. 'You two, O'Brien, Sheahan, my office, please, now.'

'Aw, crap,' O'Brien said, bending to pull on her shoes again.

20

After his encounter with the secret service agent at the gate, Brody was surprised to find the building empty when he went in. The deserted reception desk stood in the centre of the deserted foyer and had an imitation signpost next to it, painted in the regulation black-and-white stripes, just like the real thing, except in this case the signs on it were pointing to different corridors that spread out from the foyer like spokes on a wheel. One pointed to studio 3. He went down and pushed the door open and went in. It was in darkness except for an aura of light in the very centre, illuminating a desk. A voice spoke, but Brody couldn't see anyone there.

'Yes, can I help you?'
'Hello.'
'Yes.'
'I'm looking for Marie Kennedy.'
'And who are you?'
Brody told the voice.

Across the front of the desk he could make out the word *Perspective*, like it was stencilled into wood, but he felt it was probably plastic, above it the logo of TV Global News Network. A woman stepped out from the shadows into the aura of light, holding a clipboard in one hand and a mobile phone in the other.

'Is she expecting you? Wait, you look familiar. I recognise you.'

'You do?'

She reached an arm behind her, into the darkness, presumably to turn on some lights, because a second later a couple flickered to life from the ceiling.

'Yes, *Time Of Death*, you were interviewed, and you were an adviser. Jack Brody, correct?'

'Correct.'

Time Of Death had gone on to worldwide Netflix release. Sometimes people recognised him. Not very often. But sometimes. Like now.

'I'm Edith Comerford.' She walked across to him and extended a hand. '*Perspectives* director. You're working late? Nothing wrong, I hope.'

'I'm working late, yes,' he said, and they shook hands.

She waited for Jack to say something, but he didn't.

'Um, anyway,' she said, 'yes, a very interesting programme, *Time Of Death*. I really enjoyed it. Have you ever thought of doing something a little more local next time? Maybe with a little ol' station like ourselves?'

'Anything's possible. The producers approached me. I didn't choose who I worked with. But I enjoyed the experience.'

And he had enjoyed it: couple of weeks working with a scriptwriter for maybe an hour a day, and another hour with a director. Getting paid almost half a year's salary for those fourteen days, in reality, twenty-five hours' work in total.

'Very good then,' she said, 'I'll remember that. Come on, let me show you Marie's dressing room. If she's still there, that is. She might have gone home. We need to hurry. It's this way.'

She turned, and he followed her towards the back of the studio. She pressed on something in the wall, and a handle popped out. She pushed it, and a concealed door opened up onto a brightly lit corridor. It took Jack by surprise.

'This way.'

They went along the corridor.

Marie Kennedy was pulling on her coat when they went into the dressing room. She stopped, one half hanging from her shoulder, looking at them.

'Marie, someone to see you. Jack Brody... he's a police officer.'

'Is he now. Did he tell you why he was here?'

Edith Comerford shook her head. 'No, he didn't.'

Marie Kennedy's gaze settled on Brody.

'To do with that story I'm working on? Thank you for coming so quickly. I thought you'd be interested.'

'What story is that, Marie?' Edith Comerford said. 'You didn't mention.'

'All in good time, Edith. Now, let me speak with the man.'

'Yes, yes, of course... Oh and, Marie, editorial conference tomorrow at ten. If that's a little early, we can rearrange.'

'No, no, that's fine, Edith, thank you.'

'Only if you're sure? I can always rearrange if you're not.'

'Yes, for God's sake, I'm sure. Can we be left alone now, please? I'm sorry, Edith, it's been a long day, didn't mean to snap.'

'That's okay, Marie.' Her tone and demeanour like she was used to such outbursts. She crossed to the door and pulled it open. 'Look, gone.' She went out and closed it silently behind her.

Brody thought that Marie Kennedy looked even better in real life than she did on TV. Underneath her coat she wore a tight, canary yellow dress cut above the knee and a neckline that was low, but not too low. She brought to his mind a real-life Barbie doll, but one with black hair. One thing he was certain of, Donagh Hughes was punching above his weight, way above his weight. Hughes was a small, heavyset man with a comb-over. Still, he possessed what Brody guessed was possibly the greatest aphrodisiac of all – power.

'Well.' Her coat still hung from her shoulder. 'You'd better sit down?' And pointed.

'Are you a friend of Steve Voyle?' Brody asked, sitting.

'Yes.'

She pulled the coat up onto her shoulder now and perched back against the make-up counter behind her, ringed by bright, bare white light bulbs.

'This won't take long, will it? I'm really tired.' She glanced at her watch. 'It's been a long day. Although I'm not sure I should speak with you. I've already been questioned, you know... You do know that, don't you?'

'I know.'

'And it was not a nice experience. Ten minutes, okay?'

'Ten minutes. Thank you.'

Brody observed her. Marie Kennedy, the master of the political debate, wealthy, successful, opinionated and rarely wrong, appeared not to grasp the seriousness of the situation. Brody didn't believe it for one moment.

'I suppose Steve told you about me too,' she said. 'Though I asked him not to tell anyone.'

'He didn't have any choice. This is a... well, it's a serious situation, very serious indeed.'

She pouted and folded her arms. 'It's not my fault, you know,' she repeated, '... it really isn't. I had nothing to do with this. If...' Her voice trailed off.

Brody waited. 'Yes,' he said, '*if?*'

'It's not as if I hide anything from my husband. I don't. We have an' – her voice dropped – 'open relationship, okay. Not a lot of people would agree with that, or even understand it, believe me, not even in those so-called liberal media circles I move in. So I don't shout about it, and neither does he, my husband. We're very discreet. We have to be.' Her gaze became intense. 'Do you understand?'

'Oh, I understand alright. You said *if*. Just now. What did you mean by that?'

'If. Yes. I was going to say, well, if I was embroiled in this, I might, well... I don't really want to spell it out. I'm sure you can work it out yourself?'

'Actually, I can't.'

'Oh, I think you can. If I'm brought into this, I won't be happy, that's what I'm trying to say.'

'You're already in it, I'm afraid.'

'Of course, I know I am. But that isn't what I mean.'

'You're talking in riddles, Mrs Kennedy...'

'Marie, please.'

'Marie.'

'What I'm saying is I don't want to be *brought* into it, that's what I'm saying. There is a difference. My name does not need to be mentioned. Is this still a riddle to you?'

'I'd already worked that out. But it may not be possible to keep you out of it.'

Her eyes narrowed.

'I don't see why not.'

'You drove his car back from that house you both were staying in,' Brody said, not wanting to have his wheels spinning in the mud. 'Is that correct?'

She nodded. 'I drove his car, yes. I left it parked in a pub car park in Bray. I took a taxi from there.'

Brody reached into an inside pocket and took out his notebook and pen. He clicked the end, opened the notebook, and held it over a page.

'What are you doing?' Alarm in her voice. 'I already told them this when I was interviewed.'

'This investigation is official, Marie.'

'You don't need to write in your notebook. Anything I say can be between just the two of us, can't it? Your notes are archived, aren't they?'

'Yes. But it makes no difference. What was the name of the taxi company?'

Brody moved the pen from the notepad, but just a little.

She was silent, looking at him.

'Fab Cabs.' Her eyes never left the pen. 'But I really don't see the point; they already know this.'

'Is that the same taxi firm that brought you there too? Because you didn't travel down with him either, did you?'

'No, I didn't. And it was, the same taxi firm, that is.'

'I know what you said to Steve. I don't need to go over it all again. I just have one other question for you.'

'Yes.'

'Did you harm Mr Hughes in any way?'

'Jesus. What did you just say?'

Brody was about to repeat it.

'Okay. Okay. I heard you. Come on now. You don't seriously think I harmed Donagh? Me? Don't be ridiculous.'

'I don't know. I wasn't there. You were.'

'No, I didn't harm Donagh. There, is that clear?'

Brody closed his notebook, having written nothing down into it.

'Just, please, keep me out of this... or at least try. Surely that's possible. I have everything to lose, after all. I really do. Now, unless I'm under arrest, I'm going home.'

Brody did nothing to stop her as she went and opened the door and walked out, leaving him alone in the changing room. She was delusional if she thought her name could be kept out of this. Not if Hughes wasn't found, certainly, and found quickly. Brody looked around, taking in the multitude of framed photographs hanging from the walls. She was in all of them, posing alongside everybody from local councillors to US presidents. This room was a reflection of her ego, a shrine of sorts, he considered. Not once had she shown any concern for Donagh Hughes.

He thought of Ashling Nolan. It was like his mind couldn't keep her out. He thought of her eyes, those beautiful green eyes with their flecks of yellow. Where was she now? What was she doing? And more importantly, was she with anyone?

He took his phone from his pocket and brought up her number, held his finger over the call button, his heart beginning to canter, his breathing coming in short, shallow in and out takes.

Damn, he hated feeling this way.

Brody stared at his phone, his finger almost touching the green call icon button, before he sighed, removed it and replaced the phone into his pocket.

Stand still, and the butterfly will come to you.

THE MAN KNEW they were both in there. But he had no interest in the policeman. But if he had to, he'd deal with him too. No problem. Still, he was relieved when he saw Marie Kennedy emerging unaccompanied. That made things easier. He crouched low behind the bushes next to her sunset orange Jaguar. He'd make this quick. No ceremony. Like the logo said, just do it. He liked that. It was much simpler. Simple was good. Simple worked. Some people thought him simple. But you could rely on simple. It wasn't complicated; it didn't break down.

He held the weapon in his right hand. Not a knife. He'd

thought it was. But he'd been told it wasn't. It was a machete... whatever. A knife was what it was to him, a *big* knife.

He saw her coming down the steps from the TV studio, could hear the clickety click sounds of her high heels on the tarmac as she drew close.

No ceremony.

Just do it.

When she reached the car door, he stepped out from behind the bushes. The wind was blowing against him, carrying all sound and scent away. He crept up behind her. With the door open, Marie Kennedy stooped to get into her car. He swung the knife – the machete, whatever the fuck – aiming for the exposed sliver of flesh at the back of her neck just above the collar of her jacket. He swung it in a wide arc, all his weight behind it. It was sharper, this machete, this knife, whatever, and much more lethal than anything he'd ever used before; it literally cut right through skin, muscle, bone, the lot, like a knife through butter. That was how good it was. Marie Kennedy collapsed like a sack of potatoes, without even a murmur. He watched, transfixed, as her head left her body, tossed onto the ground, coming to rest near his shoe. He looked down at it, could swear he saw life still in those eyes. And then it was gone, the eyes staring up at him but seeing nothing, as lifeless as two pieces of glass. He'd never decapitated anyone before. It was much easier than he'd thought. Marie Kennedy seemed to disagree. Her body began to spasm and twitch wildly. He reached down and pressed the fingers of one hand against it, steadying the torso, and looked up.

Shite.

It was the policeman. Heading his way.

THE CAR PARK was practically deserted, just a couple of cars parked in it along with his own. He took the key fob from his pocket and pointed it, pressed the remote, and the car made its squelching sound, the headlamps blinking twice. He walked over and had just placed his hand onto the door handle when he heard it. He wasn't sure what the sound was, but it was enough to make him stand still and listen.

The wind had stiffened, rustling the trees, and the security lights about the perimeter illuminated a fine mist falling to earth like a shimmering curtain. Brody heard nothing now. He opened the door and was about to get into the car when it came again. He closed his eyes, straining to hear. Once again, the sound stopped, and he could hear nothing but the rustling of those trees. Brody shut the car door gently and walked around the back of the vehicle, stood with his hands on his hips, looking about. There was a small Toyota parked in the centre. In a corner, directly beneath a security light, was another, much bigger vehicle, a Jaguar he guessed, the light casting it into a long shadow.

A shadow that was somehow odd, because at the rear of it, instead of an angular line, there seemed to be one that was bulbous. Brody stared at it, pulling up the collar of his jacket. He watched as the bulbous shadow began to move and then disappear. He realised what it was then: someone had been crouching there.

He took off, sprinting across the car park towards it. He'd almost reached it when the world seemed to jolt and then spin before a weightlessness took hold of his body, and he felt himself floating, staring at the black sky above him, feeling the fine mist falling on his face. But only for a split second before... *umpth!* He crashed into the hard tarmac, a dull pain rattling through his entire body. He'd slipped on the wet surface. Brody took a breath and cursed, scrambling back to his feet. *Umpth!* He was sent sprawling a second time as what felt like a battering ram crashed into the very centre of his back. His cheek pressed against the wet tarmac as he looked ahead, dazed, before his feet were hoisted up and he was being dragged backwards by a powerful, unseen force. He was pulled alongside the car, and his feet dropped, plopping down to the ground. He heard footsteps come from behind as a giant moved into his line of vision and loomed above him. This giant flipped the boot lid open, crouched down and grabbed Brody's collar. For a moment they stared at one another. Brody looked at the face in the strangely misaligned head, with one eye bigger and set lower than the other, a large nose and thick, rubbery lips. The giant grunted and, with a speed belying his big, cumbersome size, swung a huge hand through the air that connected savagely with the side of Brody's head. Brody was lifted up like a rag doll and bundled into the boot. The lid banged shut, and everything became black. Brody felt like he had been tossed into a grave – his grave. And in a way, maybe he had.

The engine started, and he felt the tyres beneath him bite into the tarmac as the car sped forward before lurching to the right, sending him sprawling into the corner of the boot. A moment later he heard a voice from outside, tinny and agitated, yet one he recognised: it was the security man with the spaghetti shoulders and hat... 'Stop! You can't do that.' And then there was a snapping sound as an almost imperceptible ripple passed through the car. Brody knew what it was; the car had crashed through the boom barrier. It lurched again, and Brody was tossed into the opposite corner. He used his legs to steady himself, with one hand began to feel along the panel next to him, which was the back of the rear seat, and with the other to rummage in his pockets for his mobile phone. Damn, it wasn't there. Brody ignored the pain in his jaw, feeling along the panel, looking for the seams in the seats so he might push his hand through and pull it down. But there wasn't a seam; it was a bench seat. And the roof of the boot was the actual lid rather than what he'd hoped for, a flimsy parcel shelf.

He pulled back one leg and twisted, kicked the back of the seat in frustration. It had no effect. He knew it wouldn't, but it made him feel a little better.

'You bastard,' he yelled. 'You bastard. Whoever you are.'

That didn't help either. What he needed to do was calm down. To survive this, just calm down. He took a deep breath, held it, and released it slowly. He listened. The engine was a steady pitch, the revs high. The car was travelling fast, very fast.

A plan began to formulate in his head. He'd wait. The car had to stop eventually. He looked at his watch, fifteen minutes past eleven. How long had he been in here? A couple of minutes at most. Keep track of time, he told himself. When this car eventually stopped, he should be able to work out roughly the distance travelled at what he reckoned to be an average of one hundred kilometres an hour. Brody assumed he was being taken somewhere, to be held captive, for whatever reason.

He reckoned he would soon find out.

Sheahan and Denise O'Brien sat before the desk behind which the Old Man used to sit, but now where Superintendent Ryan was supposed to sit but wasn't. Instead, the person sitting there was Superintendent Tony Harper. He had no connection with the unit at all. Sheahan thought it all a little confusing. Ryan, who was standing by the window, folded her arms and spoke.

'Where's Brody, Sheahan? Do you know?'

Marty shook his head, turning his head away, trying to stifle a yawn but not able to.

'Tired?'

'I came here from night class, so a little, yes.'

'Get over it; it's going to be a long night.'

'He went to talk to Marie Kennedy at the TV centre is what I heard,' Harper announced, sounding smug, and looked at Sergeant Denise O'Brien. 'Undercover again, Denise?'

'Afraid so.'

'Did he say when he was coming back?' Sheahan wanted to know. 'Or if he's coming back at all?'

'I don't know.'

'Did you try ringing him?'

'What,' Harper snapped, 'you telling me how to do my job now? Anyway, I did ring him, as it happens. And he's not answering his phone. I told him to be contactable. I told everyone to be contactable.'

'Tony, if you don't mind' – it was Superintendent Ryan – 'I'll deal with MCIU matters, thanks.'

Harper sat impassive.

'We won't talk shop in front of the staff, okay, Fiona?'

She stared at him, her lips pressed into two, thin, angry lines.

'Can I ask when exactly you rang him?' Sheahan pressed Harper. 'It's just the boss always rings back quickly if he misses a call. That's all.'

'It's been over an hour.' But Harper sounded distracted.

'Not like him.'

'Then you two swing by his house.' It was Ryan. 'You know where he lives, don't you...?'

'Yes, I do. I know where he lives.' Sheahan got to his feet.

Ryan and Harper stared at one another. Harper looked like he was about to say something, but didn't.

'Come on,' Sheahan said to O'Brien.

Brody timed it as exactly seven minutes until the car came to a stop again. The engine fell silent, and there was the sound of the driver's door opening and closing. He waited, but no one came to open the boot, to drag him from it and into a locked room or somewhere. No, he was left alone, here, in this grave.

His head throbbed, and he suddenly felt tired, so tired. He just wanted to close his eyes and sleep. But he shook his head, wincing against the pain.

You can't. You must stay alert.

He reached out to the side, searching above the wheel arches for the wheel-changing kit. There had to be one somewhere. Over one wheel arch he felt the outline of a hard plastic compartment, found the button and pressed it. The panel cover fell open. Brody reached in, took out a leather pouch, opened it and located the wheel brace. Next, he ran his hand along the boot lid in front of him until he'd located the hairline gap where it joined the boot panel. He used the wheel brace to prise this apart just enough so he could place the tip of the brace in and run it along until he felt the hard metal outline of the lock mechanism. Holding the tip of the brace against it, he used his other hand to retrieve the wheel jack from the leather pouch. He took a breath and began to whack this off the end of the wheel brace. The sound of metal on metal in the cramped, sealed boot was as loud as the chiming of a church bell. Brody continued, w*hack, whack, whack.* Again and again he slammed the jack against the wheel brace, the heat quickly building, sweat forming on his forehead, dripping into his eyes, making them sting. But he never stopped. Not until…

The boot popped, and he found himself crouching in the cool night-time air. He sucked air into his lungs, feeling the misty rain like a soothing balm against his skin. Where was he? The giant, that is? In the distance he could see twinkling lights, the outline of trees and the silhouette of a long, low building, on top of it an illuminated sign:

The Dodder Hotel.

Brody knew that hotel. Between him and it was nothing but an expanse of black. Where the hell was he exactly? Another car park? He swung his feet over the boot lid, but instead of his feet touching ground on the other side, they touched... water. Brody pushed his feet down farther into it, and down again. Still, he did not reach the bottom, and the water was already up above his knees. He brought his legs back in, realised his hands were wet too. He looked down, but it was too dark to see. He became aware of something, a lightness in his belly, like a bobbing sensation. With it was a sound, of water lapping? Yes, that was what it was. He knew then. The car was in the river.

And it was sinking.

21

The luscious redhead tottered on her high heels next to Sheahan as they walked along the corridor from the unit room. Sheahan thought she was unlike any mule he'd ever worked with before.

'I've got my car outside, Rumpole,' she said. 'We'll take that.'

They went into the car park. Her car was not like any typical mule car either, a Hyundai maybe, with its hubcaps missing. Most pool cars had missing hubcaps. No, nothing like that. She stopped next to a low, sleek – and despite the unpredictable weather – open-top sports car, coloured bright purple and reflecting the lamp lights like a glitzy prize on a TV programme.

'Here it is,' she said, pointing the remote, and the doors began to open, but upwards rather than out.

'No way,' Sheahan said with boyish wonder, 'gull wings.'

The seats were low, of soft beige leather with brown trim. Sheahan tried not to look as Denise O'Brien's dress rode up to reveal a long flash of white thigh as she climbed in next to him.

'Pardon me,' she said, adjusting it back into place again. 'And um, would you mind reaching behind my seat. Hand me that pair of sneakers there.'

He did. As she was changing into them, a mobile rang. Sheahan recognised the ringtone. A state phone. She turned the ignition key to the 'on' position, flicked a switch on a steering wheel stalk and spoke:

'Yes, O'Brien.'

A voice came through the Bluetooth. Sheahan didn't recognise it.

'Denise, be advised a car left the TV centre where Sergeant Brody attended a short while ago.'

'And you're telling me this because…?'

'It went through the boom barrier. As in *through* it, you get me.'

'Oh.'

'A local unit's in attendance. Vehicle is an orange-coloured Jaguar, partial reg two two one whiskey. Car belongs to Marie Kennedy.'

'Have you an alert on it?'

'Just about to.'

'Copy that.'

She turned the ignition again, and the engine roared to life before settling into a low, rumbling idle.

'This car came from the CAB,' she explained. 'Used to belong to one of the Linihans on the northside. You've heard of them?'

'Of course.' For a time they'd been one of the biggest criminal gangs, not just in the country, but in Europe. Their demise had been portrayed in a newspaper front-page cartoon that depicted a CAB dagger being plunged through a vampire's heart with the face of the Linihan gang leader.

'Hold on tight,' she said as the car was propelled forward,

an invisible force hitting Sheahan in his chest, pushing him back into his seat, to which he was, literally, holding on.

22

Brody knew where he was, where the car was: the River Dodder. His mind churned. How far out in the water was the car? Was the tide in? If so, that would mean the water was high. And if that was the case, it was only a matter of time before this pile of metal sank into the soft silt and mud below, down to join the shopping trolleys and bicycles and whatever else was there. By morning it would be just another item of riverbed furniture. And it wouldn't take long either. No, if the conditions were right, it would be quick.

He scrambled out of the boot into the cold, black water, feeling the current immediately begin to pull on him. He thought the tide was likely going out. Brody was an okay swimmer; he began treading water, kicking off his shoes, turning in a complete circle in an attempt to get his bearings. He could see the nearest bank was perhaps twelve metres away. He started to swim towards it, had gone three or four lengths when the thought suddenly came to him: someone else, Marie Kennedy maybe, could be in the car.

He called out, but got no response, did it again, louder this time, but still there was no response. He changed direction and swam alongside the car, holding on to the roof and moving along the side, peering in. The water was up to the door handles now. There wasn't enough light to see into it properly, so he couldn't be certain if someone was in there or not. The current pulled harder at him, either it was getting stronger, or more likely, he was becoming weaker, his remaining energy sapping away.

He pushed himself from the car and started for shore.

Brody had to save himself.

23

The little sports car was beautiful, exotic and fast – oh boy, was it fast – but one thing it definitely wasn't was comfortable. The closest Sheahan had ever come to a sports car before was a friend of his father's vintage open-top Triumph Herald. He couldn't remember if that was comfortable or not; what he could remember was utter fear as the old car was buffeted about in the wash of forty-ton juggernauts. Never take a vintage car – especially a vintage convertible – onto a motorway was what he'd learned that day.

As they drove, every dip, every manhole cover – not too many potholes thankfully – sent a shock wave from the road right up through Sheahan's spine. But O'Brien was loving it, braking at the last moment on each corner, and even then only when she absolutely had to.

Sheahan tried to ignore it all by scanning the night cityscape, trying to spot a two two one whiskey Jaguar. But after fifteen minutes he'd had enough.

'You're a nut behind the wheel,' he shouted over the roar of the engine, 'do you know that? Slow down, for God's sake.'

But Denise O'Brien only laughed and tossed her head back, her long luscious red hair blowing in the wind, flicked into top gear on a particularly long and deserted stretch. Sheahan felt himself pressed back again into his seat, the wind whipping his face. But he realised there was a method to her madness, because she was covering ground in grid-like sections. And she was covering it fast. He held on to his seat and said nothing.

The man stepped off the pavement onto the roadway almost directly in front of them, a stooped figure, stumbling about, like he was drunk – which he probably was – his clothes glistening. Which was just as well, as it reflected better in the light, making it easier for Sergeant Denise O'Brien to see him, giving her that split second of time to hit the brakes and avoid running him over. The little sport car's tyres screeched, clawing desperately at the tarmac for grip and, finding it, coming to an abrupt stop. O'Brien opened her mouth, about to give this eejit her best bollocking, when Sheahan yelled: 'Jesus Christ… it's Brody.'

He jumped out of the car and ran over. When Sheahan reached him, he turned and shouted: 'Get on the phone; we need an ambulance. Now!'

BY THE TIME the fire brigade had winched the car from the river, Brody had been treated by paramedics at the scene in the back of their ambulance. He did not need to attend at hospital. As the car was being dragged up onto the riverbank, he watched on along with Sheahan and the person he now knew to be Sergeant Denise O'Brien, who, Sheahan assured him, really was a mule. The powerful searchlight on the fire engine's roof turned night into day. As late as it was, a small crowd had gathered, with just one solitary uniform keeping them back. A burly fireman unhooked the hoisting lines from the vehicle and walked to the engine. Brody noticed that still no one had looked into the car.

He took the opportunity to walk over slowly and peer in. The rear of the car was in shadow, but he thought he discerned a shape lying there. Sheahan came and joined him.

'Marty, will you go and ask them to turn the searchlight on here so I can see inside, thanks.'

Sheahan walked over and spoke with a fireman, and a moment later the searchlight was turned, shining directly into the car. Brody first noticed the canary yellow dress, it seemed to fill his vision, itself reflecting in the glow of the searchlight. Her feet were without shoes, the tights torn across the top on one foot, the toes peeping through. Her coat was open, and as before, it hung from one shoulder, falling into the footwell. It was a peculiar feeling, seeing someone so vibrant and beautiful lying dead, whom he had seen full of life only a short time before. An empty feeling, one tinged with hopelessness too, or something, Brody wasn't sure. He couldn't explain it.

And then Brody noticed, as Sheahan came and stood one side of him, the exotic Sergeant O'Brien on the other.

'Oh, shite,' Sheahan said, clamping a hand over his mouth.

O'Brien took a breath and looked up to the sky.

Where Marie Kennedy's head had once joined her body now resembled a side of salami.

24

It scurried along the bottom of the wall, stopped, turning its head up, whiskers bristling, nose twitching, small black eyes looking at a point somewhere beyond him. It may not be able to see him clearly, because a rat's vision is very poor, but the animal knew exactly where Hughes was, sitting on the stone floor, bound hand and foot by thick coils of duct tape. The foreign minister caught another movement in the corner of his eye, saw a second rat emerging from a hole in the wall. It scurried along to join its companion, and they both stood, whiskers twitching, sniffing the air, sniffing him.

Hughes pressed himself against the cold, damp wall.

'Go away,' he shouted, 'go awaaaay,' and looked to the door, what he thought was the door, a rectangular ribbon of weak yellow light. 'Who's out there? Who? And why're you doing this to me? Answer me, for God's sake.'

But no answer came. There was a sound, like a low whistling. One of the rats rose onto its hind legs. The whistling sound grew louder.

Donagh Hughes realised what the sound was then. It was

coming from one of the rats. Then the other joined in. He could almost swear they were laughing at him.

25

Brody woke later that morning feeling like he'd gone ten rounds with Mike Tyson, and then ten more. When he got up, he felt like going back to bed again, but he didn't; instead he forced himself to clear his head by jogging to Glasnevin and back. Afterwards he had a very hot shower and felt better. He arrived at the Phoenix Park just after noon. TV news vans were parked about the entrance, a gaggle of reporters swarming every car that went through. Including his. They all recognised him, calling out his name, frantically gesturing for him to lower his window. He guessed they were all perfectly reasonable people at home or at the parent-teacher meeting, whatever, but here they were like a pack of hungry hyenas sniffing around a fresh carcass.

Voices came from the unit room as he passed along the corridor outside, but none that he recognised. He kept on walking, climbed the stairs, and walked along the corridor to his office, was about to push open the door when a voice that he did recognise boomed, 'Brody!'

It had come from Superintendent Ryan's office. He went there and looked in the open door. His new boss was nowhere to be seen. Instead, the head of the KGB was seated behind her desk.

'Have you seen this?' Superintendent Tony Harper demanded.

Brody stepped over to the desk and looked at the newspaper. The headline alone took up almost all of the tabloid front page:

Foreign Minister Donagh Hughes Missing.

There was another story, reduced to a sidebar because there wasn't time or room for anything else, he guessed.

TV Anchor Marie Kennedy's Body Found Decapitated.

It was a lot to take in alright. But Brody quickly discerned the newspaper had not drawn a link between both cases – not yet, that is. But it was only a matter of time before they did.

When he looked up, Harper was staring at him.

'I see it,' Brody said.

A light tap sounded on the office door. Brody looked to see a uniform standing there.

'Detective Sergeant Brody?'

'Yes, that's me.'

The uniform held up a phone. 'This yours?'

Brody squinted.

'It was found during a search of the TV Global News Network carpark last night.'

He crossed to Brody and handed it to him. It was Brody's phone alright and looked to be undamaged.

'Thank you.'

'Your unmarked was returned to the car pool too. Just to let you know.'

'That's good.' Brody put the phone into his pocket.

'Thanks again.'

'Can we move things along?' Harper nodded to the uniform, then to the door. 'How did this get out? Huh?' he demanded when the uniform had left.

'How should I know?'

'Don't you get lippy with me, Brody. Someone had to have leaked this.'

'Calm down.'

'Don't tell me to fucking calm down.'

'I just did. You can't keep a lid on this. Like, for real? It's impossible.'

Harper looked like he was about to explode.

'W-who do you think you are, *Sergeant*? Watch your fucking mouth.'

Brody said nothing. Neither did Harper. After some seconds Harper spoke, calmer now:

'I heard you got a slap last night and almost went to sleep with the fishes... things like that seem to happen to you a lot, don't they?'

'Lately, seems so. But they tend to come in threes. It'll be someone else's turn next.'

'What's that supposed to mean? Me?'

'No, I didn't mean that.' And he hadn't. Young Harper here was getting a little paranoid.

'The shit's hit the fan, Brody.'

'I know.'

'Someone leaked Hughes to the press. I don't know who that is, but I'll do my best to find out.'

'I wouldn't waste my time, and no, not because I had anything to do with it, but because it's a waste of time; you'll never find out. It happens.'

'Okay, okay.' He took a deep breath. 'You're right.' A shadow passed behind Harper's eyes. Brody spotted it immediately.

'I have my suspicions though.'

'You do? Care to share?'

'I don't like your tone, Brody.'

'My tone?'

'Yeah, your tone.'

Again, silence.

'It was Voyle who leaked this. I just know it.' The voice sounded certain.

But it wasn't Harper who'd spoken. It was Superintendent Fiona Ryan. She came through the doorway and stood next to the person sitting behind her desk. She seemed to have no problem with that fact either, Brody thought.

'And your reasons?' Brody asked. 'You'd need more than a mere dislike of Voyle to come up with that assumption.'

'Would I? Well, I disagree.'

'Hm, we're all in trouble, then, aren't we?' Brody looked at Harper.

'I have more, of course,' Ryan said. 'Which is this, I don't trust him.'

'With respect, you don't even know him.'

Harper shook his head. 'With respect, Brody, is it? That's a good one.'

'I know him well enough,' Ryan said.

'I'd forget about whether Voyle did or didn't leak this and just deal with the shitstorm you have on your hands right now... For the record, I don't believe he leaked it. I trust him.'

Harper and Ryan looked at one another.

'He's right,' Harper said.

'What? You too? I believe he leaked it. I'll be proven right.'

'No, not that. God's sake, get over it. I agree that we need to deal with this shitstorm, that's what I mean.'

'Oh,' Ryan said, 'yes, yes, of course,' but sounding like she wasn't over it.

26

O'Brien had her wild, luscious hair tied in a ponytail. She wore tailored beige trousers with low-heel pumps and a round-neck green sweater with a zipper top. From her ears hung long dangly earrings. Her nails were painted pink. Sheahan could see why she worked undercover. Even the most twitchy-nosed gouger would never take her for a mule. They were on their way to the offices of Park Developments, to interview the property acquisitions manager, a Mr Terence Mc Gonagle: Park Developments were the registered owners of the property Hughes and Kennedy had been staying at outside Tinnock.

They spoke little on the drive over, the previous events playing on their minds...

Park Developments House, as it was called, was situated just off Smithfield Square, or Smithfield Plaza as it was known now, an area that had been on the rise for a number of years, but lately, however, the rise seemed to have come to a grinding halt, this vanguard of modernity now a meandering front line separating the new and glitzy from the old and decrepit. At one time the area had been best known for its horse market.

Park Developments HQ seemed to be caught between both worlds, a chrome- and glass-fronted edifice on a back street lined on either side by old fruit and vegetable warehouses and derelict terrace houses, still waiting for the area's phoenix to rise.

They parked in a gravel- and weed-covered cleared area opposite the building.

The girl at reception was smiling when they went in, speaking into a matchstick thin mouthpiece attached to a very slim headset... 'Putting you through now, Mr Walker, and thank you for contacting Park Developments.'

She looked at them, her smile never wavering, like it was painted onto a mask that she had fixed to her face.

'Terence Mc Gonagle,' O'Brien said, catching some luscious red hair between the fingers of one hand and pushing it back over her forehead.

The girl looked at O'Brien, and her gaze lingered, but that smile never faltered.

'We have an appointment,' Sheahan clarified, suddenly realising he didn't know if that was true or not. He pulled out his ID wallet, opened it, offering his badge for inspection.

She glanced at it.

'And you?' to O'Brien.

'Well, of course I have an appointment too. We're together.'

'No. I mean, are you a guard as well?'

'Of course.'

'Really...?'

'I know, I don't look it.'

'No, you don't.' The girl glanced ahead, out through the window. 'And *that's* your car.' She pointed. 'That can't be a Garda car... can it?'

O'Brien had her ID out. 'Yes, it can, and it is.'

'Really' – cocking her head to one side, looking at the ID – 'the guards drive cars like that?'

'Sometimes,' O'Brien said, not bothering to explain.

'Wow.' Her smile seemed to actually get wider. 'One moment...' She pressed a button on what looked like an oversized harmonica on the desk in front of her. Then: 'Mr Mc Gonagle, there's two' – she paused, lowered her voice – 'police officers to see you... yes, of course, Mr Mc Gonagle, right away.' She looked at O'Brien. 'Mr Mc Gonagle says to go right through. Take the lift behind you to the second floor; it's the third door on the left.'

'Thank you.'

'You're welcome.'

The office was practically bare, concrete floor with a huge rug in the centre. The man sitting before the window lining the wall behind him didn't bother to get up from his tubular steel and glass desk when Sheahan and O'Brien went in. He was about forty-five, slicked-back salt-and-pepper hair, stocky build, tanned skin and an expression too friendly to be genuine.

'Mr Mc Gonagle?'

'That's me; call me Terry.'

They crossed to his desk.

'Mind if we sit down?' It was O'Brien.

'Where's my manners. Of course, sit down, sit down. Forgive me.'

When they had, Mc Gonagle said: 'Forgive me too for not getting up just now, pulled a tendon in a charity game of rugger on Sunday; it's going to take at least three weeks to get better... anyway, how can I help you two officers?' He smiled, displaying two rows of teeth straight out of *Cosmetic Dentistry Quarterly* magazine.

'It's to do with your property outside the village of Tinnock in County Wicklow. We were...'

'I didn't even know we had a property in Tinnock.' He laughed. 'Just joking. We have a huge portfolio, it would be easy to lose track, but I know it.' He pressed his computer keyboard a couple of times. 'Yes, here it is.' He turned the monitor towards them. 'This the one?'

Sheahan recognised it immediately. A near identical photo of the one Voyle had sent to his phone.

'Oh shite,' Mc Gonagle said. 'It's suddenly occurred to me. This hasn't anything to do with Minister Hughes, has it? Oh my God, it has, hasn't it?'

His voice suddenly sounded very camp.

'Yes,' Sheahan said, 'I'm afraid it has.'

Marty produced his notebook, opened it and held his pen over the page.

'I don't understand...' he began.

'Believe me,' Mc Gonagle answered, 'neither do I.'

'What I mean is, this cottage looks a derelict. And the officers on the ground have confirmed it's a derelict. But despite this, Hughes rented it. From you. How is that possible?'

'Who told you all this is what I'd like to know?'

'That's not important right now, sir.' It was O'Brien, the first time she had spoken.

'Being a bit formal there, Denise.'

'You two know one another?' Sheahan wondered.

O'Brien nodded. 'Of course, Dublin is a small town, after all.'

'You never mentioned,' Sheahan added.

'Well, I am now. I worked with Terence... sorry, Terry, on a property transfer from CAB... oh, five years ago now.'

'The Leinster Stud,' Mc Gonagle chipped in, 'our first big project. Set us up, actually, here at Park Developments.'

'Really.' Marty remembered there had been a scandal

around that, suspicion of a possible sweetheart deal, of political interference. *My, my.*

'They couldn't find anything,' O'Brien said, as if reading his mind. 'Anyway, nothing to do with me, but I can't speak for present company.'

'Denise, please. We run a tight ship. Would I be involved in such a thing?'

Oh yes you would, Sheahan considered, judging by looks alone, because Mc Gonagle appeared a right smarmy bastard. He also thought it peculiar O'Brien hadn't mentioned it to him before. Why? He'd have to save that for later.

'Anyway, it doesn't look the type of place that anyone could rent,' he said.

'That's because it's not.' Mc Gonagle took a furtive look at his watch.

'No?'

'Of course not. No. You're barking up the wrong tree. I never rented that place out. Park Developments never rented that place out either. Just to be clear. Who the hell would rent a place like that from anyone? They'd need their heads examined. Also, it would be against the law; you've seen the place, health and safety and all that, fit for nothing but knocking.'

And then it came to him, as Marty realised that he had made a fundamental error of judgement for one studying law. He had just gone along, not questioning anything. He clamped his mouth tightly shut, angry with himself.

So there was only one question to consider.

'If you didn't rent the property,' he asked, 'then who did?'

Mc Gonagle grinned. Marty thought that a little smug.

'Well now, Mr Policeman, that's for you to find out.'

'You never mentioned that you knew him,' Marty said when they got back to the car.

'I didn't think it was important.'

He noted she didn't make eye contact as she spoke. She went to turn the key in the ignition.

'Don't,' he said. 'Wait.'

'What?'

'You *didn't* mention. Let's just consider that. I think it odd. Why didn't you mention it? There were political shenanigans with that stud. Do you know if Hughes was involved? By the way, do you know Hughes? Because you didn't mention that either.'

She hesitated.

'You do, don't you?'

'Now you're making wild assumptions. I don't know *know* him. I met him once or twice, that's all.'

'Where?'

'I don't know, here and there... and what about you? Did you ever meet him, Rumpole?'

Marty was about to answer, but stopped. Because he couldn't be certain. Politicians in Dublin were like bowling skittles; they kept popping up.

'Exactly,' O'Brien said, 'now, can we go?'

Sheahan nodded, and she started the engine.

27

The missing foreign minister's home constituency was in Donegal. Too far for Brody to drive. There was too much to be done here.

Instead he got onto the local station and spoke with a detective.

'Anything specific you want us to ask Monica?' the detective, his name was Tomás O'Chaillagh, asked when Brody had explained what he wanted.

'Sounds like you know her.'

'Aye, I know her, alright. He's a government minister, for fuck's sake, we all know her... you sure you don't want to talk to her yourself? That might be best.'

'I do want to talk to her myself, of course, but I want you to do the talking on my behalf, got it? For now, that is. I'd lose a whole day going there and back. We also need to keep it low-key, if that's possible. For the family's sake, until we know what this is about...'

'Aye, right enough you would.'

'I presume someone has already visited...'

'Aye, right enough they have. Loretta, our family liaison officer.'

'Good.'

'Aye. What do you want me to ask her so?'

Brody felt himself getting irritated with O'Chaillagh's slow drawl and lazy style. He took a deep breath.

'How about her favourite colour?'

'What?'

'And food. Don't forget her favourite food.'

'Aw, you're taking the pissing, right enough, you are.'

'Ask her if her husband has any enemies. You could start with that.'

'He has enemies right enough; he's a politician. They all have enemies.'

'Yes, but he might have enemies that you don't know about, disgruntled husbands, that sort of thing.'

'That sort of thing. Disgruntled husbands. Well now, that's a good one...'

'I think you know. I'll ring you back this evening. I'd appreciate it if you could have a report ready.'

'I finish at three, me. I won't be here this evening.'

Brody bit his bottom lip.

'Put a report up on Pulse, then; you know how to use that?'

'Oh, Pulse, right enough, I never thought of that. I'd better get going, then, if I have to have all that done by three.'

'You'd better,' Brody said and hung up, feeling a pain start to build at the back of his head, and not certain that it was the attack from the previous night that was responsible. After talking to O'Chaillagh, he might well have to go to Donegal. It sounded like that mule couldn't be trusted to organise a piss-up in a brewery. He tapped a finger on his desk, then stood and pulled on his jacket, went down to the unit room. Considine was behind her desk, a bunch of mules around it, but none he recognised. He thought of *Love Island*, but one for mules, except the only one who'd make the cut here was Considine. She caught his eye and stood, walked over.

'Come with me,' he said.

'See ya, fellas,' she said over her shoulder, twiddling her fingers.

'Did you really just do that?'

'Do what?'

'Twiddle your fingers like that?'

They made their way along the corridor to the fire door that offered a shortcut out into the car park.

'Aw, Brody, they're only kids; it's bringing out the–'

'Don't say mother instinct; don't tell me you're broody, because that's definitely not a sign of being broody.'

'It's not?'

'You know well it's not.'

She grinned.

'Where we going?'

'Back to the scene.'

'The cottage?'

'No. The TV studios. Last night's scene. Marie Kennedy's husband works there too.'

They reached the door, and Brody pressed the push bar down. They stepped outside, but Considine stopped.

'He won't be there,' she said.

'Yes, he will.'

'For one who just told me of the subtleties of the female brooding experience, you should know that a man whose wife has been killed – beheaded, decapitated, what the fuck – will not be at work the following day.'

'If he's not, I'll eat my shoe.'

'You're on.'

'Fine then.'

Gary Kennedy was at work, so Brody wouldn't be dining on distressed leather brogues after all. His secretary said he could spare them ten minutes. How kind. If not, they would have to reschedule for later.

Gary Kennedy was vaguely familiar to Brody, in that way that Z-lister movie and TV personalities ignite a spark of recognition that you can't remember why. He wore khaki trousers and a green roll-neck jumper inside a brown tweed jacket. He was on the phone when they went in, standing behind his desk, pacing the floor of his large office. He was a tall, slim man, slightly stooped at the shoulders in the way that many tall, lanky men are. His hair was white, prematurely so, Brody guessed. The conversation was concerned with a new contract for someone or other, '… let him go to the BBC if he wants to, but they won't want him, believe me, and when he comes back with his tail between his legs, you make sure you offer him a contract with even less money…'

What he definitely didn't sound like was any grieving husband Brody had come across before. 'Got that?' he snapped, and pulled the mobile from his ear, tossed it onto the desk. He closed his eyes, Brody could see his chest rising and falling rapidly. 'These little shites' – opening them again – 'they really think they're so fucking talented, like they're doing us all a favour by being here. This' – he stretched his arms wide in an expanse gesture – 'is the equivalent of their ego. This' – he used a thumb and index finger to measure something tiny – 'is the sum total of their actual talent. If you can call it that. Little shites.'

Brody had had enough.

'Mr Kennedy, your wife. We'd like to talk with you about her unfortunate death.'

'Hm, yes, of course.' He indicated. 'Take a seat.' When

they had, he continued, 'Look. I'm going to say something. You're going to think it odd, crazy, so prepare yourselves. Right, here it goes. I'm glad my wife's dead. Yes, you heard me; don't look so shocked. I warned you. We both hated the sight of the other, and that's no secret; ask anyone. But I didn't kill her. Why would I do that?'

Brody and Considine exchanged glances.

'I know what you're thinking,' Kennedy said, catching it.

'You do?' It was Considine.

'Yes. But I told you. I didn't kill her.'

'I'll be honest with you, Mr Kennedy, I wasn't thinking that. But I am now.'

He shrugged. 'Makes no difference. You were going to think it anyway; might as well get it out of the way right now. By the way, I saw *Time Of Death*. Excellent production. If you ever want to do anything with our studio…'

'Edith Comerford already mentioned,' Brody said. 'Really, that's not what I want to talk about right now. Okay?'

'Okay. Yes, of course.'

'Mr Kennedy–' Considine began.

'Gary, call me Gary.'

'Fine, Gary. Are you in shock? Is that it? What you just said. About your wife. Mr Kennedy, Gary, she died in the most–'

'I know, I know, her head was chopped off. Yes, yes, I heard. Well, she did upset a lot of people down through the years, after all.'

'Unbelievable,' Considine said, shaking her own head.

Brody had to agree; it kind of was.

'I admit,' Kennedy said, 'it wasn't the nicest way for her to go. I wouldn't have wished that on my worst enemy, no, I wouldn't.'

'That's good to know,' Brody muttered, and louder, 'Mr

Kennedy, sorry to have to tell you this, but we believe she was having an affair with Donagh Hughes...'

Kennedy waved a hand through the air. 'Oh, that. Yes, I know. Everyone knew except maybe *his* wife. Marie had been seeing old cocktail sausage himself for a good while.'

Cocktail sausage.

Brody didn't want to go there. This encounter with Gary Kennedy was surreal enough. His telephone rang. He took it from a pocket and peered at the screen.

'If you excuse me, I have to take this.'

He stepped out of the office.

'Hello, Mary.'

'Yes. Hello to you too.' The forensic scientist was the opposite of her colleague with whom Brody often dealt. The colleague's name was Mercedes, as balmy and bright as a summer day in her native Andalusia, while Mary was as morose and grey as October in Connemara.

'The headless cadaver brought in last night,' she said sharply. 'You remember?'

Coming from anyone else, Brody would have thought it a trick question or maybe a little graveyard humour. But not with Mary.

'Yes, Mary, funnily enough, I do remember it, as it happens.'

'Yes, well, good. Because I was told to drop everything and deal with it, so that's exactly what I've done. People don't seem to think I might have other just as urgent cases on my list. But I do...'

'I appreciate it, really,' Brody said, going along to get along.

'Hm, good. Have you a pen ready?'

Brody wanted to tell her he wouldn't need a pen if she'd bother to put her report on Pulse before speaking with him. But he knew she wouldn't do that. Pulse for her, and all the other Marys on the force, was the horseless carriage that would never catch on.

'Yes, I've a pen. Shoot.'

Which was a lie. Brody didn't have a pen ready; he'd remember all that he needed to.

Even if, as expected, it was a little complicated.

Mary explained she had expected any forensic evidence to have been washed away in the copious amounts of water that flooded in and out of the car. This was not the case. Due to the angle of the body, the water actually helped, pressing down on the body, its weight causing what she called 'percolation seepage', resulting in a single fingerprint, and within that single fingerprint a strand of DNA, located on the right shoulder of the victim.

'My guess,' Mary said, 'the killer held the victim down in a pincer grip...'

'Sorry to interrupt, Mary, a pincer grip denotes the use of fingers. Would that be enough to hold the victim down?'

'Could you let me finish.'

'Apologies.'

The line hummed with static, Mary allowing it to linger for a moment, like a punishment.

'Let's try again,' she said. 'What I was going to say is that the victim was most probably dead when the killer held her down...'

'Then why hold her down at all? If she's already dead. There'd be no need, surely.'

'Jesus Christ, Brody, you want to do this yourself? You seem to have all the answers. Will I tell Dr Mc Bain to forget about the autopsy too? You'll look after it. I mean, why bother with forensic science? Will I hang up and leave you to it?'

'No, Mary, there's no need. I got a little carried away, that's all. I do apologise. Really.'

'You've apologised once already.'

'Yes, I know. Please, Mary, continue.'

'The victim was already dead, okay. But the body – as a fan of Pulse you should understand this – by having its central processor, i.e., its brain, suddenly severed in such a brutal way from the rest of its body, caused a violent spasm of the torso for a number of seconds: think electrical short circuit, something along those lines. I would suggest this is what happened, and because of this, I suggest the killer held the body down. Now, that single fingerprint would have been lost if the conditions hadn't been just right, with a combination of water pressure, vaporisation and salt residue from the tidal water of the estuary, allowing the print to seep into the fabric of the coat. The impression was preserved in a process similar to osmosis. In a nutshell, when I dried out the coat, there it was, evident in the minute salt particles in the pattern of a fingerprint when I looked at it under a magnifying glass.'

'Great,' Brody said, only when Mary had been silent for some seconds and he was certain she had finished speaking. 'Was there a match on the system for it, for the print?'

'If there was, don't you think I'd have told you straight off the bat.'

'Yes, Mary, I'm sure you would. That's great work, Mary, tha–'

But she'd already hung up.

'Sorry about that,' Brody said when he went back into the office. He caught a look from Considine and nodded, a subliminal message to her that he had something. He sat down. 'Mr Kennedy...' He would keep this formal, no first names. 'I would like to formally request from you a sample of DNA and fingerprint. You agree?'

Kennedy's eyes widened, but he slowly nodded.

'This means I'm a suspect, doesn't it?'

'It's procedure.'

'No, it's not. My TV station makes true crime programmes, remember. I know what's what. I *am* a suspect.'

'Okay, you are a suspect. Garda Considine, would you pop out for the fingerprint scanner and a swab kit, please?'

As Considine got up, Gary Kennedy sat back in his chair. For the first time, he looked worried.

28

He had become accustomed to the poor light, his eyes adjusting to the scrap of illumination offered by the yellow ribbon around the door, making the most of it. His world was like one viewed through a weak, sepia-filtered lens, yet he could make out everything. The rats no longer frightened him as much. He had other things on his mind. He'd reached the conclusion that they weren't that interested in him, really... or at least, they appeared not to be. There were more of them now; he'd spotted six or so scampering along by the wall once. They say rats are clever, very clever. He had to agree. It took a lot to catch one in a trap, for instance. A trap had to sit in place for a long, long time before there was even a chance one might get used to it, and then another long, long time before one might, eventually, wander in and take the bait. He realised he was okay with the rats just so long as he could actually see them. A half hour ago, or was it an hour, or maybe two, a particularly big fella had strayed a little too close for comfort. Donagh Hughes had raised his two taped-together feet and stomped them down as loud as he could onto the floor. The rat had immediately scurried away. Fine. Just so long as he could see them, he could continue doing just that. But what happened when night fell, and he went to sleep? The thought made him shudder. So Donagh Hughes realised that he had been fooling himself all along. He wasn't okay with rats; he was actually petrified of them.

He hadn't noticed the door opening, so busy was he staring across at the big fella that was sitting down and preening itself now. The rat was trying to fool him, he thought, licking its front paws like that, then wiping them down across its face, like it hadn't a care in the world... but secretly waiting, for what Hughes wasn't certain, until it could creep up on him maybe, nibble on his ear, then his head, finally nibble into his brain...

Hughes shook his head, ridding himself of the image. And that was when he realised the door had opened. He looked up just in time to see a hand push something towards him across the floor before it withdrew again. The door closed with a soft plop sound. Hughes looked at the miniature metal dome resting on the floor, a sheen on one side reflecting what little light there was, on top a nipple-like bulge. Then it came to him, this was what was called a cloche, a food cover usually found in fine dining establishments, usually over a prime cut of meat on a platter. How could he eat when he was trussed up like this? And he needed to go to the toilet. Jesus, he did. They couldn't keep him tied up this way forever. Could they?

He wiggled forward, used his legs to kick the cloche off whatever it was covering. The rats scurried at the sound of the toppling metal, but he felt their eyes on him.

He immediately recognised the smell: meat, steak perhaps. For him? Of course for him. Who else? But how was he supposed to eat it?

Maybe it was roast beef. He liked roast beef. Every Sunday, each and every Sunday, until he had left home at twenty-one, that is, his mother had cooked a roast beef joint. His wife still did the same. He'd demanded it. Couldn't beat a roast beef dinner on a Sunday. But it wasn't the same, with Monica, that is, and he told her it too. Because Monica just couldn't cook like his mother. Simple as. And this was his first thought, in the faded sepia light: roast beef.

But he knew it wasn't. Maybe he had thought of roast beef because the truth was too horrible, too grotesque to comprehend. Roast beef was easier, comforting.

But he couldn't fool himself any longer.

Now that he could see it.

Yes, he could see it. Plain as – sepia – day.

On the platter before him.

Marie Kennedy's head.

He turned away, starting to gag, but unable to stop the stream of green bile seeping from between his lips. The rats began to squeal. They had reappeared again, moving closer, gathering around the platter, around Marie Kennedy's head. He wanted to stomp his feet, but knew it would be no use. They were squealing louder now; he wanted to cover his ears against that sound but couldn't. And then they moved in, swarming over it, their little teeth making a surprisingly loud munching sound as they started on the dead flesh.

29

When Brody hung up after speaking with Mary at Forensic Services Ireland, Voyle was thinking that Patrick O'Connor looked like a man with a hangover. Which was not a surprise. After all, Voyle had seen him just a little over fifteen, maybe sixteen hours before drinking his master's brandy and *then* going into that pub in Tinnock.

Voyle had come here directly from his home in Dun Laoghaire. He didn't need to go to the Phoenix Park and rendezvous with Considine first. He had been told by one of Harper's – or was it Ryan's? – minions, it was hard to tell which, that she was being held back for duties 'as required'.

'What about me?' he'd asked.

'What about you?' asked the minion, who wouldn't give his name.

'Exactly,' Voyle said and hung up.

He knew just where he stood now. On his own. That was where. *Suits me just fine.* Since Ryan had come to the unit, the natural order had been turned on its head. Unfortunately, it often happened with a new leader who was keen to impress.

One thing was certain, Ryan was not impressing – him at least.

'Um...' O'Connor began, but didn't say anything else, merely looking at Voyle, who decided that he did indeed have a hangover, his eyes puffy and red.

'Sorry to disturb you again,' Voyle began, not knowing where this was going. The afternoon air was crisp, carrying with it a sweet fragile fragrance that probably came from the gardens. Voyle had not noticed them on his first visit. He could see too in the daylight a row of neatly clipped low bushes on raised, stone-bordered beds running along the front of the house at intervals, in between them the tubular roots of wall flowers setting out to form farther up a beautiful tapestry of colour that threaded its way around the first-floor windows. A metal gardening tool of some description glinted in the weak sun next to a wheelbarrow by the fourth raised bed. Voyle imagined the upkeep of a place like this to be a constant treadmill of maintenance.

O'Connor spoke now, his voice raw and gravelly. 'How did you get in?'

'The gate was open.'

'It was?'

'Yes.'

O'Connor must have been well leathered to have forgotten to close the gates last night.

The butler, caretaker – whatever – was wearing an apron, Voyle had not paid it much attention. But he did now. It was of brown canvas, but only the top corner was still that colour; what remained was red.

'Why is your apron covered in blood, Mr O'Connor?' Voyle said.

And then the door was slammed in his face.

30

This was a nightmare. Donagh Hughes was losing his sanity. The Minister for Foreign Affairs was going fucking crazy. He roared, a proper, full-on roar, pushed up from the bottom of his belly, a hyperventilating, desperate roar of hopelessness, of fear and panic. When he'd finished, he roared again, but this time it was fused with words carried along with it...
'LET ME OUT OF HERE.'

Of course, no one did. But moments later, when he'd fallen silent, he heard a sound, like a bolt sliding back.

Because that was what it was.

The door opened.

The light from outside was bright, it hurt his eyes, and he closed them against it before opening them again, peering through partially raised eyelids, like thin blades of grass. What looked like an apparition was standing before him, the light flowing about it in rays of yellow and white, making it appear like an ecclesiastical being.

Maybe it was.

Maybe Donagh Hughes had gotten all this wrong? Maybe he was dead and had gone to heaven. Maybe this was his saviour?

Maybe.

In his delirium he raised his trussed hands as high as he could towards his messiah.

'Help me, help me, please; won't you help me.'

The voice did not sound like any messiah. 'Hold it right there,' it said.

And he did.

Donagh Hughes held his trussed hands still in the air before his face. There was a whirring sound, so distant it seemed like the buzzing of a swarm of bees or bluebottles, somewhere way off, either the bluebottles were feasting on a carcass, or the bees were busy making honey. Whatever your point of view.

He felt his hands taken in a powerful grip. The whirring noise got louder. The apparition bent, the light shifting. This was not a messiah, an apparition, nothing but a big, fat human walrus, rounded and seemingly without any shape, its grotesque, misaligned face staring intently as the whirring grew louder still. Only in that instant when the electric blade touched his flesh did he understand what was happening. The pain at first didn't seem like pain, it was more like a dunk in freezing cold water: a kick to the senses, nothing more. But as the blade met bone and the whirring changed to a dry grinding sound, throwing off a fine spray of fragments that peppered his face, the pain became unbearable. He screamed and bucked against it, but it was no use. The force holding him was too strong. Donagh Hughes could only watch in morbid fascination as the blade cut through the last resistance of sinewy muscle.

And then his finger fell to the floor.

31

It turned out Patrick O'Connor had slammed the door in Voyle's face because Debussy had been about to bolt. The tabby had only just returned from a twenty-four walkabout, O'Connor explained, and he didn't want her getting out again. The cat slinked under the hall table when Voyle entered. It didn't look like any cat he'd ever seen before. What it looked like was a yellow-eyed, hairless creature that had just alighted from a spaceship.

'It's a sphinx and rather valuable,' O'Connor said, 'belonged to Mr Gilsenan, and is part of his estate. I need to make sure nothing happens to it. I do apologise.' He was still wearing the bloodied apron. He pointed. 'I saw the way you were looking at this. Don't worry. I'm butchering a deer, that's all. I'll bag the venison and use it later. It's deer season, you know.'

'I didn't know. Really?'

'Yes. Really. Look. Come with me.'

Voyle followed him along the hall, then along a corridor, then another corridor, to a massive old kitchen with white-washed walls. Two enormous black ranges were set in alcoves to one side. On a butcher's block in a corner was the partially mutilated carcass of a buck deer, its antlered head resting in a wicker basket on the ground before it.

'I'll use that to make a broth,' O'Connor explained. 'And the antlers will be ground down into deer antler supplements, a chap in Wicklow takes them. Nothing is wasted.'

O'Connor was sweating, his skin blotchy. Voyle noticed an unopened dusty bottle of wine on a worktop next to the sinks, a couple of glasses ready beside it. Hair of the dog, courtesy of Gilsenan's personal cellar, he guessed. But two glasses. Did O'Connor have company?

A noise above him made him look up. Above was a balcony fronted by a wooden balustrade, the head of Debussy peering down from between them.

'The viewing gallery. Mr Gilsenan would sometimes gather with his guests and look at proceedings. And now Debussy is wondering just how he can get at this deer. Not that he'd eat any of it. He eats better than I do does that cat.'

Voyle looked from Debussy to the deer's head. And thought of Marie Kennedy.

'You went to a pub last night in Tinnock,' he said, and watched Patrick O'Connor go pale.

'How did you know that?'

'I was sitting in a car, eating fish and chips, as it happens. I saw you.'

'You were?' He seemed to think about that. 'Well, there's no law against that.' Although O'Connor didn't sound too sure.

'Did you go anywhere after the pub, Mr O'Connor?'

'After the pub? Like where? Why are you asking me all this?'

'Did you?'

The caretaker, butler – whatever – glanced to the side,

and Voyle followed it, saw he was looking at a large, blood-smeared handsaw. He turned back, and their eyes met.

'What?' O'Connor said. 'You think I'm going to chop you up, is that it? The way you're looking at me.'

'I'm not thinking that, Mr O'Connor, not thinking that at all.'

'I'm chopping a bloody deer, like I told you, that's all. Now, please tell me what this is about.'

'It's about the suicide of Mr Robert Gilsenan, that's what. I told you. That's why I'm here.'

'How has this got anything to do with it? This, *did I go anywhere afterwards* and all that. Actually, let me put you out of your misery. Afterwards, I came back here. Because where else would I go?'

'I don't know. You tell me. And have you any way of proving this?'

'Shite. There you go again. I will not answer anything else until you tell me what this is about, and then I'll decide if I need to see my solicitor.'

'Hm,' Voyle began, and fell silent. 'Your solicitor. Maybe that's a good idea.'

O'Connor seemed surprised. *Bingo*, Voyle thought, and wanted to say, *The truth is, I am here to look into Mr Gilsenan's suicide, but then, when I arrived just now, I see you're decapitating a deer. Well, that makes me realise you have butchering skills, and got me to thinking that last night someone decapitated Marie Kennedy. And that, Mr O'Connor, is why I can't help but think now if all this isn't maybe a little more than just a mere coincidence?*

'I came back here about 1 a.m.,' he said. 'I don't remember much about it, to tell the truth, but I remember that, just do.' He turned his head and yelled, 'Kate, come in here.'

Kate came in a moment later, dirty blonde hair, skin like old leather, in a short, wrinkled red dress.

'Who's he?' she asked, her voice scratchy, looking at Voyle.

'He's a police officer, Kate, that's who he is.'

'Is he now? And what's he doing here?'

Voyle guessed this wasn't her first time dealing with the forces of law and order. But he remembered at training college over a decade before, being warned of the dangers of making assumptions. Such an approach did not fit well with an ethos of impartiality and fairness. In short, he had been told not to judge a book by its cover.

But it was impossible sometimes not to. Voyle was judging this book by its cover.

'Kate, tell the officer when we got back here last night, the time. You weren't as smashed as me... I don't think you were, anyway.'

'And why would I do that?' Her eyes narrowed suspiciously at Voyle.

'Just do it, Kate. Tell him.'

'One o'clock. No big secret. So?'

'You met in the pub?' Voyle asked. 'Is that it?'

'We did, and we didn't.' It was O'Connor. 'We've known each other a while.'

'I was–' Kate began.

'That's enough, Kate,' O'Connor interrupted. 'We don't have to tell him our business. Okay? The time we got back here, that's all.'

'Just open the wine, Patrick,' she said. 'For God's sake.'

'Open it yourself.' O'Connor looked at Voyle. 'Now, can I get back to this?' He nodded toward the carcass.

Voyle pursed his lips. 'Is there something you don't want her to tell me, Mr O'Connor?'

'I'll tell you what. I'm getting fed up with this. Maybe I should ring my solicitor, because I'm very close to reaching my limit with all of this.'

Voyle realised he had pushed far enough.

'You can go back to your carcass, no problem. Before I leave, I'm going to look at the conservatory again. It's at the back of the house, if I remember.'

Voyle wasn't asking, he was telling.

'Why you want to go there again?' A definite change in O'Connor's tone, one Voyle had heard a thousand times before. The man was worried. *Interesting.*

'There's not a problem, is there, Mr O'Connor?'

'N-no, there's not; why would there be? But you can find it yourself. I'm busy. Just turn right out that door, next left, next right, straight ahead... no, I don't have a problem with you visiting it again. Kate, pour me a glass of that wine.'

Voyle started for the door. When he reached it, he stopped, turned, spoke softly.

'Your wife, Mr O'Connor, is back on Monday. Is that correct?'

The butler, caretaker – whatever – went pale again.

'Yes, that's right.'

'Visiting her sister, you said?'

'Yes, visiting her sister, I said. What about it?'

Voyle glanced at Kate. Who was busy pouring wine into a couple of glasses. Voyle noticed her hand was shaking slightly.

'No reason, just reminding myself, that's all.'

'Fine then.'

'They were meeting in Gort, you said. Your wife and her sister.'

O'Connor didn't answer immediately. He seemed to be thinking about it.

'Yes, Gort.'

'You sure? Gort?'

'Yes, of course I'm bloody sure. Why you giving me the third degree again?'

'Right,' Voyle said, 'just asking. Now, I'll go and find that conservatory.'

'Fine.'

He left the kitchen, started down the long corridor outside, half panelled in dark wood, arched windows along one side, portraits in gold frames along the other, an austere, almost monastic setting.

Voyle thought of what O'Connor had said just now. Which was different to what he'd said the first time they'd spoken. On that occasion O'Connor had told him his wife was meeting her sister in Galway. Not Gort.

Was that a mistake a husband was likely to ever make, hangover or not?

Maybe, but he didn't think so.

32

Brody knew he'd underestimated Tomás O'Chaillagh within one minute of his speaking with him again. It must be understood that there is a certain trait in the Irish psyche to underplay events, indeed, to sometimes come across as less knowledgeable than you actually are. That way, people will hopefully think you're stupid and leave you alone. As Brody had thought of O'Chaillagh.

'She's not feeling too bad, so she's not,' O'Chaillagh said in that slow drawl of his. 'I asked her all the questions you told me I should ask her, so I did… Oh, I did, right enough.'

'Go on.' Brody rested one elbow on his desk, leaned forward onto it.

'She's at home with her sister-in-law. That would be Mildred O'Donnell, from Letterkenny. Who's staying with Monica for a few days. Monica and Donagh's two boys are grown up now. Fine young men they are too. One is in Dubai; the other fella's in Canada. She doesn't want to worry them if she can help it, so she doesn't. You were right not to make a fuss. She doesn't want to make any fuss. Now' – there was the sound of a rustling of paper – 'there was no talk of him having an affair. So I didn't mention it either. No need to stir that up unless we need to. But I know she knows about it; she doesn't have to say it... Tell me, did you ever get the impression when talking to someone that you were discussing one thing but ye were both meaning something else entirely?'

Brody took a breath. Oh yes, he was wrong about O'Chaillagh alright.

'What do you mean?'

'Well, Monica said she spends a lot of time at home alone because her husband is away practically all the time. "Who knows what people get up to," is what she said. But the same could be said for her too, so it could, is what I hear.'

'What you mean?'

'Och, nothing specific. What people get up to behind closed doors is none of my business, provided they're not breaking the law, of course.'

'Of course. Getting up to stuff behind closed doors. Having affairs, you mean?'

'Och, I don't know, who does? Could be nothing but malicious gossip. I asked her did he have any enemies like you said, and she laughed out loud. She said he had a Garda security detail looking after him when he was at home, but there wasn't one when he wasn't at home. Although I think that suits her right fine, but she said she didn't think it was very fair. "And what good are they anyway," she said, "when he can disappear the way he has." I think she was only getting her point across that the security detail weren't always with him because he didn't want them with him. Common knowledge. So in her own way she was subtly pointing a finger at us, at the force.'

Talking about one thing but meaning another.

'So what's she actually saying?'

'That it's our fault, and she knows it, that's what she means. She could do a lot with that information if she wanted to, she said. Can you imagine? Heads would roll.'

Brody could. But he didn't care. Harper and Ryan would though.

'Can we get back to enemies…'

'Aye. She didn't seem to take any of them seriously.'

'Didn't she?'

'Except one fella.'

'Oh. Who's that?'

'The ghost, she called him.'

'The ghost?'

'Aye, because he doesn't seem to exist, yet does, all at the same time. If you get me.'

Brody was silent.

'No, I don't get you.'

'He exists in the netherworld, or Metaworld, whatever you want to call it.'

'Metaworld, you mean Facebook?'

'Aye, that's where he dwells, spewing out all sorts of vile shite. I had a look.'

Which meant that O'Chaillagh, with his slow drawl and his gormless way, was now ahead of him.

'Can you send me a link?'

'I already have. You should get it' – Brody's phone pinged in the background – 'about now.'

'Anything else?'

'I think that's enough to be getting on with, don't you?'

O'Chaillagh was right; it was enough to be getting on with.

'Thank you for your help,' Brody said.

'Ach, sure, I was only doing what you told me to do… Right so, I'll be off, then.'

There was no offer for Brody to feel free to contact him again if he needed to.

'One more thing,' Brody said.

'And what's that?'

'Did she seem worried at all, about her husband, of what might have happened to him?'

'Well, now that I think of it, she didn't, not at all. But that doesn't mean that she is or she isn't. She could be holding it in, just beneath the surface. Some people are like that. It helps this was kept low-key for a while, surely it does.'

That last comment sounded like a compliment, like it was O'Chaillagh who was in charge all along.

And, Brody thought, maybe he was.

'Okay then,' he said, about to pull the phone from his ear.

'Oh, one more thing.'

'Yes.'

'Sure, it's probably nothing, but then again... Monica was dressed for going somewhere. Not out *somewhere*, but somewhere travelling I mean, in her little pink tracksuit and Converse sneakers. I didn't see a bag or nothing, but the car was by the door, with the boot open. Course, I didn't think nothing of that when I got there, but when I was leaving, I thought to myself, Monica looks like she's going somewhere. She didn't say nothing to me, mind. Sure maybe she wasn't going anywhere at all. But it looked like she was.'

'And where would she be going?'

'Ach, sure, she could be going anywhere.'

Brody waited for another late thought from O'Chaillagh, but one didn't come.

'Do they have a Dublin home? For when he's in the City,' Brody asked.

'Um... aye, right enough, they do have.'

'And where would that be?'

'Well now... yes, I believe it's in a hotel, an apartment, they lease it, or time share, something like that, if you get me? A hotel apartment.'

Brody threw his eyes to the ceiling.

'You know the hotel?'

'Let me think. The Florence... nah, that's not it. The Lawrence Hotel... aye, that's it, the Lawrence Hotel.'

'And the car she's driving. You know the make, reg?'

'She might only be going to Letterkenny to the hairdressers or something. I didn't say she was going to stay in the Lawrence Hotel now.'

'No. But she might.'

When he'd finally gotten the make of car and reg from O'Chaillagh and put the phone down, he thought that had been a form of torture.

Which was probably the way O'Chaillagh had wanted it, so Brody wouldn't trouble him again.

VOYLE LOOKED over his shoulder as he made his way to the conservatory: it was an old trick of his, learned from tramping through unfamiliar territory, and would help him find his way back later. This big old house was a maze of stone and concrete. Patrick O'Connor had not offered to come fetch him.

Which was just as well, because Voyle wanted to be alone to try to work this conundrum out for himself.

The last time he'd been in the conservatory, he'd noticed there was an electric heater. Typical, because a conservatory, with its glass walls and roof, while being very quick to heat up when subjected to the sun's rays, was also just as quick to cool down again when the sun no longer was shining. So, this, like any other conservatory Voyle had ever been in, had a heater.

A quite big, fancy heater that took him a moment to figure out. But when he had and had turned it on, he went about and made sure the door and windows were all securely closed. Then he sat down in the wicker chair that Robert Gilsenan had been found dead in.

And waited.

33

The press had still not made the link between Donagh Hughes and Marie Kennedy. But that was about to change. The media room at HQ was packed with TV, print and digital journalists. Superintendent Tony Harper sat in the centre of the table at the top of the room, on one side of him Fiona Ryan, on the other Inspector Miriam Walker, the Garda press officer. Behind them on the wall was a huge sign that said:

> Garda Information Hotline 1-800-747-747. If You Know Something, Don't Keep It To Yourself – TELL US.

The media briefing was Harper's idea. Brody thought the investigation was beginning to take on aspects of a Machiavellian drama: The SDU superintendent was now convinced the disappearance of Hughes was politically motivated. Brody wasn't. Because if that were the case, then the police would, at the very least, have heard from his abductors by now. And also, if it were political, he, Brody, would not have survived his ordeal last night. He would, for sure, be dead.

Why had he been spared? He had no answer for that – not yet. He didn't know what this was about, but was sure it wasn't political, no. Harper thinking that it was would only waste time by going down a rabbit hole. As for Ryan, she was still obsessed with Voyle being the source of the leak, and although she wasn't saying it, Brody got the impression she thought Voyle might be somehow involved in this too. He considered her already down a rabbit hole. The real motivation for her thinking this, Brody felt, was that she simply didn't like Voyle, and that dislike had become insidious and was clouding her judgement. There was little talk of Marie Kennedy in any of it; somehow she was becoming lost to the bigger drama as the wheels of this investigation started to spin deeper down into the mud.

That was another mistake Harper was making. A big mistake. The press wouldn't see it the way he was, especially now that he was about to make a link between the two. And the woman Hughes was being linked to, Marie Kennedy, was dead, decapitated, what the fuck. That was, well, only one word would cover it...

Explosive.

The brass was about to get ensnared into a trap of their own making. Funny how those who should be able to see things couldn't, even the obvious, even when it was right in front of their faces.

But Brody could. Which was why he had given an excuse and said he couldn't be part of the press conference. He'd told Harper instead that it was imperative he spoke with the Donegal family liaison and made sure Hughes's wife, Monica, was forewarned of proceedings and that someone should be with her. Because of his actions, Monica was forewarned – but only just in time. She would not have a member of family liaison with her, however, because Monica was travelling by car somewhere, and she didn't tell the family liaison where she was going, nor was she asked.

Brody discreetly entered the media room just as the conference was about to begin, standing at the very back, just inside the door. He had to give it to Harper, he was a natural, sitting straight backed in his chair, wearing a crisp, freshly pressed shirt, hair immaculately combed to one side, gesturing with his hands as he began to speak. The room was silent, hanging on to his every word...

And then the wheels came off the wagon and careered down the side of the cliff, exploding and bursting into flames as it went, just as Brody knew it would.

After his introductions, Harper's hands gesturing like he was tossing imaginary balls into the air, he continued, 'As joint chief investigating officer on this case, I believe the disappearance of Foreign Minister Donagh Hughes is highly likely to be a politically motivated act. Also, a link has been established between Donagh Hughes and Marie Kennedy, a link of a personal, intimate nature...' And then his voice was drowned out as the room erupted. The person next to Brody said, 'Jesus Christ,' raising his Dictaphone high into the air above the din, his elbow brushing against Brody's cheek. Brody had foreseen the questions that came next... *Is Hughes a suspect in the murder of Marie Kennedy?... Did he go missing at the same time as the discovery of her body?... How long have the gardai known of this link?... Were they lovers, Superintendent Harper?...* And on and on. The Garda press officer, Inspector Miriam Walker, raised the palm of her hand to try to restore order. But it was useless. The press were in a frenzy. Harper looked like he'd stuck a wet finger into an electrical socket. Superintendent Ryan simply looked away.

The last image Brody had before he slipped out the door was of Harper with his arms tightly folded across his chest, waiting for the blindfold to be placed over his eyes before a firing squad.

Forty-five minutes later, he had arranged a team get-together in the Eddie Rocket's on Baggot Street Upper, a 1950s American-themed diner and part of a popular city-wide chain. Sheahan and O'Brien were already there when he arrived. Brody thought Sheahan looked like a scruffy student alongside the more urbane O'Brien, the two of them sitting side by side on the red bench seat. Or maybe she could be taken as his cougar lover. Brody guessed she was in her late forties.

'You look much better than you did the last time we met,' O'Brien said as Brody slid in along the bench seat opposite. He realised this was the first time they'd formally met.

'Well, that wouldn't be hard.'

'Considine's running a little late,' Sheahan said. 'She tried ringing you. But you weren't answering.'

Brody checked his phone.

'It's dead. That's why.'

'If I could politely ask,' O'Brien said, 'but why am I here? I'm not on your team.'

'I know you're not on my team,' Brody replied, 'but you've been working with Sheahan. You can at least have some lunch with us, can't you?'

O'Brien smiled.

'You ready to order?' The young waitress held her pen ready.

'A smartphone charger, please.'

'A what?'

'For this.' He held up his phone. 'It's dead.'

'Oh, I think we should have one. Let me go and check.'

While she did, Considine pushed through the door and walked down the aisle to their table.

'It's all over the news,' she announced.

Standing above the table like that, she seemed even taller than she actually was. She flicked a hand across her high forehead, pushing back blonde hair from her eyes. 'You were right, Jack, that conference was a disaster.'

Brody pushed in, and she slid down next to him.

'Now, what's all this about?'

'All in good time.'

He waited until they'd ordered before he told them. Brody didn't like the way the investigation was progressing. But there were no surprises there. Nor did he like the interference, the manipulation by Harper. In fact, he didn't like Harper either, for that matter. And as for Fiona Ryan... well, the jury was still out on her. But if someone didn't do something, and quickly, then this shitestorm would carry them all away with it.

'I feel it's like a type of stampede. You've seen the number of people in the unit room. What are they doing? They don't even know themselves.'

'And you do?' Denise O'Brien ran a long, painted nail along the edge of her lower lip, took it away and looked at it, flicked something away.

'I know this much. Hughes was being stalked by a ghost.'

'Excuse me?'

Brody looked at Sheahan. 'Check out Facebook. Donagh Hughes's page. Also that of his wife. Twitter accounts too. I'll send you a link. You'll see what I mean.'

Marty already had his notebook out, and he wrote the information down into it.

'As you said,' Brody told O'Brien, 'you're not part of this team. So I can't tell you what to do. But I can ask if you want to work on this... with Marty. Do you?' He shrugged. 'Your choice.'

She said nothing for a moment. Then: 'I'll have to run it

by my boss first...' Her effervescence of earlier had disappeared; she didn't seem so sure of herself now.

'Fine. But there's only one problem. I haven't run this past my boss either. That's the whole point. Strictly speaking, this little operation is something like what Marty will be looking for. A ghost. No one can see it. That's the way I want it.'

She folded her arms and looked pensive.

'Like seriously, you really think you can do something that this entire Garda operation can't? You can sort this out on your ownsome?'

'I didn't say that.'

'Sounded like it to me.'

'We'll be small and nimble, without any interference – that's the key. Anyway, no one should even know about this, like I said. If they do, I can cover it by saying we're following up on investigative threads, which we are. Nothing wrong with that. I just haven't told anyone, present company excepted, about it, that's all.' Brody looked at his watch. 'Now, we need to get a move on. Can we have your verdict?'

'Okay,' O'Brien said, 'I'll go along. As you say, no one needs to know. I like that. Anyway, Harper has enough on his mind; he won't be asking me any questions. But...'

'But?'

'No offence, Marty, I'd like to' – she pointed at Considine – 'work with her.'

Considine raised an eyebrow.

'Me? You would?'

'Yes. I haven't worked with a woman in over a year. The SDU is a male cesspit.'

'I noticed.'

'Only if you don't mind, of course. If you do, I...'

'I don't mind. I don't care. But personally, I find the boys easier to deal with, don't have to mind my words so much. If you get me?'

'I get you. But you should try the SDU sometime.'

'No thanks.'

'Okay,' Brody said, 'you can both work together. That leaves you with me, Marty.'

Marty nodded.

'Voyle is still out on his own on this errand he's been given, and for all the wrong reasons, I might add...'

'I'd call it out on a limb, boss, myself.' It was Considine.

'Whatever.'

The truth was, in either case, Superintendent Ryan had her work cut out to gain the trust of Brody. Voyle might be a lot of things, but he was a good mule; he didn't need to be treated like an outcast. No, Brody didn't like it.

He thought of something.

'I'm curious,' he said to O'Brien. 'What's it like on Harper's team? Despite everything, have I got the man pegged wrong? Let's hear it from the horse's mouth.'

'You haven't got him pegged wrong. No.' She half smiled, half smirked. 'My boss is a showman. Yes, he looks the part and sounds the part too. He's an absolute inspiration at any PowerPoint presentation. The only drawback is, don't ask him to do anything outside the box. That way, everything'll be fine. And it usually is. He's a yes-man.'

Brody didn't seem convinced. 'SDU jobs are all difficult, aren't they?'

'Not as you'd think. Domestic security, witness protection, that sort of thing doesn't require any investigation at all, pretty straightforward, actually. We don't deal with the stuff you deal with. And with Harper, a control freak who doesn't like to delegate, it's just as well. As you can see, these are not the traits that lend themselves to those occasions when the shite hits the fan. The emperor has been exposed as having no clothes, I think. Finally.'

An emperor, Brody thought, who was always going to

steamroller his way in on any investigation if he was allowed to. And he'd been allowed to. The SDU might have jurisdiction – although Brody thought that was open to debate – but Ryan should have maintained her authority over her own team. And she hadn't. She had a lot of work to do if she wanted to not just command the respect of the members of the MCIU, but to merely gain it in the first place.

'THIS IS RIDICULOUS,' Considine said when she and O'Brien arrived at Merrion Square and O'Brien pointed to the little purple roadster parked against the kerb. Considine thought the car looked like an insect that had crawled out from beneath a manhole cover. 'I can't even fit in that yoke. No way.'

'Aw, don't say that. Ssscchh, you'll upset it.'

Considine looked at her.

'Are you okay in the head, girl?'

'Who knows, maybe machines have feelings too. You don't know.'

'Mad as a hatter, that's what you are, if you don't mind my saying.'

O'Brien laughed. 'Only joking.'

But Considine wasn't so certain that she was.

'That hotel is too far to walk,' Considine said. 'We'll have to go back to the depot and get another car. I don't want to arrive in that yoke. It's not open to discussion. I'll take out a car from the pool that doesn't look like something from *Miami Vice*. Fair enough?'

'Fair enough. But you know what they say?'

'What?'

'Beauty's in the eye of the beholder.'

'Well, *girl*, get rid of that beaut... By the way, and I might be wrong, you into amateur dramatics, that sort of thing? Well?'

'I actually studied drama. How could you even know about that?'

'I didn't. You have a theatrical presence, that's all.'

O'Brien beamed. 'I do?'

'And only someone who loves the attention would drive a car like that.'

O'Brien beamed again and pointed the remote, popped the car boot.

'I think we're going to get on just fine,' she said, leaning against it and pulling off her high heels. 'But this work of beauty is impossible to drive in these shoes. I've got to lose the heels.'

'Why bother wearing them in the first place?'

'They're classy, don't you think? Take Elizabeth Taylor, for example. I'm a huge fan of hers, or Vivian Leigh, or anyone of that ilk, in fact. Classy ladies. You'd never catch them without their heels.'

'So you're Elizabeth Taylor now?'

'A girl can always pretend.' She pushed her small, petite foot into a pristine, little-worn Nike.

34

Who would have thought that only a couple of decades before, Dublin, long considered a European backwater, would be transformed into a cosmopolitan European city, an international hub for many industries, including hi-tech and financial services, and the world's leading player in aircraft leasing.

But it had. And when the sun shone – it being Dublin, that wasn't very often – but when it did, and the diners and drinkers spilled out of the cafés and bars onto the streets, Dublin looked like Paris or Madrid. The air hummed with a youthful, dynamic energy; the languages spoken were global. It was as if Dublin had moulted and a whole new city had emerged.

Which helped Brody now.

Because the European HQ of Facebook was situated on Grand Canal Square, a stone's throw from the city centre. Brody and Sheahan drove straight there. They parked on the double yellow lines right out front, and Brody pulled down his visor to display the official card he had taped there that said:

Garda On Official Business.

As they went up the steps towards the revolving front doors, a burly female security guard dressed in a navy-blue trouser suit emerged and stood, with her arms folded, looking down at them.

'Can I help you?' she said, her tone polite, but her expression no-nonsense, as they came off the last step and walked towards her.

'Hopefully,' Brody said, 'we'd like…'

'First off. No walk-ins allowed. If you have official business, you need to make an appointment. No exceptions.'

Brody thought her observational and interpretative skills were severely lacking for one working security at such a prestigious blue-chip company. Because two men such as himself and Sheahan, with an air about them that they possessed, *and* driving the car that they were, a two-year-old Hyundai with missing hubcaps, could only mean one thing. To anyone who should know, that is, and she should know.

'Detective Sergeant Jack Brody,' he said, taking out his ID wallet. He opened it and held it up to her. The security guard peered at it. 'And Detective Garda Martin Sheahan. We need to speak to someone in your technical department, to help us identify the holder of an account we're interested in.'

The no-nonsense expression disappeared.

'Oh well, why didn't you say?'

'I just did.'

'Yes, that changes everything.'

'I was hoping it would.'

'This way, gentlemen. Follow me.'

She led them through the revolving door into the building. A male security officer frisked them, pointed to a security scanner, and they passed through, the female security guard waiting on the other side. She made a phone call, and they accompanied her to the elevator and up to the third floor. A man was waiting for them when they alighted, mid-twenties, curly black hair, wire-rimmed John Lennon glasses, dressed in a black T-shirt and black jeans.

'Is this them?'

'It is.'

'Follow me, please.'

He led them through a set of automatic glass doors into what looked to be part railway station, part restaurant, part pub and, with an abundance of green along its walls, part garden centre. They sat in a window booth overlooking the Dublin docklands. On the table was a laptop.

'My name's Theo,' the man said. Brody detected a faint American accent. 'Security operations specialist. I believe you have a problem. I'd be delighted to help. Talk to me...'

Brody told him what they needed. Theo began tapping on the keyboard of the laptop. He spent five minutes doing so, occasionally looking up and asking a question. Then:

'I have all the details of the person behind this ghost page. But unless you have a warrant, I can't give you access to it. However, I can answer any questions you may ask me. An anomaly, yes, but I cannot divulge anything unsolicited.'

Brody wanted to tell him no one would know, but he felt certain it would be enough that Theo did.

'Well,' he began, 'name and address. Let's start there.'

'Not available.'

'I didn't think so.'

'There is no requirement for the inclusion of a name and address. Email address suffices as a means of identification.'

'We'll take that, the email address, but I don't think it'll be of much help. Marty.'

Theo gave Marty the email address, and he wrote it down in his notebook.

Fifteen minutes later they had everything there was to

know on the ghost from his Facebook profile. The account was less than a year old and appeared to have been set up solely to scattergun abuse on Donagh Hughes. Most activity took place between 6 and 9 p.m. each and every day, but sometimes, activity was registered on a Friday and Saturday night between midnight and 3 a.m. These posts could be particularly nasty. But never nasty enough to have the ghost permanently banned. So, he – Brody was referring to this person as a *he* for now – displayed a cunning measure of restraint in his behaviour. Brody assumed he worked Monday to Friday, with these weekend spikes in activity perhaps alcohol fuelled. But even if this were so, his posts were erudite, grammatically perfect, the words spelt correctly. Brody calculated the person they were looking for was well educated. He also surmised the person was one within Hughes's immediate circle of acquaintances, another politician perhaps, or maybe a business partner. This person was someone known to Hughes, but not known as an enemy. The reason for this was simple. If the person was a known enemy, then why go to all the trouble to disguise himself? There would simply be no need.

'Is it the same device each time?' Sheahan wondered.

'Same device,' Theo confirmed, 'and by the IP address, a laptop.'

'Any thoughts of how we can get a precise location address?' Brody asked.

'You can't. His location finder is off. And even if it were on, it would only provide a radius too large to cover.'

'I could be the judge of that.'

'Of course.'

'Could we ping location through mobile tower masts; it's the same technology, right?'

'Yes and no. Don't forget, this person could also be accessing Facebook via a cable connection or satellite, it happens. And even if you did ping a location, this person seems to be very security conscious. I don't think you'd get anything from it. It would be a waste of time. But I might be wrong. You'd have your work cut out is what I'm saying.'

'I agree,' Marty said, 'the clue is in the name, boss. Ghost. It's like two fingers to us. He's already thought this well through.'

Brody nodded. 'Okay, we'll move on. We don't want to spend time we don't have.' He looked at Theo. 'Can you give me your direct telephone number in case I need to ask any follow-up questions?'

'Yes, of course.'

'Shoot,' Marty said, 'and I'll write it down.'

Theo did, and it went into Marty's notebook.

'Speaking of telephone numbers,' Theo said, 'he has a video on his page. Have you seen it?'

'The meat packing plant, with the beef carcasses hanging from hooks on a conveyor belt?'

'Yes, it's the only video.'

'I've seen it.'

It had a caption that read:

To Donagh.

Nothing else. Just that. Outwardly innocuous, designed to slip past the Facebook gatekeepers. Yes, very clever. But an implicit threat all the same.

'It was downloaded from a phone,' Theo said. 'If you give me a little time, I can see if maybe I can source the number it came from. That would help, right?'

'Yes, that would help, of course.'

'Right, gentlemen, unless there's anything else, I'll get on with that and get back to you later.'

When they left the European HQ of Facebook a short

time later, they weren't any closer to locating this so-called ghost. But then again, that didn't come as a great surprise to Brody. This was a ghost, after all. What Brody needed to do was find a way to attract the entity, a digital Ouija board of sorts. And if Theo came up with a telephone number, that just might do it.

As he was thinking this, Donagh Hughes was being attacked by a pack of rats. He felt their razor-sharp teeth biting into him all over. He tried to bat one away from his face as he screamed, but too late, he felt the tickle of whiskers inside his mouth. He gagged, felt the rat's head move, its legs flailing, its nails tearing into the space between his upper lip and nose, into his chin. The rat pushed farther into his mouth, its front paws on his tongue now, as he gagged again, harder this time, as the rat moved down his throat.

Hughes's eyes snapped open, and he stared ahead. He heard the rats squeaking, heard them scurrying about, could see them in the gloom, stopping every so often to sniff the air. He felt certain it was because they could smell his blood, fresh and pungent on the stagnant air. He saw that his hands were untied, and he touched his face gingerly with one. But what he was thinking of more than anything was his face. Thank God, it was still intact. He narrowed his eyes and looked ahead. The cloche was gone, and with it the head of Marie Kennedy. He felt sick as he thought of it, as he thought of his own severed finger. Who or what was the monster behind all this? Yes, there was no other word for this entity, a monster. Then he thought – maybe he'd imagined seeing her severed head? Maybe it was all just a horrible nightmare, just like those rats nibbling his face, one going down his throat. He could try to fool himself, but he knew he hadn't imagined it. No. It was real; he could see the matted fur about the mouths of some of the rats, bloodied with fragments of bone and flesh. This was all real. And soon, he knew, he would become too weak to scare away the rats, and they would sense it. The bravest would attack; the rest would follow. And they really would start nibbling all over his body.

It was only a matter of time.

The stump of his finger throbbed with pain, but a dull pain, not as severe as before. He had no recollection – he must have been asleep, unconscious, whatever – but someone had roughly applied a tourniquet with what looked like a strip of dish cloth. Only the edges of it were white now; the rest was blood-soaked. The light seeped in around the door, and the only sound was that of his breathing, short and shallow... and the rats, of course; he could not forget those. Oh, no.

He was getting weaker...

It was only a matter of time.

THE PACKAGE WAS DELIVERED to the TV centre by van courier. The security man at the front desk signed for it and brought it to the office of Gary Kennedy. There it was handed to his secretary, who placed it into an in-tray along with the other envelopes and a couple of other packages delivered earlier that day. Gary Kennedy was having a particularly busy time of it. Understandable, really, what with his wife being dead and all. Today he was leaving early to take care of the practicalities of burying her. At four o'clock, when his last meeting had finished, the secretary brought the mail in to him, leaving the items on his desk and giving him the best saccharin smile she could muster, thinking that the man before her had a heart like a slab of granite. How nice of him to be taking time off to bury his wife. She gave one last flick through the mail; everything was expected or routine... apart from one item. She told him she didn't know where the small, rectangular cardboard box, the size of a cigarette packet, wrapped in masking tape top and bottom, had come from. Then she left the office.

Gary Kennedy debated whether he should open it or not. As head of the nation's largest privately owned TV company, he'd received some surprises in the mail down through the years. Now, anything that appeared suspicious, he usually put to one side and gave it some thought before opening it or referring it on to security.

But not this.

Something about this told him it was different. He couldn't explain it, a feeling, nothing more.

He shook the box, but there was no sound from it. It didn't weigh much. Whatever was in there had no doubt been wrapped in cotton wool or bubble wrap.

Just open the damn thing, why don't you? It's probably just a prop that someone needs advice on.

So he did, spending a minute peeling back the masking tape at one end and pulling open the flap.

He was right, there was cotton wool inside. He gripped the edges and pulled it out. It came away in one, compacted piece. He gingerly pulled the cotton wool apart down its centre and exposed the item in there, still covered by a layer of fibrous cotton wool sticking to whatever it was. He imagined it had been damp when placed inside, and the cotton wool had stuck to it. He lifted it up: his first thought, a thin, small, black crayon of some sort. Who the hell would want to send him such a thing?

With his other hand he began plucking the fibrous, clingy cotton wool from it. So engrossed did he become in peeling each strand away that the item itself lost all definition as he concentrated. Even when it became obvious what it was, he still didn't notice what it *was*. Finally, when he'd peeled as much cotton wool away as he could, he had the item more or less exposed. He held it over the box and now noticed that the cotton wool along the bottom of it was coloured dark crimson.

He looked at the 'crayon' again. And looked back at the box. Once more he looked at the crayon. And saw it with new eyes this time round. Saw the nail in the black, bloodless flesh, the thread of lines criss-crossing it beneath, puckered in the centre above the knuckle. He dropped the appendage like it was suddenly red hot, and it fell back into the box without a sound. He stared, feeling a sick, hollow sensation in the pit of his belly, and a cold prickling at the back of his neck as each follicle of hair stood on end.

But then, again, he thought...

Yes, yes, of course, you silly git...

He gave a soft, nervous giggle. It could have come from the special effects department. A prop, like he'd initially thought. Yes, yes, of course, that was probably where it came from. Gary Kennedy gave another nervous giggle, longer this time, tapering off into a deep, relieved breath. *Yeah, you got me there, buddy, whoever you are, ha, ha...*

He picked it up once more, turned it over in his hand. So realistic. He looked at it closely, gave it a gentle squeeze. He had to admit, brilliant work. Hard to tell if it was real or wasn't. He brought it close to his nose and sniffed. *Aha.* The smell like a mixture of charcoal and plastic, unmistakably moulded resin. Yes, a prop. He picked up the box. He hadn't really checked the postal frank on it. The thing could have been sent from the special effects studio in England for all he knew. They used it quite often. But it wasn't. It wasn't franked either; instead it had a stamp on it, an Irish stamp. Never mind, he'd get to the bottom of it. Most likely this had something to do with an upcoming zombie comedy series they were about to pilot. It was just that whoever had sent it had forgotten to tell him, that was all... or maybe they had, and it was he who had forgotten. Happened all the time, unfortunately.

He shoved it into a trouser pocket. He'd have to deal with this later. Right now, he had his wife's burial to organise.

Voyle wiped a paper tissue over his face. When he took it away again, it was wet and knotty and falling apart. The windows were clouded over and beaded with condensation.

That was how hot it was in the conservatory now.

It hadn't taken long either, just over twenty minutes for the temperature gauge on the wall monitor to reach forty degrees. And it was still climbing. He could feel his clothes beginning to stick to his body. He hoped he was right about this whole damn thing. If he wasn't, then he'd have a dry-cleaning bill he would be unable to claim back on expenses. Because he wouldn't be able to explain this. He was tempted to get up and test his hypothesis right now. But he didn't. It might be too soon. In fact, it probably was too soon. He had to be absolutely sure. Voyle decided to give it just a little while longer. Yes, it was hot, but was it hot enough? Just a little while longer, that should do it.

He reached into his pocket, but he had no more tissues. Instead he ran the back of his hand across his forehead.

A little while longer. To prove whether he was right or wrong. His hand was dripping wet.

35

They were sitting in a wonderfully nondescript pool car, this time an old Mondeo. The Fords had steadily been phased out, replaced by, for the most part, Hyundais. Considine had come across an interesting fact some time ago, which was this: a half day's Hyundai production was enough to satisfy the demands of the Irish market – for an entire year. Anyway, this Mondeo smelt of body odour and sweat, a little bit of vomit too, the rubber on its clutch pedal completely worn through on one side. The doorman of the Lawrence Hotel did not seem impressed. He wore a green cape with gold braid along the edges, and a top hat that had a green velvet band. He was standing by the glass-panelled entrance door with its brass handles glinting in the weak sun, looking across at them and shaking his head slightly. The Mondeo looked like a tatty street urchin in a car park full of toffs. As the doorman opened the doors of the cars and taxis dropping off, he kept glancing across at them.

Now, in a quiet moment, he folded his arms and just stared.

'What's his problem?' O'Brien wondered.

'I'll tell you what.' Considine wound down her window. The driver of the car that had just pulled into the car space next to them was getting out of his big, silver Audi.

'Excuse me,' she said.

The man wore a crumpled but well-cut suit and was morbidly obese. It didn't help, Considine surmised, that he probably spent most of his life in that fancy car of his.

'Yes.' His tone, like his eyes, was jaded, as if a part of him had given up on life.

'Do you know what time it is, please?'

Then he did something that surprised Considine. He smiled. And when he did, his whole face came alive. He looked at an expensive gold watch on his wrist.

'It's five minutes to five... well, it's actually six minutes to five, but we won't quibble.'

'Thank you.'

His eyes lingered. He was still smiling, and Considine could tell that he was years younger than he actually looked.

'Well, thanks again,' she said, but still he didn't move. Considine could have that effect on men.

O'Brien coughed, and Considine looked at her. Standing outside O'Brien's door was the caped doorman. He tapped on the window. When it came down, he took off his hat and leaned in.

'Okay, ladies. Listen up. I want you both to fuck off. Got that? I know what you're about. You can't get inside this hotel, so this is the next best thing, is it? The car park? Pathetic. You heard me. Sling yer hooks, or I'll ring the fuzz.'

The man in the crumpled suit had been listening and quickly gathered up his overnight bag and turned, waddling away towards the hotel.

'The fuzz.' Considine laughed. 'I haven't heard that one in a while.'

'Go on. Fuck off. Whatever. I won't tell you again.'

He straightened, rearranging his cape with one hand and replacing his hat onto his head with the other.

'C'mere, sunshine,' Considine called.

The doorman had been turning. He snapped back to face them, his nostrils flaring and his cheeks turning crimson. 'What did you say? *Sunshine?*'

Considine beckoned to him with a finger.

He didn't move.

She leaned across towards O'Brien and spoke out the open window. 'I should be privileged really, in a way,' she said, 'to see this side of you. Because if I were paying a thousand euro a night for a suite in there' – she pointed to the hotel – 'I wouldn't, would I? I could be as obnoxious as I wanted just so long as I paid my bill and rubbed your palm with a twenty-euro note. But here' – Considine was getting into her stride now – 'on this side of the bridge, it's what? Fuck off or I'll call the *fuzz*. For real? Listen, sunshine, I am the fucking fuzz.' She had her ID card ready, and she held it out. He saw it, and his mouth dropped open.

'I-I didn't know. I'm sorry. You don't look like any normal cops to me.'

Behind him, Considine saw a red BMW turn from the roadway outside and enter the car park. It travelled towards her before turning left down a clearway, but not before she'd noted the DL reg plates.

'Tell you how you can make it up to us,' she said, and the doorman smiled uncertainly. 'Come here, *sunshine*, and listen up.'

IT WAS HOT. The sweat dripped into Voyle's eyes; his clothes were damp. It was hot like a sauna, hot like noon in the Sahara, hot, hot, *hot*. When he closed his eyes, he didn't want to open them again; they had become as heavy as lead weights. He just wanted to sleep. He wiped the condensation from his watch and checked the time. He'd been in this conservatory for well over an hour, the heat on full blast the whole time.

He forced himself to stand, his movements slow and lethargic, and shuffled to the door. *Please don't let me be wrong about this.* He reached for the handle, the surface was wet, and he pressed on it tightly with his clammy hand to ensure a good grip.

He took a breath.

Here it goes.

He pulled down sharply, all the way, so there was no doubt, heard the latch bolt withdraw from the borehole. There was nothing now to impede the opening of the door. In theory, that is. Because the door wasn't locked. He positioned his left leg forward of his right, angling his body to allow him to exert maximum leverage. The same had happened on that night, when they'd tried to shoulder the door in, and still it hadn't budged. Eventually, they'd had to use a battering ram. Because they believed the door was locked, of course. But Voyle couldn't find any evidence that it was, or that they'd even checked. Understandable, really. If it didn't budge, they'd have assumed it was locked.

Voyle pulled the door towards him, with all his force... nothing. It didn't move even a centimetre. Not satisfied, he rubbed the sweat from his hands onto his damp trousers and tried again, his grip that little firmer now. He counted to three and yanked back, hard as he could.

Still, the door didn't budge. He tried once again, for good measure. Again, the outcome was the same.

Voyle had come across this before, on a trekking holiday in Canada when he'd stayed in a log cabin. He'd loaded up the stove with extra wood and gotten a proper fire going.

After a long day trekking and a hearty meal, he'd fallen asleep in the chair. When he'd woken, he was surprised at just how warm the little cabin had become. He went to open the front door – newly installed and constructed of wood with an aluminium finish – but it didn't budge. It was like someone had double, treble locked it. Which was exactly what he would have thought if he'd been standing outside this conservatory on the night Gilsenan was lying inside it, either dying or already dead. If he hadn't known, that is, that metal expands, especially aluminium, and with enough heat, a door can wedge itself as tightly closed as if it had been welded to the door frame.

Voyle guessed Patrick O'Connor would have known this somehow. He guessed he knew everything there was to know about this old house and everything in it. He had a feeling, a feeling he'd kept buried because he knew feelings were never enough. A cop needed evidence. And as a cop too, he was suspicious of everything. It came with the territory. So he had lots of feelings about lots of things, and most he had no reason to believe he could in any way trust.

But now, he began to trust this feeling, although he knew he still might be wrong. *Okay, I'm going with it, just for a moment. Gilsenan's death was not a suicide. No. It was the butler who did it. There, I've said it. If only to myself.*

But believing that was one thing.

Proving it was another.

THE DOORMAN'S name was James. He brought them into the concierge's office, a cluttered little space without any natural light. Once in there, he seemed to become smaller; his personality seemed to change too, even his accent. Before it had been sharp edged and clip toned, now it was of the sea and land, a country accent as natural as the soil itself. And as himself, as James, underneath the five-star persona and the elaborate uniform, he was a minimum hourly worker who could never aspire to the type of life the people he served lived.

'I didn't know,' he said, 'if I did, I wouldn't... well, you know?'

'Yes,' Considine said, 'I know, you wouldn't have acted like such a wanker. I notice that about staff in places like this, jumped-up little lord mucks. Now, the person driving this red BMW that I pointed out to you.'

'Yes, a regular, Mrs Monica Hughes... um, you know who her husband is, don't you?' He said it like it was a secret, one of many he possessed as a doorman at one of the city's most prestigious hotels, which no doubt he did.

But Considine wasn't interested. He could write a book about it, *Secrets of a 5* Doorman*. No doubt it would be a bestseller. She wasn't interested. All she was interested in was...

'Tell me about Monica Hughes.'

And he did.

Monica Hughes was a regular visitor to the Lawrence Hotel. She stayed in the same front-of-house penthouse apartment. It normally cost €1,500 a night, but the Hugheses paid a lot less. They had an arrangement with the hotel, a preferred guest something or other, the details of which were private, strictly between the hotel and the Hugheses. A quick check of the reservations database showed she usually stayed Friday through to Sunday night at least once a month. She kept herself to herself. Unlike other regular visitors, she didn't dine in the hotel or frequent any of its three bars. She merely came and went. James said he'd never seen her with her husband.

'Have you ever seen her with anybody else?' Considine asked.

James looked at her.

'We're very discreet...'

'Does that mean you have?'

'Well...' He shrugged. 'Yes, it does.'

'A man?' It was O'Brien.

He nodded.

'Describe him,' Considine said.

'Richard Kiel.'

Considine looked confused, but not Denise O'Brien.

'Really? The actor? As in *The Spy Who Loved Me*?'

'Yes, but you forget *Moonraker*; he was in that too.'

'Yes, he was, of course.'

'I like movies,' James said.

'Ditto.'

'Actually, I've had a couple of movie reviews published in my local newspaper... I mean, nothing fancy, just my thoughts, you know?'

O'Brien smiled. 'Of course, that's how you review.'

He smiled too, his eyes lighting up, holding hers. O'Brien was an attractive woman, and they were both about the same age. She held his gaze, indulging him.

'So, Richard Kiel,' she said, a business tone creeping in.

'Yes. He reminded me of him. Big... not so attractive, but beauty's in the eye of the beholder. Richard Kiel wasn't ugly, you know, he was just made to look that way. But this man' – James's forehead furrowed, like he was thinking about it – 'he was... okay. He *was* ugly. And big. Big and ugly. I couldn't understand what she saw in him... of course, there may not have been anything going on between them; that's what I thought anyway. Because he looked like, well... such a brute. But then I found out they were...' His voice trailed off.

'Were?'

'Housekeeping, they let the cat out of the bag. They know everything. Well, they would, wouldn't they?'

'Housekeeping?' Considine said, cocking her head to one side.

'Yes. They knew they were sleeping together. For a while it was all the talk of the staff canteen.'

'I don't want this to be all the talk of the staff canteen, James, our being here.'

'Of course. Of course.' He tapped a finger against the side of his nose a couple of times. 'Front of house is not housekeeping; we're a different breed.' For a moment, he sounded like lord muck again.

'There'd be repercussions if it were to get out we were here making enquiries. Serious repercussions. You understand?'

'Yes. I understand.'

'Good.' Considine felt confident that he did.

'Do you know the identity of this Richard Kiel character?'

James shook his head.

'No, I don't have a clue. There was never a name on the register.'

Of course, because that would be too easy.

'What about CCTV? Comings and goings. Is he captured on any?'

'I could look. I'll check when she last stayed, see if there's anything for those dates. But it'll take a little time.'

'That's fine. I'll give you my number, and if you get something, you'll let me know straight away, will you?'

'I certainly will. I'll ring you. Yes.'

'Good. Now, I'd like to speak to someone in housekeeping?'

'You would? Why?'

Considine glanced to O'Brien. 'Because they might have a vacancy. I know someone who'd make a terrific housekeeper.'

O'Brien's face lit up, like she couldn't wait to play her new role.

It took twenty minutes with all the windows open before the door would open again. The temperature gauge dropped from forty-two degrees to fifteen in that time. Voyle shivered when he emerged, his clothes wet, his skin feeling curdled. He made his way back to the kitchen, one long corridor after another until he heard the distant sound of voices drifting towards him, increasing in volume, reassuring him he was headed in the right direction. He approached the kitchen without sound and stopped next to the doorway, not revealing himself, knowing O'Connor and Kate were oblivious to his presence. In fact, he was certain they had forgotten all about him. Plus, it sounded like they were half pissed.

'... and I said to him,' O'Connor chortled, 'prime fillets are worth two, not one bottle of bloody Tesco whiskey.'

'Ha, ha, Paddy. That's a good one. But what a cheapskate, eh? Tesco whiskey. And you too, for taking them in the first place. You'd better make sure you don't tell Andrea that story; that would change things for her. Lord of the manor, my arse.'

Patrick O'Connor stopped laughing. 'I told you not to mention Andrea. You're not fit to talk about her, you auld hag.'

'Aw, hurt your feelings, did I.' She chortled back. 'Poor Patrick, he's in love with his little Esmeralda. But she doesn't love you, you know that, don't you? She's only using you, you auld eejit.'

'Shut the fuck up,' O'Connor shouted.

'Truth hurts, does it? *Sir* Patrick.'

'You shut your mouth, I told you.'

Voyle thought it best to make his presence known. He stepped out from the wall and stood in the doorway. The scene was like one straight out of a Victorian novel, the shafts of light from the high windows carrying motes of dust and casting shadows onto the whitewashed wall, a sense of dark grimness to everything. Patrick O'Connor was standing by the carcass of the dissected deer, wine glass in his bloodied hand, a trickle of the liquid running down from the corner of his mouth. Take away the glass and it would give rise to the suspicion that it was not wine trickling from his mouth, like the villagers had warned Voyle not to come here, to the Count's lair, high up in the Transylvanian mountains. Kate was laughing, standing by one of those huge, black ranges set into the wall, her hair falling down over the front of her face.

Still they hadn't noticed Voyle standing there.

O'Connor put down his glass and took a step towards her. Kate pushed her dirty blonde hair back from her face and stared at him defiantly.

'I told you,' he said.

'You told me what? What you going to do?' She raised her glass and drained the contents, then drew her arm back and flung the glass across the room. It shattered on the wall next to Voyle. He stepped into the kitchen.

'That's enough, you two.'

O'Connor swung round, his eyes wild.

'Remember me?' Voyle asked.

O'Connor's expression softened. 'Jesus. No, I actually forgot all about you, really. This crazy bitch. You've seen what she's like yourself just now. I should never have invited her. You try to do the right thing and help people, and this is what you get.' He turned to her and pointed a finger. 'Go on now. Get out. Leave.'

'What's this all about, anyway? Why're you two arguing?'

'It's nothing,' O'Connor said, angling his body so Voyle couldn't see his face. 'Isn't that right, Kate?'

But Voyle could see Kate's face, could see the cloud pass

behind her eyes as she looked at O'Connor, unmistakeable: fear.

'Yes,' Kate said, 'it's nothing.' She gave Voyle an uncertain smile. 'Sure, we're always like that.'

'Yes, Officer, we're always like that.' O'Connor's eyes ran over him, taking in the stodgy clothes, but he showed no reaction. 'Will there be anything else, Officer?'

Cocky bastard. Then Voyle thought of something.

'No. I'll be on my way,' he lied. 'Thank you for your help.'

'Oh, you're welcome, Officer, anytime, anytime at all. You take care now.'

A LITTLE LATER, Voyle was sitting in his car parked in the gateway to a field – waiting. He didn't have to wait for long. The automatic gates to Ash Hall opened, and a small, rattly old car came out and started down the road towards him. Once it had passed, he swung round and followed, after a minute turning on the flashing grille and dash lights. When that didn't work, he gave a short *whoop* of the siren and watched Kate look back at him in the rear-view mirror. She pulled into a clearing at the side of the road.

Voyle was out immediately. He didn't want to give her any time to get on the phone.

'You,' she said, her window coming down. 'What's this all about? Why did you pull me over?'

'Come and sit in the back of my car for a moment, please? I want to talk to you a moment.'

'You do? Um…' She appeared to be thinking about it. 'I don't think that's a good idea. What're you up to? Tell me why first, and I'll think about it. You're a cop. I don't trust cops.'

'And I don't have time for any sales pitch, Kate… Tell you

what, I'll just get the alco test kit, and we'll do it here at the roadside.' He made to turn away. 'Won't be a sec.'

'Wait. You mean you're breath testing me?'

'Well, it wasn't iced tea you were drinking back there in that kitchen, was it? Or we can, you know, just talk about it.'

She bit her lower lip. 'Talk about it? Talk about what?'

Voyle said nothing.

'Whatever,' she said, and opened her door.

SERGEANT DENISE O'BRIEN was going undercover.

'Don't you think I should run this by my manager first?' James the doorman asked.

'Nah,' Considine replied, 'don't worry about it. This'll all be over before you get the chance. We just want to get the lie of the land, that's all. Okay, James?' She smiled.

'Well, yes, of course... alright then.' He gave an uncertain shrug, said to O'Brien, 'Fine. Come with me, then. We'll get you kitted out.'

The uniform was a little tight, and O'Brien was without the regulation black flat-heel shoes: instead she wore her Nikes. But who'd notice? No one, they hoped. She was playing the role of hotel housekeeper, not restaurant hostess. As Considine stood back and appraised her by the counter in the hotel uniform room, she thought the amateur actress looked to be in her element.

'Remember,' she said, 'you just knock, say "Housekeeping", tell whoever answers that the last guest has just rung in to say she's left her make-up case behind and can you please have a look to see if it's still there? Clear?'

'Well, that's hardly a line I'd fluff. I played Eliza Doolittle in the Ranelagh Players production of *Pygmalion* in 2009. We received a favourable review in the *Irish Times* too. I got this, girl.'

'Great,' Considine said, and, looking at James, 'You think she's in there now?'

'I'd say so,' James said. 'But I can check... look, are you sure I don't need to run this by the manager? The more I think about it...'

'No, James, we'll be gone before you know it. Why make a fuss? Impromptu is best.'

'I agree,' O'Brien said, 'but this is improvisation. That's what they call it when you have to ad-lib, you know.'

'Whatever,' Considine said, 'let's do it.'

THE WOMAN who opened the door in answer to O'Brien's knock was wearing a bathrobe, on her face a green gooey face mask, big pink curlers in her hair.

'Sorry to trouble you, ma'am,' O'Brien began, taking to her role, switching on her best smile. 'Did front desk contact you about a make-up bag? It was left here by the last guest. I've come to have a look for it.'

'It wasn't the front desk. It was James, the concierge.'

'Oh...'

Monica Hughes moved to one side. 'Come in, will you. And just to let you know. I'm in a hurry. Don't delay. I haven't had time to unpack properly.'

'Thank you.'

O'Brien stepped into the room. Monica Hughes turned and walked along by the side of the bed into the bathroom. She didn't close the door. O'Brien crossed to the dresser on her right and casually opened a drawer. But she didn't look inside. From where she was standing, she had a clear view into the bathroom. The wife of the Minister for Foreign Affairs was standing in front of the mirror. She rolled the dressing gown off her shoulders, and it fell to the ground. Beneath she wore a transparent, short, thigh split black nightdress, and through it O'Brien could see a tiny black G-string underneath. Not what she had expected. Not what she had expected at all. Something more sombre at least, considering the occasion.

O'Brien moved from the dresser to the window on the other side of the room, turned and scanned the bedroom. It wasn't large; the bed took up most of it, along with the dresser, that is, and the sliding wardrobe. The carpet was deep and the wallpaper embossed, enough to give it the appearance of five-star luxury. But beyond that it was nothing special.

'How are you getting on out there? Did you find it?'

From where she was standing, O'Brien could no longer see directly into the bathroom, but she could see a sliver of it in the dressing table mirror, could see the tap running, Monica Hughes rubbing the face mask from her face, beginning to dry it with a towel.

'No,' she said, 'I can't see any sign of it.'

She watched Monica Hughes throw the towel away and appraise herself in the mirror. She was not wearing a bra, and two fulsome breasts were visible beneath the nightdress. She cupped them in her hands and looked at them, then her hands dropped away, and she picked up a blusher brush. At that moment she turned her head, and she caught O'Brien looking at her in the mirror.

'What? What are you looking at?'

'Sorry, I didn't mean to stare. I was just wondering where the case could be, that's all, because it's definitely not out here.'

Monica Hughes had already looked away, busy applying blusher to her cheeks. The cop in O'Brien wanted to ask her what *she* was up to. Why she was dressed the way she was dressed... but then she thought that she wasn't, dressed, that is. Not only did it look like she was getting ready for bed, but it also looked like she definitely wasn't getting ready for sleep.

'You can look in here if you want.'

O'Brien was hoping she'd say that.

The bathroom was nothing fancy, a stand-up shower in a bathtub with a pull-around curtain. Basically, the same set-up as a bedsit. But the floor and walls were expensively tiled. Monica was still busy concentrating on applying blusher.

O'Brien spent a moment pretending to look about.

'I don't see anything,' she said.

Monica Hughes leaned over the sink, having just finished with the blusher, now engaged in the more intricate procedure of applying eyeliner.

'Oh really...' like she wasn't really listening.

But what O'Brien did see was a black garter belt with red trim and a pair of fishnet tights draped over the stool next to the sink. Of course, just like Voyle trying not to make assumptions about something, O'Brien too had been warned of the dangers of false assumptions. Maybe it was just the way Monica Hughes liked to prepare for bed, even if she was going to bed in the late afternoon. After a long drive, maybe that made sense. And Monica Hughes could wear whatever she liked when climbing beneath the sheets. Why assume anything? But then she reached the same conclusion as Voyle had reached. Sometimes you just had to judge a book by its cover. Sometimes you had to just accept that if it walked like a duck and quacked like a duck, then...

Monica Hughes was getting ready to have sex.

Of course.

Nothing wrong with that either. It was a free country; thank God it was; you could do whatever you wanted, even if your husband was missing, even if he was the Minister for Foreign Affairs. Still...

'I'll leave you in peace, ma'am,' O'Brien said, stepping out of the bathroom.

Monica Hughes blinked at herself in the mirror, her lashes long and vampy. She raised a hand to her lips; in it was a stick of lipstick. She began applying it; ruby red, it made her lips appear even bigger than they were.

She puckered them, said, 'Fine.'

O'Brien left the bathroom and went to the front door. She placed her hand on the handle and lingered there for a moment, having one last look around. Nothing but assumptions in this room, she thought. So what if Monica Hughes was having a little fun? In fact, she envied her. In any case, her role was over, nothing to do now but exit stage left.

She was about to press down on the handle when it moved as if of its own accord. O'Brien looked at it and realised someone was opening it from the other side. She took two paces back and waited for it to open. When it did, she thought it was true what they said.

Richard Kiel, the Richard Kiel without the silver teeth and bad-guy make-up, was actually quite handsome.

But the man standing before her, no matter what way you cut it, definitely wasn't.

36

Brody got the call on the way back to the Phoenix Park. He'd never spoken to the commissioner before, but he recognised his voice immediately. 'Jack,' the most senior officer in the force said.

Jack didn't answer right away. More than anything, he was confused. Why was the commissioner ringing him? And why was he addressing him by his first name?

And then he thought maybe this wasn't the commissioner at all. Maybe this was a scam call, someone who sounded like the commissioner, pranking him on one of those funny radio programmes he'd listened to so many times.

Still he didn't speak.

'Jesus, man, are you there?' the so-called commissioner said.

'I'm here.'

'Good. Can you be in my office in ten minutes?'

'Um, can you make it fifteen?'

'Yes. Just be there.'

The phone line went dead. Jack felt stupid. If that was a prank call, it was the shortest ever one in history.

It wasn't, of course, a prank call. When Jack arrived at the commissioner's annex at HQ with three minutes to spare, he was immediately ushered into reception. A secretary sat behind a desk on the other side of the room, beneath a window. She was a middle-aged woman with grey hair and spectacles dangling from her neck on a gold link chain. She smiled and asked Brody his name. Then she told him her name was Mrs Phillips and that the commissioner had overrun on a call but should be with him soon. 'Would you like something while you wait? Tea, coffee?'

Before he could answer, a door in the panelled wall opened, and the man himself was standing there.

'Jack.' He raised a hand in greeting, as if they were long-lost friends.

Brody had never even met the man before.

'That's me.'

'Thanks for coming. Come on in.'

The commissioner's office was enormous, an oval-shaped conference table with a green velvet inlay in the centre, a picture of the president of Ireland on the wall above Commissioner Mc Kay's desk in the centre along the front-facing wall beneath a high, narrow bay window. The legs of the desk were intricately carved, and two pale green glass-shaded lamps were on top, one in each corner. Brody had heard about this desk; it was of historical significance, having once belonged to the commanding officer of the old Dublin Metropolitan Police based at Dublin Castle, for so long the centre of British power in Ireland. A display cabinet stood beside the desk, inside it another item of historical significance, an old Dublin Metropolitan Police inspector's helmet. Ireland was an independent country for just over one hundred years, yet for hundreds of years before that it had been a British colony. Such small historical tokens as were in this office were like tiny brush strokes on a much bigger historical canvas.

Despite it all, the office had all the trappings of modernity about it, alongside a sense of mature authority, strong and enduring.

The commissioner was a slightly built man, with heavy eyebrows that did nothing to lessen a natural sense of intensity about him. He wore glasses that made his eyes appear small and somewhat sunken into his head. This lent him a removed, distant appearance, like he was present but not present, both at the same time. He went and sat behind his desk.

'Take a seat, take a seat. Thanks for coming once again, Jack, especially at such short notice.' He pointed, then swept his hand through the air. 'There's no one else here. Just us. Aye, so I want you to be candid. Okay, Jack, you got that?'

'Okay, I got that.'

'Good. Let's get down to it, then. We just have no clue where the Minister for Foreign Affairs is. As for Marie Kennedy...' He shook his head. 'Aye, this is a mess, Jack. A great big pile of steaming shite, that's what this is.'

Brody blinked. The commissioner was not known to be one for the crude vernacular. In fact, he was known to be a bit dour. A legacy perhaps of his northern Presbyterian upbringing. But Ireland had come a long way. No one cared about such things anymore... well, most people anyway.

Jack said nothing... after all, what was there to say? But he was also wary. He didn't trust senior officers, even the commissioner himself. He wondered, *Am I to be a sort of blowback repellent for him?* Because every senior officer carried a can.

'Harper is a bollocks,' the commissioner said, as if reading Brody's mind and trying to reassure him. 'But I think you know that already... Jesus Christ, Jack, don't look so worried.

It's okay, I'm not asking you to comment on it. You don't have to agree or disagree. I'm just making a statement, okay.'

Jack didn't believe he looked worried, and would be disappointed if he did. Instead, he took it as a little bit of deflection on the part of the commissioner.

'Superintendent Ryan?' Jack said, his voice lilting at the end into a question mark.

'Yes? Superintendent Ryan. What about her? All I can say is what a mess they've made, both of them, herself and Harper.' And Brody imagined the singling out of 'herself and Harper' at the end to be a little squirt of blowback repellent. 'So I want to ask you, and there's nobody else around, remember... what do *you* think? Don't dress it up now. I can take it. Tell me.'

Brody pursed his lips. 'Right then. Here it goes. I agree. It's a mess. But I want to ask you a question... do *you* also think it's political?'

'What? You ask do I think it's political. You hedging your bets now? Is that it?'

'You said yourself, there's no one here. I can say what I want. No, I'm not hedging my bets. I'm just asking a question.'

'Okay. To tell the truth, because there's no one here, I don't know what to think. In all my years of policing, I've never felt as helpless as I do now. I hate to admit it, but I just do. It's painful. It makes me appear weak. Where I come from... well, never mind that. I like you... okay. Yes, I've never met you before, but everyone says you're a man who can be trusted... talk to me. Tell me what you think.'

Ask a sergeant from way down the food chain what he thinks. Yes, you must be stuck, Jack thought. But still, Jack liked the commissioner too, or he liked what he was trying to do, trying to change the system from within, to make it more transparent, get rid of the cronyism and the backslapping old boys' network, dig deep and root out the corruption. Not the big-time corruption, mind. There wasn't any – generally speaking, that is. No, but the mostly small-time stuff. But from acorns do mighty oaks grow. Yet, some didn't see it as corruption, but that's what it was: the favours for friends, or friends of a friend, the tearing up of infringements for people with connections, that sort of thing.

'Just before I came in here, I spoke with some people,' Brody said.

Among them was Voyle, but he wouldn't be mentioning that. Because Voyle wasn't making much sense, telling him he was locked – yet not locked – in a conservatory, that he had the heat on full blast and the place was sweltering. He'd sounded excited, told Brody he was of the opinion Gilsenan's death wasn't a suicide, that the man had been murdered, and it was the butler who had done it... But he couldn't prove it, mind, just a feeling, but a very strong feeling nonetheless, along with some circumstantial evidence too. Brody had thrown his eyes to heaven. Maybe the man was suffering from heatstroke? So no, he wasn't going to mention this to the commissioner. The commissioner wouldn't be interested anyway. Not now.

Instead he told him of Sergeant O'Chaillagh, who reminded Brody of Columbo, the 1970s TV detective who would slap his forehead and say 'one more thing'. He told him what he'd said, and not said, about Monica Hughes. Then he told him what Considine had said about the man she called Richard Kiel. Then he paused for effect while this sank in, and then gave the big reveal: Monica Hughes and Kiel appeared to be lovers.

The commissioner slapped his own forehead.

'Wait, what are you saying?'

'I'm not saying anything, just stating a couple of facts.'

The commissioner drew in his cheeks, his heavy

eyebrows knitting together, his lips pouting, like he was sucking on a wedge of lime.

'B-but...' he began before falling silent. Brody could almost hear his brain start to whirl, processing what he'd just heard.

Brody didn't answer.

'Well?'

Still, Brody didn't answer.

The commissioner bit his bottom lip.

It was all in the silence.

37

He wanted to die. He'd had enough. Donagh Hughes didn't care anymore. He didn't care about rats, or this filthy, darkened room, or whether he lived or died... Well, yes, he did. He wanted to die. If there was a button on the wall offering him instant death, he would press it without question.

Beneath the filthy piece of cloth wrapped around the stump, the pain throbbed. It throbbed like it had a sound all of its own, a drumbeat pulsing through an auditorium, fed through speakers, amplified, filling up every space and reaching beyond to infinity. No, he couldn't take it anymore. He couldn't fucking take it!

He opened his mouth to scream, but he was too weak, and no sound came out. He'd not been given any food. He'd been given nothing but some water. He was no longer even hungry, like he was too weak even for that. Still, he imagined it, that he was screaming at the rats, at the bastard who'd put him in here and was responsible for everything. He screamed at the world that somewhere out there was going about its business like it didn't care.

Because the world didn't care. If it did, he wouldn't be left to rot in here the way he was, at the mercy of some mad fucker. The guards would intervene, the UN would intervene, the European

Council of Foreign Ministers would intervene, Interpol would intervene, the stupid security detail of his that he was always trying to lose would intervene.

Well, wouldn't they?

Yes, they would. They would. They would.

Well, where the fuck were they?

He opened his mouth even wider, his silent scream combining with the throbbing of his finger; both seemed to have sounds of their own, like a soundtrack to the dire situation he found himself in.

But he knew his finger, or the stump that was left of it, just like his silent scream, did not really make any sound. The only real sound to be heard was the screeching of the rats, low and persistent, as if sensing his ebbing strength, readying for the moment when they could pounce.

It was only a matter of time.

And he knew there wasn't much time left.

38

Up close, Kate looked like an alcoholic. But Voyle knew you could be an alcoholic and not look this way too. Some alcoholics were lucky; they still looked after themselves, ate right, slept enough, still managing to keep a balance. But not Kate. Her face was red and blotchy, broken capillaries like a spider's web spread across her cheeks. Alcoholics often have red and blotchy faces just like this, a sign their livers were overworked, forcing the body's largest organ, its skin, to help by getting rid of the toxins that were overloading it. Her eyes were a little yellow too. If she didn't stop drinking soon, Kate'd be in trouble, real trouble. If she had a pressure gauge on her forehead, it would be in the red zone, hissing wildly. And Voyle didn't think she'd stop, didn't think she could stop. In fact, he felt certain of it. In the closed environment of the car, she gave off a sweaty, minty, stale yet sweet aroma of alcohol.

She asked if she could smoke, and Voyle nodded his head, just told her to make sure she cracked her window open first. She did. Her teeth were small and matched the slight yellow of her eyes. All in all, it was a shame Kate was the way she was. Voyle guessed she was no more than late thirties, but she looked a lot more, maybe even fifty. She still appeared to have a good build, but Voyle guessed it was partly because she was malnourished. Yes, he thought, a great pity.

'I want you to tell me about Patrick O'Connor. We can start with what's going on in his life. Tell me what you know. And what was I overhearing back there? When you two were both arguing. And who's this Andrea?'

The tip of her cigarette flared as Kate drew on it deeply. She held the smoke in for a long time before blowing it out in a thick stream through the crack in the window.

'That's a lot of questions. And you know what? I'm not going to answer any of them. I'm no rat. You're wasting your time.'

'A rat. I'm not asking you for his bank account details or anything. Jeez, just a bit of background, that's all.'

'No. I'm not.'

'Fine, Kate, we can do this one of two ways. It's up to you. Have you forgotten our little arrangement?'

Kate gave him a blank look, and Voyle decided that she already had. Yes, it was a great shame alright. So he took out the foil-wrapped breath-test kit from the door pocket and turned it over in his hands. She didn't speak, so he made it look like he was about to tear it open.

'Once I open this, I have to account for it. I have to use it. So put out that cigarette, I'm going to arrest you on suspicion of drink-driving, and prisoners aren't allowed to smoke. Come on, put that fag out.'

She took a series of hurried puffs on the cigarette; it disappeared down to its tip before Voyle's very eyes; then she flicked it out the window. He took it as a sign she was not going to co-operate; he would indeed have to arrest her. He was wrong. As he was just about to tear the foil wrapping on the alco meter open, she said: 'Don't. I'll tell you what you want to know. Where'll I start? Andrea? She's the biggest thing in his life right now. His girlfriend.'

'Okay. Start there. His girlfriend.'

'That's not her real name... I don't think it is, anyway. It's hard to tell, she has so many.'

'So many?'

'Yeah, names. She goes by Cindy Bone on Twitter... honestly. Cindy Bone. You can guess what that's all about. She lives in Amsterdam. I'm certain of that.'

Voyle gave her a look, and she caught it.

'Hm, I know,' Kate said, 'a bit of a pattern forming, isn't there? But he can't see it. I know something else for certain too; she's less than half his age; she thinks she's bagged a rich old bastard, a real lord of the manor. Now, as for what we were arguing about back there...'

'Whoa, whoa, back up. Stay on Andrea. She thinks he's lord of the manor, you said. What'd you mean by that?'

'Exactly what I said. I just told you. He's told her he's Lord Brown. A makey-up name. He told her he keeps a low profile, in case she checks on Google, which I'm sure she has. That'd impress any girl, especially someone like Andrea, or whoever she really is. He never tried any of that on me, I can tell you.'

'No.'

'No.'

'You'd like him to?'

'I would have. Maybe. In the beginning. But not now. Now that I know what a bastard he really is.'

'Have you met Andrea? Tell me more about her.'

'Tell you more about her? I don't know much more about her. I've met her twice, that's all. But I had to keep my mouth shut both times, only speak when I was spoken to. Because I was serving them; he had me pretend I was the maid. He paid me to do it. Do you know she gnawed on a bone? I saw it with my own eyes. While he nipped out to the kitchen to take a sneaky snifter... when he was with her, he only sipped on a wine or maybe a sherry or port, like he was Lord Brown, a refined gentleman... It was me who cooked the food too. I was cook and slave to them both. But he had to pay me for that... cash in hand.'

'Where's his wife, Kate? They're supposed to be a caretaker couple.'

'They are too, when she's here, that is. But she took off about a year ago. Poor Judith didn't have it easy; he treated her like shite. And it wasn't beyond him to give her the back of his hand. See, I told you, a bastard.'

'Then why the hell have you anything to do with him?'

'I ask myself the same question, believe me. One of these days I won't. I... I...'

You're going nowhere, Voyle thought, *because you're getting something out of it, free booze and cash in hand.* That was enough.

'He told me his wife was visiting her sister,' Voyle said softly.

She scoffed. 'He tells everyone that.'

'You think it's odd she's gone such a long time?'

'None of my business. She took off. I told you. I don't blame her.'

'Andrea is young and pretty, is she?'

'Oh, she's young and pretty alright. What do you think? Of course. He's in love with her. And she's in love with what she thinks he is. He's loving it all... but it won't last forever, yet he doesn't want to know about that. He thinks he can keep fooling people. He's not thinking straight. He's thinking down there.' She pointed to her crotch. 'But you didn't hear any of this from me, you got that?'

Voyle nodded. 'Of course. Don't worry. And he's up there in that big old hall all by himself. Tell me, doesn't Gilsenan have a family? Aren't they wondering too?'

'Someone showed up one day. I think it was a solicitor. Mr Gilsenan has family, of course, but an Anglo-Irish family; they're spread about England and the world. Old money, this isn't top of their priority list, not yet anyway, but they'll get round to it, believe me. The likes of them always do.'

'Surely one of them is a debauched gambler addicted to opium who'd take a keen interest and like to sell it off.'

'A debauched what?'

'Never mind,' Voyle said. This jigsaw was getting more intricate with each new piece he tried to click into place.

'And his wife took off, hm. I'd like to speak with her. Any idea where she might be?'

'Nah, she just fucked off.'

'How convenient,' Voyle said, tapping a finger against the steering wheel. 'Thank you, you've been a great help.'

'I can go?'

'Not exactly. I'll drive you home; you can collect your car tomorrow. That's the way it works.'

She didn't like the sound of that and started to object, but he gave her a look, a look that comes with the job, a look that says simply, *don't*. She closed her mouth again, and he drove her home. Afterwards he parked on Tinnock's main street and took a piece of paper from his inside pocket with a number written on it, punched it into his mobile phone. It took a time for it to ring.

He had to go through some hoops to actually speak to the man, and repeat more than once, 'Yes, that is correct, a police murder investigation.' But finally he got to speak to the man himself, Bart Ingram, the CEO of ATW International, at the company's headquarters in Columbus, Ohio, five hours behind and still part of the working day.

'Yes, this is Bart Ingram.' The accent was a hybrid of home counties toff with refined American twang, but mostly toff.

As Voyle began to outline the circumstances necessitating

his call to him, and which he was mostly making up as he went along, Bart Ingram interrupted: 'What's that got to do with me, old boy?'

'I was just about to get to that, Mr Ingram...'

'Yes, cut to the chase, please. I'm a very busy man.'

'I'll cut to the chase, yes. You were involved in a very bitter takeover battle in your bid to wrest control of ATW from Robert Gilsenan, correct?'

'Sooo? That's business. It doesn't mean I'd want to kill anyone, for God's sake. If that were the case, we'd have a lot of dead bodies on boardroom floors. Anyway, he wasn't murdered; he killed himself... isn't that right?'

'Maybe. That's why I'm ringing you.'

'Then get on with it, old boy.'

'How well did you know Mr Gilsenan?'

'I knew Robert very well. I learnt everything I know about this business from him. He was a wonderful mentor, I must say. And we were friends, for a time, that is, until I ousted him. What a horrible word that is, don't you think? I do, ousted. But Robert himself has done similar in the past – numerous times too. Like I said, it's business. He didn't get to be the cardboard king for nothing. But I do think we could have become friends again at some time in the future, if he hadn't died. I mean–'

Now it was Voyle's turn to interrupt.

'Was he the type to kill himself, Mr Ingram? That's what I'd really like to know.'

'Good God. No. But then again, who can tell? I know they say that about a lot of people, "oh, he wasn't the type," and all that. But I certainly didn't think so. With Robert, here was a man who loved life. If you ask me, he was too bloody practical to kill himself. And he was also a tough old bastard. Not the type to kill himself. Not at all. No. Also, old boy, remember that car he waited a year for, that he never even got to drive. You heard about that, did you?'

'Yes. I heard about that. Where is that car now, by the way?'

'How should I know? Did you speak with any of his family?'

'No.'

'Don't you think you should?'

'All in good time.'

'Speaking of time, will there be anything else?'

'Did you ever stay at Ash Hall, Mr Ingram?'

'Yes. A couple of times. A beautiful old pile. Last time was just before things went sour between Robert and me.'

'When was this exactly?'

'Well, I don't know, not exactly, must be a couple of years ago now, something like that.'

'And you would have dined there, with Mr Gilsenan I mean?'

'Of course. Yes, I would. And did. He was my host. Where's this going?'

'Do you remember anything about it? Any little details. The food? The staff? The servers? Stuff like that.'

'Actually, I do. I have a good memory. The food was merely passable, and that's being generous. His cook had recently left, apparently.'

A klaxon sounded in Voyle's head.

'His cook had recently left?'

'Yes. That's what I just said. And good household staff are hard to find, believe me. Listen, why are you asking me these questions, about food and staff? Is there something fishy up?'

'Thing is,' Voyle said, 'I just visited the house, Ash Hall. Met the butler, caretaker, Patrick O'Connor…'

'A shifty-looking character as I remember him. Robert thought he was great, however.'

'... but he never mentioned his cook leaving. That would be his wife. They were a caretaker couple.'

'Yes, I know. She was a cordon bleu cook, by the way. He didn't mention it, did he? That's a bit odd alright.' Ingram laughed. 'Maybe you need to look at him, then. They always say it's the butler, don't they?'

Voyle didn't answer.

And Ingram stopped laughing. 'Oh, I get it. I see now where you're going with all this. Why you're asking me these questions? You really do think it might be the old boy–'

'Thank you for your help, Mr Ingram.'

And Voyle hung up.

39

As the sun went down, the clouds drifted in from the east, heavy black clouds shutting out the starry night sky, sitting on the city like a big black chicken. And then the rain came, not particularly heavy at first, but steady and unyielding. Brody stopped at traffic lights, the windscreen wipers slicing back and forth, the sound rhythmic and strangely almost hypnotic. He watched a stream of pedestrians scurry across the road in front of him, heads down, hands in pockets, nothing seemingly but a determination to return to the shelter of their nests. As he was doing too.

Brody was tired, knew he needed sleep, to recharge. Because if he didn't, he would be no good to anyone, not himself, certainly not the man he was looking for: Donagh Hughes.

The lights changed to green, and he drove through. Up ahead was O'Connell Bridge, and he could see the flashing blue lights of what he knew was a checkpoint. These were everywhere now, all over Dublin, all over the country, the logic being they could deter whoever was holding the Minister for Foreign Affairs and stop them from moving him about. The logic in turn being that if this could be achieved, then it would buy more time, give rise to the possibility of a lucky break, the possibility that someone might notice, someone might lift a phone, someone might tell the police about it. Because that's what it often boiled down to. Solved crimes were statistically proven to be overwhelmingly down to lucky breaks, usually information received or gardai literally stumbling across something – as was the case in the UK when the police literally stumbled upon the Yorkshire Ripper – more than anything to do with solid investigative work. Or sometimes a game of bluff, a game of poker of sorts, when an investigator pretended to hold a hand that he or she didn't. That could work too. Right now, the investigation had very little to go on. They needed a lucky break.

He reached the tail end of traffic at the checkpoint. When he got to the top, the blue revolving lights of a Garda 4x4 coupled with the murky, damp weather added a *Walking Dead* malevolent feel to the world outside. The garda looked at Brody. Brody didn't recognise him. But he was waved through.

His phone rang, the shrill sound jarring him from his reverie. Brody flicked the Bluetooth on the steering wheel stalk.

'Detective Sergeant Jack Brody?' a voice said before he had time to speak.

'Yes, that's me.'

'This is Theo, at Facebook.'

An image of an elbow came into Brody's mind, and he felt it right in his stomach.

'I have good news, Detective Brody.'

And nudged him sharply again into his stomach.

'I have a phone number for you.'

As Brody was receiving this news, Gary Kennedy picked the two drinks he'd ordered from the counter of the Liffey Bank pub and carried them to the table in a discreet corner. It is an out-of-the-way pub near the river, busy during the day with office workers, but mostly quiet at this time. More importantly, it was where no one was likely to recognise him. Not that he had anything to hide, he hadn't, especially not now... but at the same time he did. Because dear old Marie was dead, just not dead long enough, that's all. Indeed, she wasn't even in her grave, nor would she be for some time to come. Not until they'd found her head and the police had completed their investigation. It was almost comical in a way... almost. What was important was that Marie was dead. And what a relief that was. Still, it would help if he could appear like he was at least just a little upset. However, so far he wasn't. Never mind, he still had plenty of time to play the role of the grieving husband. For the moment, it was best to stay low-key, so the Liffey Bank pub it was.

Bethany, the cutie Trinity media studies student, was the perfect companion for this evening. Gary taught a media module at the esteemed old college. She was American, and like most Americans, very upfront about everything. She'd made no secret of her interest in him: call me Beth, sir, with a flutter of her eyelashes. Gary was more than happy to oblige. She, Bethany – oops, Beth – was exuberant of personality with a permanent wide smile fixed to her pretty face... all as saccharin as a doorstep politician at election time, of course. He knew that. Not that he cared. He didn't.

He placed the drinks onto the table and sat opposite Beth

in the shadowed alcove. She took a sip of her Negroni – he'd had to instruct the barman how to make it – then pressed the glass against her bottom lip, turning it white. He knew that outside the world of autocues, of teleprompters and scripted words, all of which she excelled in at his teaching module, the girl struggled to string two words together. But he was one step ahead of her. He knew she had as much interest in him as it took for her to get a work placement at the station, preferably as relief news anchor. Gary knew that would look impressive, really impressive, on her CV when she went looking for something at the America TV networks. Fox News maybe, he reckoned she was a Fox News type of gal.

Right now, Bethany – oops again, Beth – had a look in her eye that he'd never seen before, a suspicious wariness. He knew where that was coming from. Gary decided it best to release the air from the balloon. After a ponderous sip of his twelve-year-old Irish, he said: 'Thanks for meeting me, Beth. I just couldn't face being alone this evening. You'll have heard what happened to my wife. Terrible. I'm a little in shock, to tell the truth. Forgive me. I haven't processed it fully; that will take time.' At least that last part was true.

She smiled, displaying two rows of perfectly even teeth like sculpted marble bollards. She looked at him like he was the only person in the entire world. Still, she didn't speak.

'I have something to ask you, Beth. In fact, it's the reason I wanted us to meet this evening.' Which was a lie, he'd only made up his mind on the matter this very second, but lies rolled off his tongue like salt sprinkled from a cellar.

Bethany beamed at him like he was a Roman emperor. She really had a way of looking at you, like you *mattered*, like you *really* mattered. Gary Kennedy knew that *he* mattered, and thought how she would make viewers feel when she looked out at them from their TV screens, like *they* mattered.

Beth lowered the glass from her mouth and flicked her tongue across her lips. He felt himself stir. She was playing with him.

'We'll need someone as a stand-in on *Perspective*.'

He let that hang.

She held his glance and said nothing, then smiled and placed her glass onto the table.

He realised he was staring. Bethany – Beth – stared back. Her eyes were a deep azure, mesmerising blue. He felt she was communicating with him in some way, like she understood him, telling him, *It's okay. Everything's going to be okay.* He suddenly felt like she was the cat, and he was the mouse.

He blinked, no longer able to maintain the intensity of the stare, and broke the spell.

'But tonight, Beth, God, I'm so lonely, so *lost*.' He leaned forward onto the table.

Bethany – Beth – leaned forward too, her smile so wide it threatened to rip her face in two. They both were so close to each other that he could smell her delicate perfume, the soft aroma of alcohol on her breath. But from him it was rather different. He was conscious of a whiff of something, something stale. Well, it had been a long day, after all. He'd noticed it earlier and had applied extra body spray and that expensive cologne he kept in the office. But he detected it breaking through again. Bethany – Beth – gave no hint that she had. That was all that mattered.

God, he could kiss those lips of hers right now, so soft and sensuous. They were lips that demanded to be kissed.

Steady on, he told himself, *get a grip*. He imagined a cat toying with a mouse, flicking it into the air with its paw, but the mouse was him. Then he saw Beth's eyes suddenly look down, and her eyebrows knit together, then knit together tighter still. The effect was like a scene break in a script, everything suddenly shifting. Her eyes glanced to his and then down again, a silent communication for him to follow her. He did, cocking his head to one side like an inquisitive puppy. What the...?

He blinked and shook his head. It was no use. Maggots really were crawling out of his pocket.

40

The news from Theo at Facebook gave Brody a powerful boost, pumping high-octane adrenaline through his veins, overpowering every trace of tiredness and fatigue. With that came a clarity of purpose, a hope that this first real break in the case might lead somewhere. He now had a telephone number for the ghost, the man who went to such lengths to hide himself, who seemed to hate Donagh Hughes more than anyone else. Did that mean something? Could that mean something?

Right now, it meant that Brody had stopped thinking of Ashling Nolan. He'd take that.

But as Brody considered this potential break in the case, a little voice whispered in his ear, a little voice he'd tried his best to ignore, but couldn't. Because he knew, even if he didn't like what that voice said, he would listen to it anyway. The voice said: *Come on, Brody, if this ghost is so careful, so fucking good at hiding himself, and he is, do you really think he's going to link his actual telephone number to his Facebook account? Well, do you? I know the answer. And the answer is, Brody, no, he fucking wouldn't.*

The adrenaline rush ebbed and became a trickle, but strangely, even without it, Brody wasn't tired again. Because he knew the most critical voices are often our own. Instead, he remained energised, with the conviction that this information *did* mean something. He told that inner critic: *Fuck you.*

He did a U-turn as soon as he was able to, and headed back to the Phoenix Park. He rang ahead to the unit room. The person who picked up was talking to someone. Brody waited, then: 'Yeah.' He was also chewing gum, and loudly too with a slurping sound. Brody took a breath. The quicker he got this done, the better. You pick your battles. And this battle wasn't worth it.

'This is Detective Sergeant Jack Brody. Who am I speaking to?'

'Me.'

'You a smart arse? Who am I speaking to?'

'Jason Cawley. That was an in-house joke.'

Jesus.

'Let's start again. I have a phone number. I want you to contact Eir. Find out if it pinged any masts in the last forty-eight hours. Got that, Cawley?'

'Um, yes, I got that. Thing is…' *Slurp, slurp.*

'Yes, the thing is?'

'I've already been detailed a job, and, um… you're Brody, right?'

'Yes, Jesus, I'm Brody. I just told you.'

'Okay, yes, but you're not attached to my unit. Me, myself, I'm attached to Pearse Street. And this investigation is under Superintendent Harper. He gathered us specific like, very specific. Everything goes through him. No exceptions.' *Slurp, slurp.*

Brody was on the verge of exploding like an overheating boiler. He imagined a heavy, sending a flurry of punches into it, rattling the chains on the hook it hung from. He closed his eyes, concentrating, and it was enough to clear the steam.

'We'll talk again, Cawley; you can count on it.'

Brody pulled in abruptly when he spotted a free parking space at the roadside. The driver behind leaned on the horn.

'If you weren't tailgating, it wouldn't be a problem, you prick,' he muttered, the radiator beginning to steam again. He killed the engine and banged on the steering wheel. Damn Harper. He thought of Fiona Ryan. Maybe he should reach out to her? No, he wasn't going to do that. Damn her too.

Instead, he rang Marty Sheahan. The phone was answered on the second ring.

'Boss.'

'You home, Marty?'

'Yes.' A wariness to Sheahan's tone. 'Just getting a bite to eat. Marissa made pizza. Why?'

'Sorry to intrude. I'm on my way back in...'

'Uh-oh.'

'Yes, uh-oh. There's been a development. I've decided we are the only ones who can deal with it. I need everyone back at the ranch. Okay?'

Marty didn't sound too pleased, yet there was no hesitation. 'I'll get my jacket and leave straight away, boss.'

'Thank you, Marty. You can start making phone calls right away too. I need something done. Listen up.'

THE TWO UNIFORMS who answered the call at the Liffey Bank pub looked like they should be wearing school rather than police uniforms. As was increasingly the case lately due to a spate of early retirements. Duty sergeants now had the difficult task of making what was once routinely possible, the pairing of old-timers with less experienced younger mules.

The old-timers had hung up their boots and were wearing slippers instead, drinking wine or pints of Guinness, out on the golf course or pruning roses. Whatever.

The two rosy-cheeked youngsters came through the door and stood, surveying the scene. They saw a man on the ground, slumped against the wall next to an upturned table, holding a tissue to one side of his face, blood seeping through it. By him on the floor there was a large smudge in the carpet, purple and black at its centre, with a large and irregular outer circle, off white in colour. Next to the smudge a couple of maggots crawled about in the tufts of carpet.

'What happened here?' one of them asked, puffing out his chest and placing his hands on his hips like General Patton.

The other fella crouched and peered at the floor, seemingly oblivious to Gary Kennedy slumped beside him.

'There's some bone in there, Kev,' he said.

'Is there? Bone?'

'Yes, bone.'

'What happened, I asked?' the one who was standing said, finally looking at Gary Kennedy now.

But it was the barman who spoke, stepping out from the behind the counter, who said, 'He got a couple of digs, that's what.'

'He did? And why did he get a couple of digs?'

'I dunno. There was a young one with him, nice-lookin' one too. Something happened. I looked over, and he was taking something from his pocket. Honest to God, there was maggots on it. She screamed, and he dropped it to the floor. Then when she tried to leave, he grabbed her, he says to her, "It's okay, it's not what you think, honest to God, it's not what you think," and then she really tried to leg it, but he wouldn't let her, he kept holding her and she kept trying to push him off her, and he kept saying, "It's not what you think, Beth, please, it's not what you think.'" The barman shrugged. 'I dunno. Next thing, the two fellas who'd been drinking at the counter were down, and one of them gave him a couple of slaps. I dunno, they must have thought he was slapping her around or about to slap her around. I don't know what they were thinking.' The barman pointed. 'Yer man there just went down. The other two legged it then. I don't know the one who slapped him, but the other bollocks, I recognise him, Lenny's his name...'

The two rosy cheeks looked at him curiously. 'And what's this on the floor?' the one who was still crouching, nodding his head towards it, said.

'Jasus, shoulda told you that from the start. It looked like a finger to me. A bleedin' finger.'

'A bleeding finger? Whose bleeding finger?'

'No, not a bleeding finger. A *bleedin'* finger. Haven't you ever heard? It's only a figure of speech. Never mind. A finger, a real finger, there on the floor, like in the song... a mouse, where? There on the floor. The same, only a finger, see. You following?'

They didn't look like they were fully following.

'Where's it now? This finger.'

The barman pointed. 'There. On the floor. That there. Don't know how I'm going to clean it. In the panic to get out of the gaff, I suppose, one of them – not Lenny now, the other fella – squashed it under his boot.'

'You taking the piss, fella?'

'No, I'm not taking the piss. A finger. I told you.' The barman held his hand up and twiddled his own. 'One of these. Are youse two slow or what? No offence.'

'Christ,' one of the rosy cheeks said, 'where? what? I mean, whose finger was it?'

The barman shrugged. 'I don't know.'

'Well, where did it come from?'

'My pocket,' Gary Kennedy piped up with remarkable calmness.

They both looked down at him.

'Your pocket?'

Despite everything, he seemed to have regained his composure. He extended his hand.

'Will you help me up, for God's sake. Has anyone called an ambulance? Why are you both standing there like two buffoons? Help me up, I said.'

They began helping him up, as if relieved someone was finally telling them what to do.

41

If Voyle was correct, Patrick O'Connor would return to the same pub he'd been in the other evening when he and Considine had been watching while eating fish and chips in the car. So he tidied himself up as best he could and went there, took a stool at the counter and ordered a pint of zero alcohol Guinness. He didn't think it would taste very good, but was pleasantly surprised.

To tell the truth, he didn't know what he hoped to achieve by being here. But he'd find out.

The pub was old, with a public bar and lounge, the décor 1960s. He reckoned O'Connor would favour the public bar, with its plain wooden floor, wall seating like church pews, a high counter and mirrors running the length of the wall. So that was where he sat.

Pubs like this were rare now. The rise of the Celtic Tiger had meant a clean sweep, out with the old and in with the new, the swank, the big and the brash. Now the trend had come full circle, and the trend was in reverse, with considerable sums being spent converting pubs back to the way they used to be. Old was chic.

It was Sunday evening, the place was busy, but not that busy, the clientele a mix of young and old, and mostly male. The younger punters were unusually subdued, Voyle thought. He put it down to frayed nerves from a weekend's drinking. The older clientele, it was just another night for them.

Voyle was aware the barman was looking at him. He was standing at the other end of the counter, polishing a glass. He put this down and sauntered over. 'Howya,' he said.

'Howya,' Voyle answered.

He was a young fella too, a smidge of a moustache above his upper lip, with an open, smiling face.

'You're not from around here? Dublin?'

And talkative.

'Yes,' Voyle said. 'Dublin. To tell the truth.' He looked to his left and right, dropped his voice an octave and said, 'Can I let you in on a little secret?'

'A secret.' The barman raised an eyebrow. Now he looked wary.

Voyle knew a barman would know the lay of the land. Anything there was happening, he'd know.

'I'm a detective, a garda detective. Okay?'

'A detective. Go on owra dat...'

'Here,' Voyle said, and plopped his ID onto the counter, cupped his hands around it. The lad peered at it closely.

'Oh, well now...'

'Patrick O'Connor. He drinks in here, doesn't he?'

'Lord Paddy. Yes, he's a regular. You're interested in him, are you?'

'Maybe.'

The barman said nothing. Voyle caught it, a look.

'What is it?'

'Am I the only one thinks it's strange his wife took off and never came back? Just like that. Gone. Last time they were in here, I saw him slap her.'

'You did?'

'He was drunk, they were rowing, nothing unusual for them, and he just slapped her across the face. He didn't think anyone could see. But I did. Now, when he comes in, it's like she never even existed. He never mentions her. I think that's weird.'

Me too, thought Voyle.

'You think something happened to her?' the barman asked.

Voyle didn't want to answer that one, and was relieved when someone called for a drink. The barman turned and nodded. 'Another pint, Jimmy, coming right up.'

The barman looked back at Voyle. 'One other thing,' he said.

'What's that?'

He leaned onto the counter, said almost in a whisper, 'He's selling stuff from the big house.'

'What kind of stuff?'

'All sorts. Antiques. Furniture. Not cheap either, from what I hear.'

'How did you hear?'

'He meets punters in here, sometimes. They talk; they don't know, think it's all legit. He doesn't talk about it... for obvious reasons.' He glanced along the counter. 'Yes, Jimmy, coming right now.'

Voyle drained his glass and stood. 'Thank you for the information.'

'It's not information. I'm no informer. We were just talking, right?'

'Of course. Yes, just talking.'

Voyle went outside and sat in his car as the taxi drew up. He watched Patrick O'Connor get out and head into the pub.

He had an idea. One that would not have made much sense a short time ago. But it did now.

He started the engine and turned the car around, headed back in the direction of Ash Hall. He might as well give this a go. He had nothing to lose. If he was wrong, then he was wrong, and no one would be any the wiser.

But if he was right...

42

I'm going to die. I'm going to die here in this filthy hovel, lying on this filthy floor; no one will ever know... only the person who put me here, that is. I will die alone. The rats will eat me. Though not all of me. When they've finished what they want, my body will appear as a macabre Swiss cheese. They will eventually waddle away, having gorged their fill, disappearing through holes they first slipped through with ease but now have to contort and push themselves through to fit. I know the end is coming. I know it. They know it. That's why they're getting more and more restless, more hyped up; they can smell it, almost taste it, the death on the air. Now they've started nipping at one another, jockeying for position. Soon they will get into a frenzy; they won't be able to contain themselves any longer. They might even start on me before I've died. The biggest ones have already marked me out. I know it because I felt them piss against me, designating which piece of meat belongs to whom. Rats are clever, after all, very clever. The smell of that piss is vile, disgusting. The biggest rat of them all, he's literally as big as a small cat, has now taken to sitting close in front of my face. He just sits there... watching... waiting. He may soon give up waiting, might just stretch that big neck of his out and take a bite... and another bite... and another.

Donagh Hughes opens his eyes and realises he was dreaming. There's no rat as big as a cat sitting in front of his face. He no longer knows what is exactly real and what's not. He is confused. He turns his head and realises he is back home, he is lying in his own bed, and lying next to him is his wife. He is so rarely at home now. He has neglected Monica for so long. She is a good woman, she really is, the mother of his children, the best mother in the world.

'I'm sorry, sweetheart,' he mumbles, and lifts his hand to stroke her head, stirring up the hornets' nest that is the stump of his finger. But the pain jolts him from his delirium and into reality... but only briefly. And briefly he remembers where he is, the hovel he is lying in. He remembers the big rat, the one as big as a cat. But there is nothing there. He was dreaming. But he knows it makes no difference. Hell is hell. All he can be sure of is he's alive, nothing more.

He shivers. It is cold, so cold. Yet he is hot too, a burning-up hot, but at the same time cold, so cold.

He feels a sudden tickle of whiskers on his chin and recoils in horror, hitting the back of his head on the wall behind him. He sees it pass in front of his face. It's the one, the cat rat. He has not been dreaming. Everything is real.

Donagh Hughes opens his mouth, wanting to scream, to roar, wanting to do... something. But he can't.

He can't do anything. Nothing at all.

43

By the time they'd worked out what's what, by the time they'd talked to their skipper and he in turn had talked to his, by the time they'd worked out that Gary Kennedy, the man found sprawled in a pub who admitted to having a human finger in his pocket, was the husband of Marie Kennedy, the woman found decapitated in her car the night before. Well, by the time they'd worked all that out and someone had finally picked up the phone to ring the Phoenix Park, it was almost midnight.

As the officer at Pearse Street dialled Brody's number, Brody, Marty Sheahan, Nicola Considine and Sergeant Denise O'Brien were ensconced in his office. None of them were unduly tired; they were all being carried along on the adrenalin thermals, fuelled by coffee and energy drinks.

'I'm expecting a call as soon as they have something,' Marty said. 'They have a couple of people in India working on it.' They were discussing the tracking of the phone number Theo at Facebook had given them.

'India?' Brody said.

'They don't work nights here, in Ireland I mean.'

'Whatever.'

'Any word from Voyle, boss?' Considine asked.

Brody smiled.

'Why? What did I say?'

'Nothing, it just sounded like you cared, Nicola, that's all.'

'He's an irritating little man. To be generous, maybe a bit misunderstood too... Any word from him, boss?'

'No. Maybe I need to give him a call.'

His desk phone rang. Could it be Voyle? Think of the devil and he's sure to appear and all that.

He snatched up the receiver.

'Detective Sergeant Jack Brody,' the voice said.

It wasn't Voyle, it was a detective at Pearse Street. He listened to what the detective had to say, then: 'Will that be on Pulse soon?... Good.' He nodded and hung up. 'Gary Kennedy,' he announced to the team, 'husband of Marie Kennedy, was assaulted in a pub and has admitted to carrying a human finger around in his pocket.'

O'Brien spluttered.

'Yes, you've heard correct,' Brody confirmed, and thought of Voyle. He made his mind up. To hell with this Gilsenan wild goose chase, he needed Steve here right now.

44

Voyle parked in the same gateway to the field he'd parked in earlier while waiting for Kate to emerge from Ash Hall. How much time did he have? He didn't know. Maybe hours, maybe all night. But he reckoned he probably had at least ninety minutes for definite. If he didn't hang around, that should be more than enough. And he didn't plan on hanging around.

It was dark and moonless, but some clouds were backlit by stars like a 3D animation. Voyle was an outdoorsman, and it was just enough light for him to see. He jogged from the gateway back along the road. At the entrance to Ash Hall he hardly hesitated, bounding up the lattice of metal work on the gates with the grace of one accustomed to scaling sheer rock faces. On the other side he dropped to the driveway, ran towards the house, pausing at the top just before emerging into the wide, open clearway before the house. As he jogged across it, he felt exposed, the big old house brooding in the darkness before him. He tensed, waiting for motion sensors to detect him and illuminate security lights. But none did. He couldn't be certain there was no one in there. He made straight for the fourth raised bed and stopped, turned in a full circle, his eyes scanning all directions and seeing nothing out of the ordinary.

Voyle walked quickly down to the fourth stone-surround, raised bed. As he'd hoped, the wheelbarrow was still there, the implement he'd spotted reflecting the weak sun earlier still leaning against it. He saw now that it was a spade. He stood over the raised bed, a section of its wall missing, a pile of stones lying on the ground next to it.

Voyle picked up the spade and rested the blade against one of the raised bed stones. He nudged it gently, and it came away like a loose tooth. He considered the wall had become compromised by the number of stones already removed. The least nudge would send the whole lot crashing to the ground. He used the spade to take away another stone and another, and finally most of the remainder came down in one clump. He jumped onto the raised bed, dug the spade into the centre of the bank of soil. It was compacted but came away easily. This might not take as long as he thought.

The weak light began to fade as the clouds gathered. Voyle never eased up on his task. Fifteen minutes later he'd almost all the soil out. And decided this had all been a waste of time. There was nothing here. O'Connor could deal with the mess and wonder how it got there. As he thought this, he placed his foot onto the step of the blade for what he decided was to be the final time and pushed it in. But on this occasion, the blade hit something solid. *The bottom*, he thought, *that's all, I've reached the bottom.* Still, he was curious, and dropped the spade to the side, flopped down onto his knees, and using his hands, he scooped back the remainder of the soft soil. Taking his phone from his pocket, he turned on its flashlight. The beam of light revealed something that made him snap back onto his feet and reach for the spade again. He placed the phone between his teeth and cleared away around the outline, scooping back the last residues of soil. When he stopped, he took the phone from his mouth, panting gently. In the powerful beam of light, the cadaver's bones stood out in relief against the black clay. And with it there was the smell of putrefying flesh. Voyle made out fragments of clothing, a watch strap, an earring, a row of buttons clinging to a strip of material that he imagined had once been a blouse. There was a strip of crumpled, stiff canvas, a broken strap in one corner. This was an apron, he imagined, just like the one Patrick O'Connor had been wearing when Voyle had called and found him cutting up the deer carcass. Voyle crouched down and peered closely at the skull. The impact of the spade's blade had, unfortunately, damaged the eye socket. However, above it there was a large, untidy hole, a web of cracks along its edges. This had been caused by a blunt instrument, he surmised.

Voyle came to a conclusion.

The body lying here was that of Patrick O'Connor's wife. He surmised too that O'Connor had been trying to repair the wall when stones had started falling out. He thought that maybe he'd been in the process of moving the body and had disturbed the structural integrity of it.

Just as Voyle had been about to give up, he had made this discovery. It was true, it was always darkest before the dawn.

Out of the corner of his eye, Voyle spotted something. He watched as a beam of light filtered through the trees, moving quickly along the driveway. A car was approaching.

The taxi dropped O'Connor at the front door, and in the light offered by its headlights, he opened the door and went inside. The taxi departed, and all was darkness again. Voyle was about to breathe a sigh of relief when the exterior lights came on, his shadow stretching out before him. He quickly crossed to the wall of the house and pressed himself against it. What he needed to do was call this in. Right now, however, he needed to stay concealed until he worked out exactly what he was facing, that is. He realised his shadow was draped over a portion of the wall next to him like a huge example of street art. He dropped to the ground and crawled across and flattened himself behind the raised bed, the back wall of which was still intact.

He didn't have long to wait before he knew what he was facing.

A voice shouted. He recognised that voice. It was O'Connor's. 'I saw the shadow. It's you, isn't it? Mr Policeman. Come on, where are you? You hear me, Mr Policeman? Where are you? Come on out.'

Voyle thought about that. Not a good idea, he decided.

'Do you hear me?' O'Connor shouted again. 'Where are you? Come on out.'

Voyle heard a sharp, metallic cracking sound. And knew what that was. It was the sound of a shotgun being snapped shut.

And then his telephone rang.

45

Brody listened to the phone ringing out and hung up without leaving a message. He'd ring Voyle again later. It was late, and Voyle was likely in bed. It being Voyle, he probably wouldn't be alone either.

'Nicola, can you go to Pearse Street and have a chat with Gary Kennedy? He's agreed to an interview. Even if I'm not sure that it's him, that whole thing sounds... implausible.'

She nodded, getting to her feet.

As she walked to the door, Marty Sheahan's mobile phone rang. He answered, placed a hand over the receiver and said, 'It's Sanji in Mumbai.'

'Put it on speaker,' Brody said.

He did and placed it onto the table. Sanji informed them there'd been a hit on a mast just a few minutes ago for the number they were interested in.

'Which mast?' Marty asked.

'Sector 1A. Ring End?'

'Ringsend, with an *s*.'

'Pardon me, yes, Ringsend.'

'Other hits?'

'Yes. There are. I will email you through a complete list. The phone was travelling today too; there is a track from one side of the country to the other.'

'And where was the first hit recorded on that track?'

'A place called. Let me get this right...'

'Donegal,' Marty said, 'is that it?'

'Aha, that is how you say it. Yes, that is correct.'

'Thank you, Sanji,' Marty said. 'Please forward me the list.'

Marty glanced at Brody, who nodded. Marty terminated the call.

Brody yelled, 'Nicola.'

She appeared back in the doorway a moment later.

'I was halfway down the stairs. What's up?'

'Change of plan. I want you to go to the Lawrence Hotel... Detective O'Brien, can you go with her?'

Denise O'Brien smiled. She seemed very at home with the unit. 'Of course.'

'Thank you.'

'And how will we play this, boss?' Considine asked, stepping back into the room.

Brody nodded to her new colleague.

'I'll let Sergeant O'Brien come up with something. You think you can do that? A good improvisation maybe?'

Her eyes twinkled.

'Already have one in mind. I'm thinking of a scene from *The Return of the Pink Panther*. That should do it. Inspector Clouseau wasn't the complete idiot you'd think he was. He always got his man, after all. Yes, that should do it, suitably adapted of course.'

'Of course,' Brody said, 'but make sure you arrange backup. This isn't a movie, after all.'

Voyle heard the footsteps approaching across the gravel, coming towards him. He knew now what he was facing. And also knew that O'Connor would despatch him with the ease he would a deer he'd cornered in the forest, having tracked the petrified beast for hours.

I've got to do something.

He swivelled his eyes to the corners of their sockets, taking in a portion of the façade of Ash Hall that was next to him. There was a drainpipe there. An old-type drainpipe, cast iron, strong and sturdy. It would take his weight easily. He could make short work of that, shimmy up onto the roof in no time. But he wouldn't be able to make short enough work of it. O'Connor would have him picked off in seconds, pepper him with buckshot, turning him into a sieve. The exterior lights had turned night into day. Voyle knew he would be a sitting duck. *That won't work, no way.* Of course, he could take his chances and simply run for it. He'd at least have a chance then. *Nah, won't work either.* If he was going to die, he didn't want it by being shot in the back *and* while running away.

So, really, there was only one choice. One choice only.

Voyle took a deep breath and sprang onto his feet.

It was one fifteen in the morning. Considine and O'Brien were in a small seating area at the end of the corridor just down from Monica Hughes's room. This was an area for residents to come and do whatever, read their newspapers, make private phone calls, drink tea or coffee or gaze out onto Grand Canal Dock through the big bay window there. Considine and O'Brien were standing by the window, gazing out, thinking. Below in the darkness a light shone in the window of one of the houseboats that was moored there. But all else was in darkness.

Considine was the only one who could attempt to get into that room. It had to be her, not O'Brien, not again. She'd already played a role as a member of the housekeeping staff and would likely be recognised.

This was where the Pink Panther came in.

O'Brien had whispered what she had in mind, and Considine was thinking about it. She didn't look convinced.

'That's...' she began, but fell silent.

'What? Stupid? Is that what you mean?'

Considine said nothing. The more she thought of it, the more she thought that maybe this wasn't so stupid after all.

'You just turn your jacket inside out,' O'Brien told her, 'and hide the Garda name; then you'll look just like a member of security.'

Considine ran a hand through her long, blonde hair, still doubtful.

'But,' she said, 'if I do, won't that blow *my* cover? If we need to do something again I mean.'

'Maybe not. It's only a small cameo, after all. Anyway, there might never be an "again". When you go into that room, if I don't hear back from you after, let's make it five minutes, I'm going to call it in.'

'Sound,' Considine said. 'Okay, let's get this over with before I have time to think about it.' She turned, facing down the corridor. 'Stage left.'

O'Brien grinned.

'You're a natural, girl, you really are.'

VOYLE COULD SEE the shock on O'Connor's face when he popped up from behind the raised bed. *Surprise!* The time it would take the butler, caretaker – whatever – to make sense of the situation and for his brain to send a signal to his finger to pull the trigger was only the blink of an eye. That was how long it would take before Voyle became a heap on the ground. But that might be just enough. Voyle sprang up onto the back wall of the raised bed, bending his right knee as he came down, then springing forward, head low, arms outstretched, sweeping them through the air, giving him extra thrust, enough to clear the space over where O'Connor's wife's putrefying body lay, and land on the gravel of the forecourt on the other side. Then he shimmied left, shimmied right, O'Connor swinging the shotgun wildly as he tried to follow him, but not quite managing to, those brain neurons, addled by his earlier intake of alcohol, no doubt having difficulty computing the fact that Voyle was not doing what was expected of someone with a double barrelled pointed at them. Voyle was not standing rigid like a poor, petrified deer. No, O'Connor's eyes widened like he could scarcely believe what he was seeing. Voyle was *not* running away; he was *charging* right at *him*. O'Connor was too slow, and Voyle too quick. By the time O'Connor pulled the trigger, by the time both barrels flared, by the time the weapon boomed and bucked, Voyle was no longer standing where he had been. He'd gone, travelling like a missile beneath the radar, crashing into O'Connor, both of them crumpling to the ground. Voyle was up again before the stupid, dazed look had left O'Connor's face, his foot swinging through the air, kicking the shotgun away and to the side. O'Connor began to fumble his way back onto his feet, managing to raise himself up onto one hand before Voyle swung his foot again, sending it into O'Connor's belly and dropping him like a skittle. O'Connor slumped back down again and rolled over onto his back, staring up at Voyle.

'You're not going to win this, O'Connor, are you, prick?'

The butler, caretaker – whatever – made a low grumbling sound and rolled onto his side. Once again, he began trying to raise himself up. And this time he succeeded, because Voyle allowed him to. Standing up, O'Connor clenched his fists and started to slowly advance.

Voyle shook his head. 'You're not getting the message, are you?' He stiffened his right arm and sliced it through the air, snapping it against O'Connor's windpipe like a billy club, in what was called a chop board karate slice.

This time O'Connor went down again and stayed there, coughing and spitting and gasping for breath.

46

The list came in an email attachment, and Marty Sheahan printed out two copies, brought them to Brody and spread them on his desk: one for himself, and one for the boss. They drank cold coffee as they looked over the track line of the telephone number over the previous forty-eight hours. A pattern was detected very quickly.

'Mast Zulu Three.' Brody stabbed a finger against the printout. 'It spent a lot of time there, didn't it?' He checked the time attached to each contact. One was registered early on the morning of the day Donagh Hughes was believed to have gone missing, with multiple pings thereafter for the same mast. What was really interesting with mast Zulu Three was that it was located in... drum roll, County Wicklow, specifically, cue another drum roll, please, outside the village of Tinnock.

'Well, well, boss,' Marty said.

Brody sat back and rubbed his eyes. He wasn't tired, adrenaline and energy drinks were still giving him wings, but his eyes were dry, and they made a squelching sound like someone was cleaning one of the office windows.

'But why?' Brody said.

'Why?'

'I'm thinking. We've gone over this before. He's called the ghost, isn't he? He's been covering his tracks all along, hasn't he? And yet...' He tapped a finger onto the printout. 'There he is, his movements for the last three days, as if he hasn't a care in the world, like a tourist sharing his itinerary with everyone. Nah, something's not right.'

'But, boss, these *are* his movements, whatever the reasons for them. That's the whole point with this. He can't disguise his movements.'

Brody looked at the printout again and traced his finger across it.

'And this mast here, Oscar Nine, it registers a ping three hours later. In Donegal. Where exactly in Donegal?'

'The middle of nowhere, boss, looks like, literally.'

'Is it near a motorway? Something? Anything? What?'

'No, that mast provides coverage to a very rural, sparsely populated area. The telephone company get a tax break for doing it.'

'We need to check it out.'

'I've already given it a quick once-over on Google Maps.'

'And?'

'I'd say if you wanted to hide somebody, it'd be the perfect place.'

Brody said nothing, thinking that over.

'And what's that mean? The perfect place to hide somebody?' The voice belonged to Superintendent Ryan.

Brody looked up, and Marty looked back over his shoulder.

She walked through the open doorway into the office.

'I haven't seen much of you lately, Jack. You avoiding me?'

'Just getting things done.'

'And what's that supposed to mean?' She stopped by his desk.

'Where's Superintendent Harper?'

'Don't change the subject.'

'I'm not. It's all connected, that's all. Where is he?'

'He's gone home. A bad migraine. He gets a lot of them.'

I bet he does, Brody thought.

'I repeat, what do you mean? "Getting things done?" What's that mean?'

Brody told her.

'Oh.' She sounded surprised. 'So you just went off on your ownsome, did you? Freelance. Didn't think to mention it to your commanding officer.'

'Does it matter?'

'Yes, it does, and you know it.'

Jack pointed to the door.

'Until you walked in here, did you even care? Wasn't it the priority of Harper to–'

'Superintendent Harper to you.'

'Okay. Wasn't it the priority of *Superintendent* Harper to limit the fallout from his car crash of a press conference? Wasn't that the priority? And he'd elbowed you aside to take over authority of this investigation, remember, and I haven't heard anything from him in a while on that, nor you.' Brody shook his head. 'You just let him take over.'

'How dare you? How bloody *dare* you. And what you say is simply not true.'

But Brody knew that it was. He said nothing. Now was not the time. But it was coming close to the time. When this was over, that is. And Brody had a feeling that it soon would be.

She dropped her voice. 'The priority of this investigation has always been the safe return of Donagh Hughes. Nothing else.'

'Whatever,' Jack said, 'like I say, I was getting things done. I also spoke to the commissioner.'

'What?' Her eyes widened, taking up half her head.

'*He* summoned me to *his* office.'

He waited while that sank in.

'He did? Um, and what did he say?'

'Right then. What did he say? Well, I've nothing to hide, so I'll tell you. He was concerned about the course of this investigation. He asked me what I thought about the way it was progressing. So I told him. There.'

Jack knew by Ryan's expression that the commissioner hadn't spoken to her. She leaned down onto the desk, resting on her palms, looked slowly from Marty to Brody.

'You're the clever one, Jack, aren't you? The clever dick. And what am I? Just the slimy super trying to grovel her way to the top on the career totem pole, is that it? Like all the rest of them. That what you think, Jack?'

'I didn't say any of that. You did.'

'Okay, Jack Brody, I admit there's a little bit of that in me. But there's a bit of that in everyone on the job, isn't there?' Her eyes narrowed as she looked at him. 'Or maybe not. But maybe you should try it for yourself sometime too, *Sergeant* Brody. And then you can talk to me the way you are. How dare you.'

'No thanks.'

'The pinkie,' she said, like she'd plucked the word out of a clear blue sky.

'The what?'

'The little finger, the halfway house for maggots, that Gary Kennedy had been carrying around in his pocket.'

Brody burst out laughing, like a sudden release of tension.

'The halfway house for maggots. That's a good one, that is. That's funny.'

'It is?'

'I think so...' Brody looked at Sheahan. 'What about you, Marty?'

Marty stuck his lower lip out in a Gallic, non-committal way, like Brody imagined he would do down the Four Courts someday.

'It came from Donagh Hughes,' Superintendent Ryan said, all sombre, 'the finger. Didn't you know that, Jack?'

'No. I didn't.'

'The lab rang me, just like I told them to.'

'Good. I'm glad to hear it.'

She looked at him curiously.

'You don't care, do you? You don't bloody care that they rang me and not you.'

'Jesus,' Brody said, 'you told them to, didn't you? You just said so. And where are we? The playground? You're being childish. No, I don't care. Why would I? All I care about is that Hughes without his finger won't last long. Not if it was chopped off. That's bound to be what happened. He won't last long at all. He'll be a dead Minister for Foreign Affairs before much longer. And that has ramifications.' He raised his eyebrows. 'If you know what I mean?'

She opened her mouth, about to say something, but closed it again.

Yes, she knows what I mean alright, Brody thought, imagining a guillotine coming down onto a neck, and her head plopping into the waiting wicker basket.

He jumped to his feet, grabbed his jacket from the back of the chair, and started pulling it on. 'Marty, come with me. Gary Kennedy. We're going to Pearse Street.'

'Oh no you're not.' Ryan placed her hands onto her hips.

'No?'

'The SDU are interviewing Gary Kennedy as I speak.

They've been with him for almost two hours now... you didn't know that either, did you?'

Brody threw his eyes to heaven and shook his head. Christ, what was it with this woman, Superintendent Fiona Ryan?

'No, I didn't know. What does it matter? Just so long as we know the outcome.'

'Because I am the unit commander. I have to lead. Not you.'

Brody sighed loudly.

'Give me patience,' he muttered.

'This will be all over very shortly, Brody. We have our man. I can feel it.'

'Glad to hear you feel that way. I don't.'

'We'll see, then, won't we?'

'Yes, we will. By the way, I can't contact Voyle.'

'Dead wood. Don't worry about him. He'll be transferred out of this unit first chance I get.'

'Why?'

'Because I don't like him, that's why.'

'No other reason. You just don't like him. Is that it?'

'Yes, that's it.' Her eyes flicked to Marty, then back to Brody. 'And that's enough.'

'What,' he said, 'and we might be next, is that it?'

'Dead wood,' she repeated, and left the office.

47

Considine was so accustomed to giving business knocks that she was about to give one on this occasion too but managed to stop herself in time, freezing her fist in mid-air centimetres from the door, turning the flat end towards the floor and placing the knuckles against the panel, tapping on it gently but sharply instead.

'Yes.' A muffled female voice from inside came back almost immediately, soft plodding sounds following as Considine imagined Monica Hughes approaching. The voice spoke again, much clearer and louder this time, right on the other side of the door, 'Who is this?'

'Security,' Considine said. 'I apologise about the time. We tried ringing but got no response, I mean no sound from the phone; maybe it's off the hook or the connection is out of the wall or something.'

'Nothing is wrong with the phone. It's not off the hook. What's this about?'

'Hopefully, probably nothing. It's just our computer monitor is showing red for this room.'

'Red. What's that mean?'

'I'm sorry, but could you open the door, please. I don't want to disturb the other guests. I'm sure you can understand.'

Considine took a step back and placed herself squarely in front of the peephole. She could feel a pair of eyes on her. Then she heard the lock click back, and the door opened.

Monica Hughes stood there before her, in a sheer negligee with nothing on underneath but what the good Lord had decided to give her. Her hair – on her head – was ruffled, and her face glistened.

'Do you really? Have to come in, I mean.'

'I'm afraid so. I have no way of knowing if there's smoke, or whatever, in this room or not.'

'There's no smoke... and what's *whatever?*'

'Well, I don't know. That's why I need to check.'

'One minute.' She turned.

Considine averted her eyes from the surprisingly pert arse beneath the sheer material as Monica headed back and disappeared into the darkness of the bedroom. She slammed the door shut, and she could hear muted voices from inside, couldn't decipher what was being said. The door opened again, and Monica Hughes emerged, this time wearing a red satin dressing gown.

'I'm sorry, but I really need to get a move on,' Considine said, stepping into the room without an invite, like the time had expired on waiting for permission. 'And yes. I will need to see all rooms.'

The plan was for Denise O'Brien to ring the number when Considine went into the room. . The phone number to be called was the one Theo had given Brody, of this so-called ghost. The thinking was it might be in this hotel room. If it was, they'd hear it.

But there was no sound of any telephone ringing anywhere in this room that Considine could hear. The lights were still off, yet there was enough light through the door to see what was what. Still, she wished she had brought her flashlight with her. If she had brought the flashlight, there'd be no need for lights. It was only a matter of time before Monica Hughes switched them on, and that would afford her an opportunity to have a good look at her. Considine didn't want that.

Best to make a speedy exit, she decided. Maybe there was a phone, and maybe it was on silent, or maybe it was turned off. More likely, she felt increasingly certain, the phone had nothing to do with the people in this room. Because Monica Hughes had nothing to do with the disappearance of her husband. Yes, she might be having an affair with whoever was in that bedroom. But there was no law against that. Anyway, this had been a long shot.

'Everything seems to be in order,' Considine said. 'Thank you. I'll be on my way. So sorry to have disturbed you.'

'You didn't even look anywhere. And all after you made such a deal about looking around. Now you haven't... where's your card?'

'My card?'

'Your identification. You never showed it to me.'

Shit.

The bedroom was straight ahead of Considine, and she could see the door opening. A dark outline materialised, standing there, big, muscular, a man so big he had to bend his head to stop himself hitting the top of the doorjamb.

And then the light flickered to life.

And *then* a phone began to ring.

And *then* Monica and Considine stared at one another.

The phone sounded again, shrill and loud, and both

women turned towards the coffee table where it lay, the screen lighting up each time it sounded.

The giant who'd been standing before her moved quickly past and picked it up. Then she heard him cross to the door, and she heard it close.

Then she heard it lock.

48

The big old kitchen was cold. They sat in it; a side lamp was on, but not sufficient to light all of the room, shrouding it in shadow where it could not reach, all the rest black like the mouth to a great cave. O'Connor sat slumped forward, his elbows resting on his knees, a beaten man. Or so he looked. But Voyle wasn't so sure and sat a distance away after first snapping a pair of cuffs on him just so he wouldn't have to worry about it. But he still did. O'Connor was a devious bastard, after all. Right now he was subdued and dazed, and in that condition, Voyle deemed it a good time to ask him questions.

'Robert Gilsenan,' he began. The butler, caretaker – whatever – raised his head. Voyle nodded towards the front of the house. 'The body. Is that it? You thought I'd ask about that. That's your wife, isn't it?'

O'Connor dropped his head again, shuffling his feet, pushing himself back into his chair.

'I know what you did to Gilsenan. You killed him, didn't you? Made it look like a suicide.'

Voyle fell silent. There was the sound of a dripping tap. It echoed through the kitchen. O'Connor cocked his head to one side and shrugged.

'What?' he said. 'Me? I killed Mr Gilsenan? Is that what you're saying?'

'The door was never locked,' Voyle answered, 'was it? In the panic of it all, to get inside, they had to ram the door, didn't they? What they use, a key? The big red key? I never saw it mentioned in any of the reports... that little detail was overlooked. Being a suicide and all, they probably thought it wasn't of much consequence, which it wouldn't be if it was a suicide. The door lock would be effectively destroyed, not that anyone looked; far as I know, they didn't.'

'It *was* a suicide.'

'No, it wasn't. No. No. No. Come on now...'

O'Connor was silent.

'But they thought it was locked,' Voyle said. 'Anyone would have assumed it was locked. It was hot in there, stifling hot, for a reason.'

O'Connor gave a wincing *you're talking rubbish* look. Still, he remained silent.

'Of course, maybe, in the heat of the moment, excuse the pun, no one noticed the heat, but I doubt it. Still, even if they had, the conservatory would have cooled down again within minutes. And by then you'd have turned the heater off, wouldn't you? Conservatories are designed that way; they warm up and cool down quickly. I checked. And a funny thing about conservatories, it doesn't take much to heat them. Even on a winter's day, you ever notice how warm they can be without a heater on, just a bit of winter sun through those big glass panels, that's all. People don't generally heat conservatories, they're terrible at retaining heat, so why would they? Generally speaking, that is. But I know what happens if you do heat a conservatory. The metal contracts, I mean, like really contracts. The glass doesn't break either, you'd think it would, but it doesn't because the sides of the frame are far enough apart and the outer surfaces are in the open air. Now the door, that's different, that joins to the interior of the house, and it's of thicker metal, all aluminium, which is important, as is the doorjamb, thicker too, and what happens is it wedges together, almost fuses, depending on just how hot it is. If it's especially hot, like it was on that night, I bet, then that door would be absolutely immovable, wedged tighter shut than if it were double padlocked and triple bolted, like the door to a nuclear bunker... and you'd have known that, wouldn't you?'

O'Connor didn't answer.

'Oh yes, you'd have known that, O'Connor, wouldn't you? To get in that door, no way could they do it without a big red key. But even then, I'd say it took them a while. So yes, of course, they were going to assume that damn door was locked. It had to be. There could be no other explanation. You're a clever man alright, aren't you? The lord of the manor knew all this; he had it all worked out. As Sherlock Holmes would say, "When you have eliminated all which is impossible, then whatever remains, however improbable, must be the truth". And that, my dear fellow, is how Robert Gilsenan died. What did you do? Put powdered sleeping pills in his drink and have him pass out, then crack some more in there, hold his mouth open and pour in the alcohol... something like that, pinched his nose, was it? So his mouth would open like a moat. Robert Gilsenan never woke up again. I personally don't think you used single malt whiskey. Why would you? You'd have kept that for yourself. Some own-brand shit, was it? Yes, I'm right, aren't I?'

O'Connor looked remarkably relaxed about it all. Voyle guessed his brain neurons were all singing from the same hymn sheet now. Which was not what he wanted. He wanted him subdued and confused. That way he might say things he didn't mean to.

'Hah,' O'Connor spat, 'Sherlock Holmes, is it? I bet you think you're Sherlock Holmes. And what? A structural engineer too?'

'That *is* what happened,' Voyle said, a statement, not a question.

The butler, caretaker – whatever – made a slight movement, like he was about to lean forward again, but stopped.

Say something, you bastard, Voyle thought, *say it.*

But O'Connor fell silent again.

Shit.

'Why did you do it?' Voyle asked. 'For Andrea? Is this all because of her? From what I hear, big guy, she doesn't love you.'

Bingo.

Voyle saw O'Connor's expression change like he'd just pressed on an open wound. Voyle kept pressing...

Ouch.

He saw the tears start to well in O'Connor's eyes. It never failed to impress him how some of the cruellest and most depraved bastards he'd ever come across often turned out to be the most hopeless romantics, turning into blubbering mushy heaps in the blink of an eye. And he thought it odd that O'Connor had never come to police attention before. How was that possible? A devious bastard alright.

O'Connor sniffled and ran the sleeve of his jacket across his eyes. 'She's something else, she really is. She's beautiful. She's alluring. She's young.' He blinked back the tears, gave a crooked smile. 'And she makes *me* feel young, you know what I mean?'

There was a trace of smugness there now, the tone one of arrogant pride, his fleeting phase of hopeless romantic having passed. Now it was *hey, look at me.*

Voyle did just that and decided on something. This man was pure evil.

WHEN THE DOOR locked behind her, the giant moved across the room and stood next to Monica Hughes. He was naked except for a pair of blue boxers. They made an odd couple, the two of them, she small and petite, less than half his size, standing there in her red satin dressing gown. Considine guessed he was at least six feet five tall. And unlike a lot of tall men, not lanky either. Instead he was wide shouldered and barrel chested, with thick arms and firm legs. But it was his head that really grabbed her attention. A very large head, even taking into account his overall size, a head without any natural symmetry to it, oddly shaped, with outsized ears, long square chin, black frizzy hair like tangled wire. Stand this man in a field of crops, and he would be the perfect scarecrow. And a mean one too, close-set eyes that were deep and dark. He lurked behind Monica Hughes, saying nothing.

Beauty and the beast was Considine's first thought, and her second... well, she didn't have a second. He remained like that for a moment, not speaking, before he slowly put the phone to his ear, not speaking, then removed it and turned to Monica Hughes. He gave her an odd look, like a big shaggy dog looking to its master because it doesn't know what to do.

'They hung up,' he said, his voice high pitched and strangely childlike.

Monica Hughes darted over to Considine and grabbed hold of her arm just as Considine had discreetly been reaching in for her state phone to try to call this in without being noticed.

'What?' Considine said. 'What are you doing?'

Monica Hughes opened her mouth. For a moment

nothing happened; she just stood there with her gob open catching flies; then she shrieked: 'Help me. For God's sake. Help me. He's going to kill me. I'm being kept prisoner.'

'Yes, I suppose I do,' Voyle said, 'I understand. She makes you feel young.'

O'Connor nodded. 'Here,' he said, 'any chance of a cup of tea before we go? I'm parched.'

'Tea?'

'If you unclip these for a couple of minutes, I'll make it myself, for both of us, put a little something in it too. What do you say?'

Voyle laughed. O'Connor must really think him stupid. *Good.*

'I'm taking you in. I don't think so.'

The butler, caretaker – whatever – shrugged.

'Worth a try. Here, take my wallet from my pocket, then.' He half turned. 'This one here, go on. Don't worry, what am I to do when you've me trussed up like a chicken?'

'What's in that wallet?'

'Go on. You'll see. Take it out.'

Voyle got up and walked slowly over, warily put his hand in O'Connor's back pocket, felt the soft leather outline of a wallet there and took it out. He stepped back.

'Open it,' O'Connor said. 'Go on. It doesn't bite.'

Voyle did, and in one of the clear plastic pouches was a photograph of a young woman smiling out at him. She appeared striking with even features and black raven hair, wearing a tight latex T-shirt and skintight jeans, every curve of her hourglass figure accentuated. He brought the wallet closer to his face, peering at what she wore around her neck...

'Is that a...?'

'Yes, that's an emerald'
'Looks expensive.'
'It is.'
'You bought it for her?'
'I *got* it for her.'
'What's that mean?' Voyle felt he knew very well what that meant.
'It's not important,' O'Connor said.
Oh, but it is, old sport, it is.
'Come on, what difference does it make now?' Voyle nudged.
'Exactly,' O'Connor said, 'so why're you asking?'
'Fine, I won't.'
Shit.

A restless silence settled between them. Voyle needed to call this in, but he knew that when he did, it would be over; he wouldn't get a chance alone with O'Connor again. Not like this he wouldn't.

He thought of something.

'Just so you know, I have no problem with rich bastards losing their shit either.' His words were like the lyrics of a bad rap song, he thought. 'How do they get their shit anyway? Did you know that the top one per cent of the world's population own ninety per cent of the world's wealth? That's not fair.'

Voyle had expended his arsenal of knowledge on global social injustice and exclusion in that one statement. There wasn't much more he could say to follow on from that.

'What?' O'Connor said. 'You Che Guevara now?'
'Just saying.'

They became silent again, but Voyle sensed a change.

'If you know it, you know it,' O'Connor muttered, and louder. 'Clever, eh?'

Voyle realised O'Connor was seeking affirmation, recognition, praise even, at the very least a little credit for his great work, his ingenuity, everything he'd been having to keep secret.

Well, that's about to change, sunshine.

'I knew you were a clever bastard the minute I set eyes on you. I just didn't realise how clever.'

'Ha.' O'Connor guffawed. 'The butler did it. You'd never guess.'

I know.

'Did he really do it though, the butler I mean?' A touch of incredulity in Voyle's tone, bait to a fisherman's hook.

'Well, you worked it out so far, didn't you? So you must be clever yourself... somewhere. We could make a great team, if you're interested.'

'What's that mean?'

'Ah, don't act stupid *stupid*. You're acting stupid, aren't you? I'm beginning to think you've been acting stupid all along. You can't be stupid, 'cause you worked it out.'

'Well...'

'I did it. Okay? Of course I fucking did it. My wife, it was a release, for her, for both of us. Jesus, she was hard to put up with, she was. And Gilsenan, the rich prick. Yes, yes, I did it. I doped him up and turned on the heat. It was hotter in there than the Gobi desert... really, it was. I checked, fifty-four degrees, baby; it was a wonder he didn't combust, ha ha. "Get me my single malt, Patrick," he used to say in that plummy voice of his. The bottle would be sitting right beside him. But would he lift it up and pour it himself? Would he fuck. I had to come all the way down and do it for him. He liked that. I knew he did. I was his poodle. Sometimes I used to spit in his food. I really did, mix it up real good so he wouldn't notice... here, you really believe in all that Che Guevara stuff?'

'Everyone believes in it; doesn't mean we want to change anything though, does it? Not when people think they might be able to get a few crumbs for themselves. That hope is just enough to keep everyone on the treadmill.'

Yes, a very bad rap song.

'Well, I took a slice for myself, didn't I? And for a brief time I was, I *am*, lord of the manor. Andrea believes it. That's enough for me. That's all I want. That's everything I want. You know what it feels like to have someone like her look at you the way she looks at me? It's almost orgasmic, that's what it is. She's... she's in awe. Of me. That's a feeling better than any drug, I can tell you, and I can't get enough. No, I can't. And lemme tell ya, in the bedroom, wow, I have no words to describe, she whispers in my ear, *Go on, you rich bastard, I like it, rich bastard, no one does it better than a rich bastard, harder, you rich bastard.* No, I don't know what that's about either. But I do know she wouldn't piss up against me if she knew who I really was. No, I'm not stupid either.'

'No,' Voyle said, and thought, *But still, you're stupid enough*, taking his phone from his pocket, switching the record function off, not mentioning that every word he'd just said had been recorded. The oldest trick in the book, and one that kept on giving. A trick the boss had used on his last case, which had made Voyle think of it.

Instead, Voyle said: 'I've got to make a phone call.'

MONICA HUGHES PULLED on Considine's arm like it was all that was keeping her from plunging down a sheer ravine. She couldn't make sense of any of this. In fact, she was completely baffled. There was simply no sense to it at all. She stood, buffeted by Monica Hughes pulling on her, yet, despite this, she thought the woman didn't look like anyone who was being kept against their will to her. She cursed to herself that it was she who was here and not O'Brien. O'Brien was the actress. Monica Hughes grabbed her other arm now and began pulling on both of them, shrieking: 'Save me. Please save me. You've got to save me.'

'Save you from what, Mrs Hughes? Tell me. And you're being kept prisoner here by whom?'

The wife of the Minister for Foreign Affairs pointed a long, perfectly manicured finger at her presumed lover.

'Him! He's keeping me prisoner.'

Considine grabbed Monica Hughes's hands and yanked them off her.

'What the hell is going on here?' She remembered the door was locked, and took a step backwards, bumped into something, a table it felt like, with a potted plant on it, a cactus or similar; she could feel it prickle against her arse.

'Mawnica...' The man said in that childish drawl, the pronunciation weird, like he was uttering the name of the little city state in the south of France, Monaco, not the name of the woman standing before him. More than anything, Considine detected in that voice a sense of confused hurt.

The man stepped towards Monica, who crossed again to Considine and pressed herself against her, looking at the man as he started to advance. Monica Hughes smelt of sweat and sex.

'Pleeeease,' she beseeched, 'pleeease...'

'Mawnica...' the man repeated as he took another step until he was right in front, towering above them.

Considine looked up. It really did seem like she was looking at a giant, his head almost touching the ceiling.

'You two,' Considine said, her voice rising, summoning all her authority, 'I don't know what's going on here, but something is.' She pointed at the giant. 'And you? Why'd you lock that door? It's an offence to stop me from leaving.' She threw back her shoulders in a display of false bravado.

The giant ignored her.

'Why, Mawnica?' he said instead. 'Why?'

Then, with a speed belying his great size, he grabbed Monica's wrists and pulled her towards him like a rag doll. His hands were sides of ham with yams stuck on for fingers; they could easily snap Monica Hughes's arms clean from her shoulders if he wanted to.

'Leave me alone,' Monica Hughes shouted, 'leave me alone,' pulling furiously against him, something as useless as a toddler attempting to break free from the grip of a determined parent.

'Why, Mawnica, why?'

The giant's lips, like two seals lounging above the escarpment that was his chin, pressed together, and he moved the entire country that was his head, trying to press those two seals against Monica's sweet, pink lips.

She gave another of her piercing, glass-shattering horror-movie-soundtrack shrieks that seemed to hit the giant like a baseball bat full in the chest. He froze, his face, all its rivers and ravines, its gorges, its cliffs and valleys folding in on each other, a Richter scale ten earthquake, collapsing everything. He began to quiver at first, then shake, then convulse, his great bulk slowly toppling forward, threatening to bury her beneath him.

Monica Hughes's hands clawed at the air, so small in comparison to the hams and yams that they looked like a bird's, but ones she brought up and dug into his cheeks, drawing them down, four thin lines of blood erupting as the pretty little bird dug her talons in – deep.

Considine moved sideways towards the door.

'Help me,' Monica Hughes screamed when she saw her edging away. 'He wants to kill me. You must stop him. You must help me.'

The giant's ham hands with their yam fingers began to awkwardly caress Monica Hughes's face, and down to her shoulders, along her arms, oblivious to the four rivulets of blood moving down his cheeks, oblivious to the hands that had now begun pulling at his fuzzy hair... The giant made deep, rumbling sounds, and Considine realised he was sobbing. He remained like that, clutching Monica Hughes to him, frozen into a twisted, bent pose.

Considine didn't stop; she was almost at the door now. Monica Hughes was no longer looking at her; she'd stopped moving too, her head bent against the giant; they both appeared to be lost in their own world, a modern version of Esmeralda and Quasimodo. All that was missing was the ringing out of the bells of Notre Dame Cathedral.

Considine turned and reached for the lock lever on the door, was just about to turn it when she felt a heavy weight settle onto one shoulder. The weight pressed down, at the same time squeezing like a vice grip as she folded beneath it.

Then she was kneeling on the floor. The giant released his grip and backhanded her across the face, spinning her round and down onto her back. She lay still, the stinging pain in her cheek like scalding water had been poured over it. She felt the ham hands foraging over her body, finding what they wanted in the pocket of her windbreaker. She saw the state phone plop to the floor next to her face, and an enormous shoe like a rowing boat without its oars crash down onto it, squashing it to pieces.

She thought, *Now I'm really in the shite.*

49

Two things happened almost simultaneously. The first was a phone call. It was from Voyle. Brody listened to what Steve had to say, and could scarcely believe what he was hearing. He'd actually written off the whole Gilsenan caper as just that, a caper. He didn't know if it was or it wasn't a suicide, no one did, and he felt sure no one ever would. The coroner would sign his signature to the form that said it was, and that was what it would officially become for evermore. A suicide. Robert Gilsenan, he who was filthy rich, who had waited a year for the delivery of his Italian sports car – which he had never even gotten to drive – had killed himself. Except that he hadn't. And as he listened to Voyle, Brody regretted his believing that too. Voyle said he could prove it. The news was like a sucker punch. Brody felt he'd been flung across the room. He hadn't seen this coming.

And Voyle wasn't finished.

'There's a body, what's left of it anyway, at the bottom of a raised bed at the front of the house.'

This second punch threw Brody across the room again.

'It's his wife. I just know it,' Voyle said.

Brody sat there with the phone pressed to his ear and shook his head in disbelief. 'His wife?'

Voyle gave him a synopsis of everything so far. Brody was quiet for a moment, then: 'Okay, I'll get onto Wicklow, have someone get out there ASAP.'

'That's already looked after, boss. I rang ahead. They're expecting us.'

Brody was silent. 'What you mean,' he said, '"expecting us"?'

'I'm bringing him in myself.'

'I thought that's what you meant. You can't bring that prisoner in yourself. It's bad enough you're down there on your own. Steve, you hear me on this now? Do not bring him in. Not on your own. You wait.'

'I'd have him in Wicklow in less than an hour. Instead of waiting here.'

'You think he wouldn't try something on the way, just the two of you sitting in the car? Come on, Steve.'

Voyle said nothing.

'You're right, boss. I hear you.'

'You just wait. And make sure he's in a secure room.'

'Come on, boss, I know the drill. I'm with him at all times.'

'And when you get to Wicklow, you let me know.'

'Yes, mammy... only joking, come on, boss. It's fine. I'll wait.'

'And Steve?'

'Yes?'

'Good work.'

'Thanks, boss.'

Brody put the phone down. Damn Ryan, putting Voyle in a situation like that. Then again, without Ryan, no one would ever have known. The result of unintended consequences, as they said. A head came round the door. Brody didn't recognise the head; there were so many heads around this place lately.

'Superintendent Ryan,' the head said, 'says to tell you O'Brien rang...'

'Yes.'

'She hasn't heard from Considine. She was supposed to...'

'The hotel?'

The head nodded.

'O'Brien thinks she's in trouble.'

Brody was already halfway across the room, Marty Sheahan following right behind.

CONSIDINE HAD her head slightly raised from the floor, watching Monica Hughes, who was sitting huddled by the open French window in the centre of the room, the lace curtains billowing gently in the breeze, the giant next to her, sitting on the floor, his back against the wall. From here he had a direct view across to her, but his attention wasn't on Considine. Even sitting down, he was enormous, she thought, with Monica Hughes, the little bird, next to him. The blood on both his cheeks had congealed to leave four smudged billowing outlines like boat sails. He held one massive hand lightly on Monica Hughes's shoulder, the thumb stroking her neck beneath her ear.

Considine shifted her gaze to see that Monica Hughes was looking at her as she suddenly jumped to her feet, brushing the giant's hand away. Her dressing gown fell open, and she secured the robe tightly again, stepped over to the French windows and pulled one open. A narrow balcony was outside, and she went onto it. She leaned over the wrought-iron railing and looked down, pressing herself against it, leaning across it farther still. It looked like she was about to topple over.

The giant scrambled awkwardly to his feet, too, and stood still, like he didn't want to spook her, watching on.

'I'm going to escape from you if it means killing myself,' she said, raising one long, very shapely leg over the railing and straddling it. 'My life is nothing. You've taken me. You've taken my husband from me. You've destroyed me. I don't want to live anymore if this is how it is.'

The dressing gown fell open.

The giant moved with that surprising speed of his and grabbed her by the upper arm.

'Mawnica. No, please. I love you. You told me you loved me too. Mawnica, you said you loved me more than anything in the world. What's happened, Mawnica? What?'

'I never told you that, you crazy bastard. Take your hands off me.'

'The baby, Mawnica. It could have been, it could have been...'

'SHUT UP! I said.'

The door burst open, and they tumbled into the room, six armed SDU officers shouting at the top of their voices, a cacophony of conflicting commands that would confuse anyone... 'Don't move'... 'Take your hands off her'... 'Get down on the ground'... 'Freeze'.

Standing behind them, in the doorway, was Brody, Sheahan and O'Brien.

And then everything fell silent. The six SDU officers formed a half circle in front of the window, weapons trained on the balcony.

Considine was on her feet now, and she went and stood next to Brody, Sheahan and O'Brien, all mere spectators.

The giant took his hand away, and Monica Hughes

lurched to the side. It seemed she could no longer defy the laws of natural physics. This time she was gone.

Except that she wasn't.

The giant's arm sprang out again just in time, and his big hand gripped her, yanking her backward, the momentum threatening to swing her onto the balcony and to safety, but her hand snapped onto the railing, stopping her like a clamp. The giant reached forward, and this stirred up the posse of mules, who all began shouting again. Brody cursed; that would achieve nothing but to spook her even more. '*Stay where you are*'...'*Don't move*'... '*Step back*'... '*Put your hands in the air*'...

BRODY BEGAN to make sense of what was happening. He saw the look in Monica Hughes's eyes, eyes that never left the giant's, the intensity of her stare, eyes that never blinked, not once, a snake charmer, but of people, not snakes, or of one person in particular, this person whom she seemed to have complete control over, who would do her bidding, whatever she asked. She knew exactly what she was doing, how far she could push this. But the giant didn't.

Brody thought the star of this show was Monica Hughes. He could swear he saw a trace of a smile cross her face as she opened her mouth and...

Screamed.

The mules became apoplectic: '*Move away... I said move fucking away... Go back, go back*'... A sharp clicking sound cut through the air, and silence again. Someone had cocked their weapon. Things could go very wrong, very quickly now. Monica screamed again and began writhing as if in a frenzy, but not to fall off the balcony, Brody could see, as he saw her instead slide onto it. The giant released his grip, standing before her, blocking her way to the French window. She ran to the nearest end of the balcony and pressed herself against the wall. The giant stepped towards her, looking dazed, hurt, *wounded*. He called out her name in that high-pitched voice of his that was both beautiful and frightening at the same time... *Mawnica*.

She screamed again... 'Help me. Stop him. For God's sake. HELP ME!'

The giant took another step, almost upon her now, raising both his arms, about to touch her. And then all hell broke loose.

The sound of six handguns all discharging their rounds at the same time was like one coordinated explosion of sound, enough to shatter panes of glass in the French windows, shake the partition walls, and send a miniature shock wave through the room. It came again. And again. On the third and final time, the air was thick with nitro and graphite, and the giant, tossed about as if by an invisible puppeteer, ended up sprawled on the floor, his legs protruding onto the balcony, upper body lying on the hotel room floor. Steam rose from his chest, torn open to reveal what looked like a blood-soaked bucket of offal, and from the half of his head that was still intact, one eye dangled at the end of a long sinew of muscle. The giant was a mess.

Brody shook his head, trying to restore sound, but this had no effect on the ringing in his head. He looked back to the giant, saw one intact eye staring at him, frozen, on it a look of utter confusion. Then it blinked. Somehow, the man, this indestructible creature, was still alive!

50

There comes a point when you just have to give up. When you have no other choice but to. When it's the easier option, when it's just too damn hard to continue to hang on. Donagh Hughes was dipping in and out of consciousness; when he came round, he was confused and quickly retreated back to oblivion again, where he found himself strangely at peace. It was at these times, those brief conscious times, when he thought of her, his wife, Monica. That time they went to Bundoran, when the kids were young, it was a blistering hot July day, and they'd all sat on a park bench near the seafront and ate fish and chips out of brown paper bags. Such happy times. Such wonderful times. And yet she had never been enough; that had never been enough. He'd always wanted others, wanted more. He thought of his wife with a sense of overwhelming love and affection, realised he had not thought of her in this way in years, if ever. He wanted to make things right again. He desperately, more than anything else, wanted to make things right again. And then he'd slip back into unconsciousness, and each time when he came round, he was weaker than he was before... And yet, he thought of her, of Monica, with a powerful, irrepressible sense that he wanted to make things right. But he *couldn't, because at the same time he knew it was too late, he had broken her heart, and now he was to die, in this filthy, squalid place, and he would never be able to make things right with her again.*

This was the end. Just let me die, Lord, don't let me suffer any longer.

His eyes were growing heavy again, they were so very heavy, the thin string of yellow light around the door fading, becoming smaller and smaller, almost gone now...

51

A couple of hours or so after he'd first rung Wicklow Garda station, Voyle rang back.

'Detective garda who?' the voice on the other end of the line said.

'Steve Voyle.'

'Oh, yes, I remember someone mentioned you rang. Sergeant Andy Maloney here. Listen, Voyle, I haven't had time to deal with this. You're going to have to hang on a little while longer. I'll get somebody out to you just as soon as I can.'

'I've already been hanging on for way too long.'

There was the sound of a slow, rattly intake of breath. Voyle guessed the man was either a smoker or had recently given up. He went with the former.

'Listen, Voyle, I'm dealing with a gathering of the clans here. In honour of Big Jimmy, the bare-knuckle king or some such *ráiméis*. As a mark of respect, they're literally pummelling each other on the streets down here. I'm just about holding the line. You're going to have to wait.'

'And you know what I'm dealing with, don't you?'

Sitting on the high-backed wooden chair in the very centre of the big old kitchen where Voyle could keep a good eye on him, Patrick O'Connor cocked his head.

'A double murderer, that's what. Kinda trumps what you've got on your hands, wouldn't you say.'

'Oh, by the way, on that...'

In the background, Voyle could hear doors banging and a drunken voice shouting some – to use the Irish term for nonsense as the sergeant had just done – *ráiméis* or other.

'Yes?'

'You say he killed his wife. Robert Gilsenan too. That that wasn't a suicide at all. That he killed him too. Have I got all that right?'

'You've got that all right.'

'And you were sent down from Dublin, the Major Crimes Investigation Unit no less... that right too?'

'That's right.'

'All on your ownsome.'

'Well, I'm all on my ownsome now, yes.' Voyle didn't want to get into the details.

'That's quite a story, fella.'

Fella. The term Voyle himself used for anyone he came across on the job whom he wasn't sure of.

'Listen,' Voyle said, 'you think I'm making all this up, don't you? Didn't anyone call my boss, Detective Sergeant Jack Brody. I gave you his number.'

'I told you what it's like down here.'

'So no one did, did they?'

Maloney didn't answer. And Voyle knew he was right.

'Ring my boss, Maloney. And get a car over here. Now!'

Voyle hung up and walked to the end of the long kitchen table and sat down.

'What you grinning at?'

O'Connor seemed to be looking past Voyle, and his expression was like the cat that had gotten the milk.

Voyle became aware of a sweaty, minty, stale yet sweet alcohol aroma. He turned slowly. Kate was standing there in the doorway, in her hands the shotgun Voyle had left propped against the wall by it. Voyle's first thought: *I should have secured the room, just like the boss told me to.* Then relief. Because the shotgun was pointing at O'Connor.

'Kate.' He stood up and took a step towards her. 'What're you doing here? And give me that, please.'

She shifted the weapon. It seemed she was about to hand it over to him. But he was wrong. She was merely repositioning it until the barrel was pointing at... *him*. And it stayed that way.

'S-stop,' her voice slurred, her eyes swimming about in her head. Kate was pie-eyed, but her grip was remarkably steady. 'Or you'll g-get this, though not the way y-you, hic, want to.' She gave a soft, drunken chuckle, like this was all great craic, great craic altogether. And to her, maybe it was.

But not to Voyle. Who didn't move. Because one thing he was certain of: someone as drunk as she was was about as predictable as a bad-tempered bull on a hot day.

52

The unadorned bulb was made of clear glass, the filaments inside visible like the antennae of an insect, the tips glowing yellow. Brody had seen something similar on sale at Brown Thomas, the Dublin department store equivalent to London's Harrods or New York's Saks Fifth Avenue. It was part of a collection called the avant-garde premium and cost €100 a pop. The KGB – oops, SDU – mules had objected to himself and Considine bringing Monica Hughes here to the hotel manager's office. They said they needed to run it by their commissar first. Brody said he'd prefer to run it by the commissioner, and what was the problem, he only wanted a quick word? No problem, they said when they heard that. Anyway, they had enough problems. They would soon have to explain why they'd pumped so much lead into the giant to the team from GSOC, the Garda ombudsman commission's office, when they got here. What was left of the giant's body had been strapped onto a gurney and taken to hospital by ambulance. He'd died on the way. No one was surprised. Not even an ox could survive those wounds. What was surprising was that he had lasted for as long as he had.

Brody now didn't know how much time he had before Harper came barging in here, probably with Ryan towing right behind. So he needed to be quick. If he did this the right way, if he hit the chestnut at just the right angle, he might crack it open. He also needed to be careful – very careful, like manning the tiller on a sailing boat traversing a dangerous lagoon, a light hand was required, a little nudge here, a little nudge there, but never too much of anything.

Monica Hughes didn't know the giant was dead. And that was how he wanted it. The answer to that question would be important for her, so Brody was not surprised when the first thing she said to him was, 'Is he dead?'

Brody nudged the tiller just a fraction, avoiding the jagged rock that had appeared dead ahead in the water.

'He was alive when he left,' he said. 'Yes, he was alive.' Which was perfectly true and could withstand scrutiny. It would be difficult to prove that Brody, at this moment in time, knew for sure the giant was dead. He'd heard it over the radio, after all. Who could prove that?

'Alive,' she said, alarmed, but something else was there too... a tenderness, and that same regret he'd heard earlier. Which didn't surprise Brody, not one bit; it fitted in perfectly with his thesis.

But then, her eyes narrowed into those of a fox, cunning and suspicious. Those eyes took in Considine.

'You. You're a guard too?'

'Of course.'

'Am I under arrest?' She swung an arm around the room. 'And why have you brought me here?'

'To talk, that's all,' Considine said, 'before the others get here.'

'The others?'

'The brass,' Brody said with great solemnity, 'the heavy hitters, it gives us a chance to have a quiet chat, to get things into perspective.'

'Perspective?'

'He was alive, Monica,' Brody said, putting things back on track, glancing to Considine.

'It all makes sense, you know,' Considine said.

'It does?' Monica Hughes asked.

'It would be best,' Brody said, 'if you told us. So I'm going to ask. Do you know where your husband is?'

Monica Hughes blinked, and the colour seemed to drain from her cheeks.

With that comment, Brody had picked up his cards from the table and raised the stakes, pretending to hold a hand that he didn't hold. Had he played it right? Or would she call his bluff?

'We know...' Brody added, but let that hang, knowing he knew very little at all.

'No, you don't,' she snapped.

Shite, Brody thought. She was seeing him *and* raising the stakes.

Monica Hughes slung an arm over her face, covering her eyes. Brody could see bruising on her wrist where the giant had grabbed her. She held her arm like that for some seconds. For Brody's benefit, he felt certain.

'That man kidnapped me. You know that, don't you? I told you.'

'Yes, you told us.'

'And he tried to kill me. You saw it yourself. He was going to kill me right out there on that balcony. But you don't believe me?'

'We didn't say that.'

'It's in your voice. You sound like you don't.'

They fell silent for a while; then Monica said, 'So he's

alive, is he? Well, if he tells you any different, don't believe him. You can't believe him.'

She took a deep breath and closed her eyes, exhaling. Brody took it as a sign of desperation, but also as a desire for release. A time for him to push.

'Stop trying to fool both yourself and us.' He stiffened his voice into a heavy, business edge. 'I saw the way you looked at him when you were out there on the balcony that time, and the way he looked at you... It was a game of some sort to you, wasn't it?'

Now, he laid down his best worst card. 'He told us, Monica. He told us everything.'

A comment that could be construed in many ways, a ball of mercury that would be impossible to pin down, to know exactly what Brody meant. Especially as the person purported to have said it was now dead. Whatever it took, Brody thought, whatever it took. He had nothing to lose. He held his other cards close to his chest, like he had something, but knowing they were nothing but duds.

And then Monica Hughes did something he had not expected. She burst out crying. But he wasn't going to fall for that one.

'Where's your husband?' he demanded. 'Tell me. Before it's too late. Where is he?'

And then, just like that, she did.

53

The words tumbled out of Monica Hughes; she hardly stopped long enough to draw breath. All from that one question, *Where's your husband?* When she'd answered that question, Brody's voice had lilted in surprise, *But that's where he went missing from*, and she nodded, said, *I know.*

Brody stepped out of the room and called that information in, went back in and resumed his seat, hoping Monica hadn't become tongue-tied. She hadn't.

Brody: I've sent a unit round to check.

Monica: He's there.

Brody: But we already looked. We didn't find him.

Monica: You didn't look too closely, did you? He's not in the actual house. A shed, at the back, towards the sea, corrugated iron, ten-minute walk. That's where he is.

Brody: We'll see... That man, in your hotel room. Who is he?

Monica: Sean Dowding. We go back a long way. Went to school together. They called him the elephant man, some of the local kids, I mean. That's cruel, don't you think?

Brody: Yes, Monica, I do think that is cruel.

Monica: And no. He didn't kidnap me. I can't hide anymore. I don't care. The poor bastard loved me. He really did. I didn't love him. I used him. Look, I'm sorry about it all, I really am. You know something...?

Brody: What? Tell me.

Monica: He may be dead, my husband, and I don't care. Good riddance. He deserves it. Will I tell you what he put me through? He put me through hell, that's what. Running around for years with other women. I put up with it, more fool me, yes, yes, I know. You know too, he got a woman pregnant. There may have been others. I don't know. I wouldn't be surprised. She's the only one I know about. You know how I know about it? Because she rang me, that's how. A couple of months ago. She sounded so young, so I asked her her age. Twenty-six, she said. The child was eight, which meant he'd gotten her pregnant when she was just eighteen. Dirty old bastard. Like, really, *ugh*. And you know why she rang me? She wanted to know about bone marrow. The kid has a health issue, she needed a donor, a match, and she thought... When I put that phone down, I said to myself, *I'm going to get you, you bastard.* And I did. I hope he's dead. Fuck him. I mean it.

Brody: And did you help her? With the bone marrow.

Monica: What? Oh, no, I told her to ring him and then hung up.

Brody: Marie Kennedy, Monica.

Monica: What about her?

Brody: Exactly. She was...

Monica: I know, I know. She was decapitated. He shouldn't have done that. I didn't think he would. I didn't tell him to do that. I just told him, you know, give her a fright, that's all, not to chop her fucking head off. Still, when you think about it...

Brody: Yes, Monica, when you think about it.

Monica: Well, for him to do that. Well, I mean, that took a lot of... *passion,* didn't it? He must really have loved me.

Brody: You could call it that. But it didn't work out for her, did it? Dying the way she did.

Monica: It should never have happened, like I say. Sorry.

Brody: Sorry.

Monica: Yes. Sorry. Sorry. Sorry. What else can I say? What?

Brody: Well, *I* have to say, Monica, you don't sound too bothered.

Monica: Don't I?

Brody: No, you don't.

Monica: Well then.

Brody: I'm curious.

Monica: Of?

Brody: The, what would you call it? The cottage, let's call it that, where Marie Kennedy and your husband...

Monica: Don't call him that. Call him anything you want. Whatever. Just don't call him that. *My.* He's not *my* anything.

Brody: Okay. *Him,* we'll call him *him,* how's that?

Monica: Fine.

Brody: We spoke with the owners of that cottage, a property company in Dublin. They never rented it out to anybody. It's not fit to be rented out. They couldn't have rented it out. There's no electricity. No running water. It's a hovel, Monica. How did you manage that?

Monica: Oh, no problem. I gave him a cock and bull story. Said it looked like a lovely place for us to go and stay sometime. I showed him pictures of somewhere else. He didn't question it. I knew what he was after, what he was thinking, that it was a lovely place for *them* to go and stay. I'd seen the place when I was down in Tinnock last summer. That's when the idea came to me, and when I saw that it had a basement too, that you could just walk right in to the place... well, that's when I *really* got the idea. I've a second phone he doesn't know anything about. Oh, two can play at that game, so they can. I gave him that number, told him he could text only. That way, I could communicate with him and pretend I was the owner. I made it as easy as dropping his zipper. He even gave me his credit card number without my asking. As if I could do anything with it. I told him it wouldn't be ready until after ten at night, to make sure it was dark when they arrived. I sent Sean down just to do the bare minimum to fix up the place. Jesus, he fell for it. They both did. They didn't care. They just wanted a place to fuck.

Brody: Sean Dowding. Tell me about him.

Monica: He's a peach.

Brody: What's that mean?

Monica: You don't know? He's soft on the outside, hard as a nut on the inside. Just what I needed. He lives in Letterkenny. Alone. A bit sad. But I was, I was everything to him. I really was. He had nothing else in his life. Just me.

Brody: Did anyone put two and two together?

Monica: Are you serious? I never worried about that. I told you what the kids called him. No one thought I'd ever have anything to do with *him*. Not like that. Come on. They thought it was something to do with my charity work. I did a lot of charity work; it came with the territory of being married to *him*.

Brody: The baby. He, Sean Dowding, mentioned a baby. Remember? What was that all about?

Monica: I got pregnant. I don't know, fifteen years ago. I went to England for an abortion. Sean came with me. It broke his heart. He wanted me to keep it. He thought we could finally get together, become the family he'd always wanted. I mean, what a fairy tale. As if. I couldn't have that. I just couldn't. What about my two boys, my sons? I had to think of them. How would they take it? It was crazy. Not that I ever would anyway. But I thought, if I didn't, that would turn him against me. But you know what? It made him cling even closer. That's why...

Brody: That's why?

Monica: When I got that telephone call. Out of the blue. From that woman who'd had *his* baby, I, I...

Brody: Yes, You...?

Monica: Something snapped. I couldn't have *my* baby. Not that I wanted to, but still... Yet he had no qualms. So I wanted revenge. I really, really wanted revenge. I wanted him to suffer. I hope he's suffering. I hope he's dead.

54

He saw it, a strong light that filtered through his closed eyelids, stirring him awake. He opened his eyes slightly, a light that was dazzlingly bright flooding in. He realised a door had opened. But... something seemed different. Was it the same door? He didn't know. Or was it the door like his mother had mentioned, a door to the other side, when you pass from this world to the next. Was that what it was? Would she be waiting for him there, on the other side? Would she? Please, please, Mammy, I'm coming.

'Let me through,' he wanted to roar, 'let me through, let me through.'

But no words came from him. He was too weak. He could only watch through half-closed eyelids. Who were these people who were tumbling through now? His uncle Cyril? His mother? But not his father, please don't let it be my father, not him...

'Donagh Hughes...' a voice sounded from above. It sounded like his uncle Cyril. Yes, it did. It must be him, it really must. The sound of it gave him renewed strength, so that he was able to open his eyes fully, watching as they gathered round him. He counted at least four.

'Donagh Hughes...' But surely not his uncle, because his uncle Cyril would know who he was? He wouldn't have to ask.

And then he knew.

'Angels,' he whispered, 'you're angels?'

'Yes, Mr Hughes, in a way, guard-ian angels. We're the guards. Relax. Everything is going to be alright. We're going to take good care of you. Everything is going to be fine, Mr Hughes, sir.'

It was all too much for Hughes to take in.

He began to cry.

55

Kate was completely bombed, drinking shots of neat, own-brand vodka, but spilling most of it, barely able to hold her head up, while O'Connor sat blissfully ignoring her, looking at Voyle, plucking his lips, thinking. Kate pointed a finger, half at O'Connor, half at the floor... *I did t-this for y-you...* strings of spittle hanging from each side of her mouth like icicles... *you o-owe me f-for this, P-Paddy, y-yes, you d-d-do...*

Great craic altogether, Voyle thought.

The roles had been reversed; now Voyle was the one sitting in the chair in the centre of the room while O'Connor was keeping a good eye on *him*.

The butler, caretaker – whatever – scraped his chair on the flagstone floor as he stood, walked over to Voyle, and stepped behind him. Voyle heard his footsteps retreating to the other side of the kitchen. Kate, oblivious to the fact he was no longer there, continued her slurred, spittle-drenched conversation with a vacant chair.

Voyle turned his head all the way to the side, twisted his eyes right into the corners, could just about make out

O'Connor standing by the butcher's block, running a hand along the knives, cleavers, and bone saws hanging from the wall there in a neat row. He looked away again, his neck beginning to hurt.

His neck hurting was the least of his problems. At least his head was still attached to it.

Brody awoke with a start. He'd been dreaming. The office lay in a blue-tinged semi-darkness, the light from the car park outside filtering through the half-shuttered blinds in a reflection of chequered stripes along the wall. In his dream Ashling Nolan had been standing at a bus stop. He'd been pleading with her not to leave. But she did anyway.

The carnival had moved on to Harcourt Street, HQ of the SDU. He was surplus to requirements, it seemed. He'd played a pivotal role, and now the main lead, Harper, was taking centre stage again. The SDU was a travelling trope.

His office door was open, and the corridor outside was in darkness. He'd come back to the Phoenix Park to return the pool car and to collect his own. Forty winks, he'd told himself. The sound of his phone again pierced the silence. He realised it must have been that that had woken him up. He groped about and picked it up from his desk, peering at the time: 5:25 a.m. He'd been asleep for a little over an hour.

'Brody,' he said, his voice thick with sleep. His eyes stung; his back was sore.

'Sergeant Andy Maloney. Wicklow Garda station. Hello... you say your name's Coady, that right?'

'No, Brody.'

'Sorry, Brody. It's the end of the night shift. We've had a crazy one. You know what we've had...? Anyway, I don't think you do. Tell me, you have a fella down here by the name of Steve Voyle, detective garda?'

Voyle!

Shit. Brody hadn't heard from him. He shook his weary head, trying to shake out the tiredness. Voyle had not contacted him like he was supposed to.

'What's happened?' he asked, in the pit of his stomach feeling a gnawing sense of dread.

'Well, you tell me, he your boy or not?'

'Yes, he's my *boy*. Now, where is he? With you?'

'No, he's not with me. But he rang earlier. Wanting a unit to go collect him and bring a prisoner in.'

'And did you? That must have been hours ago now.'

'Jesus, no, we didn't. You any idea what it's been like down here? Every cell in the station is full. But I'll send someone in just over half an hour, okay? B watch can look after it, all fresh eyed and bushy tailed.'

'Maloney, listen, I want you to shut up and listen…'

'Whoa, whoa, Brody, let's keep this civilised. We're both sergeants. You're the same as me. No better, no worse. You don't get to tell me to shut up and listen, or how to listen, or anything else for that matter. I've–'

'Maloney!' Brody shouted. 'If you don't fucking shut your mouth and listen, the commissioner himself will take those three stripes from your arms and shove them up your arse. Have you got that?'

Maloney didn't say a word. He'd got that.

O'Connor selected a boning knife and held it lightly, approached Voyle and stood before him. He held the knife like a musician might hold a prized instrument, a sculpture might hold a favoured chisel, a painter the brush he preferred for his most delicate work. The knife was streamlined and a beautiful piece of craftsmanship. O'Connor was a professional, after all, and in a place such as Ash Hall, his tools could only be the best. Its blade was slightly curved, tapering to a fine point. As Voyle looked at it, despite his predicament, he thought of a cheetah, sleek, streamlined and beautiful. O'Connor held it up between both hands, balancing the tip of the blade and the end of the handle between the index finger of each hand.

'What am I going to do with you now, eh, Mr Policeman?' he said, his eyes looking over Voyle, sharp and sombre, yet clinical, *weighing* him up. 'I'd say you're eighty-four, eighty-eight kilos, something like that.'

Close. Voyle was eighty-seven.

'A buck deer is about seventy. I reckon you'd take about three and half hours to bone and boil... except I don't have the time. Get up.'

THEY RAN on lights and sirens. Three cars, one unmarked, two marked, Brody, Considine and Sheahan, both of whom he'd roused from their beds, travelling in the unmarked, two uniforms in each of the marked. He'd left O'Brien out of this.

Ordinarily, Dublin metropolitan officers rarely responded to emergencies outside of their area: they had more than enough to do on their own patch. But there was nothing ordinary about this job.

They sped along the M11 to Wicklow, the motorway practically deserted at this hour, and the sky a cold, clear, early morning blue, the fertile lands of Leinster stretching out all around them. The gnawing sensation in his stomach was still there – only worse. He had the feeling of being in a tunnel, a dark tunnel, one he didn't know where it led, or what he would find when he got there.

As it happened, the Wicklow mules were sitting in their car when they arrived, parked outside the gates of Ash Hall. They didn't even bother to get out of it. The driver merely wound down his window and rested his elbow there on the door.

'Howya,' he called out to no one in particular.

Brody ignored him. It was when the Pearse Street mules had taken their extendable ladders, now carried in the back of all mobile units, and were carrying these towards the entrance gates to Ash Hall that the Wicklow mules hopped out of their vehicle. They didn't look so friendly anymore.

'Wait a sec,' one said, holding out the palm of his hand like stopping traffic at an intersection. 'What's going on here? Who's in charge?'

'That'd be me.' It was Brody, and, to the two uniforms with the ladders, 'Don't stop, lads; get these things set up.'

Brody walked over to the Wicklow mules. The one who'd been driving had a heavy middle but was trim everywhere else; his eyes looked rested and jaded both at the same time. The other fella kept a hand in one of his pockets and looked like he'd do whatever he was told to do. He didn't care. Brody concentrated on the driver, was about to speak, but the fella got in first.

'How would you like it,' the fella said, 'if we went waltzing into your patch, telling you what to do? Huh? You wouldn't like it. Well, you wouldn't, would you?'

Brody turned, pointed to the ladder being hoisted against the front entrance gate.

'Fine then. After you. You lead the way. Fully involved. Sorted. We don't have time. Get a move on.'

'W-what? We weren't told anything about going over gates. You don't have a warrant. I don't think you do.'

Brody started walking towards the gate. 'Don't need a warrant,' he said over his shoulder, signalling for the fella to get a move on and go ahead of him if he wanted to, 'not in a double murder case.' The fella didn't move and didn't say another word. 'Fine,' Brody said when he'd reached the foot of the ladder, 'stay there and secure the area... Unless you have an objection to doing that too?'

Again, Brody got no reply. It looked like they didn't have any objection to that, no, not at all.

With the Wicklow mules outside, Brody, Considine and Sheahan, along with the Pearse Street mules, advanced along the driveway. Seven of them. A small army. Plenty.

Just before the main entrance door, they stopped. Brody looked about.

'Is that where Voyle said he found those remains?' Sheahan asked in a low voice, nodding in the direction of clumps of soil and stones piled on the ground off to their right, a shovel lying next to them.

'That's the way he described it.'

'Sscchh, listen.' It was Considine, and they all did.

'I can't hear anything,' one of the uniforms said.

'Exactly.' Considine looked at Brody. 'I don't like it, boss.'

'Neither do I,' Brody admitted, 'neither do I.'

Ash Hall was not so much a collection of bricks and mortar, a house, a mansion, or whatever you wanted to call it. No, it was much more than that. It was an enigma, an architectural Rubik's Cube, full of long corridors and more than one double door and secret passageway – a reflection of the era when it was built, an era when a landlord and his family might have had to flee in the dead of night when torch-carrying agitators arrived to burn the place down – and everyone in it.

The front door was locked, a stout, heavy, wooden affair.

Brody stood back, looking up and along the vast façade, like a living thing, impenetrable and brooding.

Then.

He detected something carried on the air, thinking of those torch-wielding agitators from the past, his nose crinkling. But this was not the past, this was now. Brody identified what was causing it.

Something was burning. But he couldn't see exactly what.

'Marty, take a couple of lads and go round the back.'

Marty did, and once he'd rounded the first gable, the smell became stronger – much stronger. Rounding the second, back gable, he saw a geyser of smoke billowing from a window on the ground floor, towards the centre. He ran down and stopped some distance back from it. Or what had been a window, it looked like it had been blown out, thick, black smoke curling up into the still, cold air.

'Don't,' a uniform said as Marty pressed a sleeve against his mouth and moved closer. He ignored the uniform, stepped closer, close enough to see through the smoke into a huge kitchen, a figure slumped against a table, a woman, looked like, her head resting on her hands as if she were sleeping, the flames licking around the floor at her feet.

Marty had on a blue sweater with white stripes. Marissa, his girlfriend, had knitted it for his birthday. He pulled this off and held it over his mouth, leaned into the dense smoke, jumped onto the high windowsill, and slid down the other side onto the kitchen floor. He didn't stop, not for a second, spotting two side-by-side large sinks in the wall. He went and turned on the taps in one, took a deep breath, removed the sweater and held it beneath the flow of water, saturating the material with it. Then he pressed the sweater over his face, peering through the thick stitches to see his way. He crossed to the table, coiled one arm under the right armpit of the woman slumped there, and hooked the hand around the back of her neck in a tight S-hook fireman's grip. He stepped backwards, catching her weight, her body sliding from the chair, continued, dragging her across the floor, a dead weight. But Marty, wide and strong, powered on like a locomotive until... his feet stumbled against something, and he almost fell over. The dead weight acted like a ballast, helping to keep him upright. He turned his head to the side and peered downward at what was there.

A body!

Despite the black, acrid smoke that even with the wet sweater pressed against his mouth made it almost impossible to breathe, he recognised immediately who it was.

Voyle!

For a split second, the time it takes to merely blink an eye, he was tempted to drop the body he was holding. Forget about her, whoever it was, and instead concentrate on rescuing his pal and partner.

But Marty didn't. Marty couldn't; he never would do that. And Voyle wouldn't want him to either. Instead, he gingerly sidestepped around Voyle and resumed moving towards the window. When he reached it, he shouted out at the uniforms. He could just about see them standing there like spectators in the stands at a football match during intermission. He knew they couldn't see he was holding someone: they could just about see him. 'Hey,' he shouted, 'both of you! Over here. Now!'

Marty hoisted the woman up onto the windowsill by the shoulders, where they grabbed her.

'Is she dead?' one of them shouted. They dragged her off the windowsill and laid her on the ground. 'No, she's not,' the one who'd enquired shouted, holding two fingers to her wrist. He pinched her nose shut and bent down, unceremoniously plonked his lips onto hers.

But Marty was already turning away from the windowsill.

'There's someone else in here,' he said, disappearing back into the smoke-filled kitchen, flames dancing like orange and red waves ahead of him. It was suffocatingly hot, but the flames offered him just enough light to see his way. But he found himself gagging on each breath, could feel a lightness in his head, spreading through his entire body, knowing practically all the oxygen there was in this room was going to feed the voracious appetite of those ever-increasing flames.

He didn't have much time. He moved forward, knowing he would only get one chance at saving Voyle – if he was alive, that is. And that if he got things wrong, he might not be able to even save himself.

It would have been easy to miss it. Brody almost did. When he stabbed in the speed dial number for the comms room at Dublin South Central – which would circumvent the requirement to go through an emergency 999 call centre – the sound was nothing louder than the buzzing of a bee.

It would have been easy to miss it.

But Brody didn't.

Because this was February, and there were no bees in February, global warming besides.

And it would have been easy to ignore it and concentrate on Marty Sheahan instead, whose blackened face could be glimpsed at the window, only because his two eyes glowed like white beacons through the swirling smoke.

The uniforms were pulling a body out. He could see another on the grass, a woman, lying on her side, coughing, waving a hand through the air. Marty was coming out too.

The buzzing-bee sound was morphing into something else, a growl or grunting noise. Brody looked at the uniforms, at the body they'd just pulled from the window, kneeling beside it, one starting chest compressions. The body was that of a man. And Brody saw who it was.

Voyle. Even as he saw all this, wanting to run forward and help, he stopped himself. As if dazed, he cocked his head to one side and didn't move. The sound was growing louder, yet strangely, palpably powerful, and refined, like a rock guitarist lulling an audience with a low riff before blasting out an ear-splitting chorus. There was a sense of expectation to it.

He thought of O'Brien's little sports car; it was beginning to sound like that. And then, just like that, it did sound like that. It was the throaty, husky roar of a powerful engine in high gear.

Brody looked along the rear of Ash Hall, towards the trees running in a thick line by the edge of the manicured lawns there, that even at this time of year held colourful flower beds, pruned trees and green, clipped grass. It seemed to be coming from there. Was there a road on the other side of those trees, or through them? The noise was reaching a crescendo, as Brody saw a flash of yellow through the foliage, moving fast, very fast, the sound beginning to fade again. As he looked, he could see the high perimeter wall of Ash Hall just beyond. He knew where that car was going. It was heading for the gate.

Brody heard Voyle cough, then cough again and splutter, saw him spit out a gob full of blackened phlegm. He knew he was going to be alright.

And then he thought of buses. You wait for one forever, and then two or more come along at the same time. Except in this case it wasn't buses, it was sports cars. First there was O'Brien's. And now… putting it all together, Brody was prepared to bet a week's salary, no, a month's… okay, make it a year's, that that car was a Maserati, specifically the Maserati Robert Gilsenan had waited a year to take delivery of, and had never gotten to drive. It would soon be at the gate.

Brody took off, running fast, pulling out his phone as he went.

He'd make another wager, his house this time. That the person driving it was the butler, or caretaker – whatever – one Patrick O'Connor.

Of course, he knew he was never going to be fast enough to make it in time. Impossible. So halfway across the gravelled forecourt of Ash Hall, he was not surprised to see the tail lights glow as the driver hit the brakes, and the tyres squealed, the car banking sharply to the right as it sped off again. Now, all Brody could do was hope.

He ran through the open gates onto the roadway. It was down to the Wicklow mules now: they either had or they hadn't. He'd given them enough warning. They had. A spike strip lay across the road, just in front of the tyres of a yellow car, sideways across the tarmac, the back end against a ditch: a saloon, Brody saw, gleaming and beautiful. But he had no time to appreciate its aesthetics. Not now. Its engine was running, a person in the driver's seat sitting slumped over the steering wheel.

One of the Wicklow mules approached it and stood by the driver's door, attempted to pull it open. But the door appeared to be locked. The other mule began hauling in the spikes.

'He's unconscious,' the one by the door shouted to Brody.

How convenient, Brody thought, *too convenient*.

'Don't,' he shouted to the one hauling in the spikes. But too late – almost. The spike strip hadn't quite cleared the road in front of the car completely: the end of it lay just before the left front wheel. And suddenly, the driver was sitting straight up. The engine growled, a V8 Brody guessed, or a V6 at the very least, as the car sprinted forward, the automotive equivalent of a racehorse. The driver couldn't see that the road wasn't cleared, not completely, and so drove straight over the spikes, which caught the edge of the tyre. A horse can't run on three legs, and a car can't drive on three wheels.

It was only a matter of time.

'Sorry, lads,' Brody shouted to the uniforms, darting towards their car, 'but I'll need this.' He was sweating, and he wiped the back of his hand across his eyes.

'You can't.'

'I can.' Brody got into the marked. The engine was running. He rammed it into gear.

'But I took it out. If anything happens to...' The words trailed in through the open window as Brody took off. He hadn't invited them to come along. If he was to stand any chance of catching that car, even with one tyre slowly losing its air, he needed this squad weighing as little as possible.

He brought the car up to 120 kilometres per hour in no time. He was impressed. But there it ended. Once the needle reached 120 kph, the steering wheel began vibrating in his hands... However, let us freeze proceedings here for a moment. Something needs mentioning. It is Oscar Charlie 6, the particular patrol car Brody was driving. Needless to say, considering its role, Oscar Charlie 6 had had a hard life thus far. Still, it was bearing up well, especially considering that underneath its roof lights and bells and whistles it was nothing but a bog-standard Mondeo. Three months earlier, while being driven at over 80 kph, *in reverse*, by a mule chasing a gouger, the gear stick had come off in the driver's hand. In a scene reminiscent of the movie *Alien*, the drive shaft had come up through the floor, breaking through between the rear and front seats.

Which explained why, as Brody pressed the accelerator all the way to the floor, a loud clunking noise came from somewhere beneath the car. Brody didn't know it, but the drive shaft had started to separate from the gearbox. He ignored the noise, he ignored everything, pushing the car, the needle reaching 140 kph and miraculously passing through it, the car beginning to shake so badly that Brody expected it to disintegrate at any moment. But something he had not expected happened then, just like an aeroplane passing through turbulence and emerging out the other side. The shaking stopped; the car steadied, no trace of any vibration, nothing – anywhere. Brody pushed on, bringing the needle higher and higher, sliding the car through the bends, sirens screaming, lights flashing. The Mondeo levelled out at 180 kph, on a country road with scarcely enough room for two cars to pass. A couple of times, on long stretches, he caught glimpses of yellow, but nothing more. He wondered – had those spikes worked at all? Like, really? But he knew they were designed for a slow release of pressure rather than one devastating blowout. He could only drive on and wait. Seconds became minutes, minutes seemed like hours.

He had a feeling this wasn't going to end well. Car chases like this seldom did. Brody became even more certain of this fact when he saw the tractor towing a flatbed trailer. They came round the bend, the trailer sliding out from the back, churning up the ditch as its wheels ploughed through the soil, starting to concertina in against the side of the tractor, a gigantic flip-top phone. Brody was still managing 180 kph, the tractor roughly fifty metres away when he slammed on the brakes. Yet he knew. He wasn't going to make it. He didn't have enough time – or enough road. He'd either hit the tractor, maybe head-on, or get sandwiched between it and the trailer.

And that was what would have happened. But it didn't. Because two seconds after he'd rammed his foot down onto the brake pedal, at that very moment the drive shaft snapped, twisting the steering rod and sending the car into a gut-wrenching spin, but one that was going nowhere except, as Chuck Spalding would say, turning on a dime.

It possibly saved Brody's life. Ironic really, because if the car had been in the condition it was supposed to be in, Brody wouldn't have walked away. The coupling connecting the trailer to the tractor appeared to snap, so that it swung in and struck the side of the tractor, shaking it like a toy. Brody might have been the meat in that sandwich.

He jumped out of the squad car. But he didn't walk away from it. Rather, he ran. And as he did, a shaken-looking tractor driver pointed from his cab back down the road. 'There's a car on its roof round the bend. I couldn't help it, honest. He just came out of nowhere straight at me. It's not looking good either, it's not...'

'Stay there,' Brody shouted over his shoulder, not stopping.

He rounded the bend, it was narrower than the rest of the road, passing a road sign in the verge that said: *Dangerous Bend, Beware.* You don't say.

First thing he noticed was the sun reflecting on a chrome emblem, remarkably untouched, in the centre of the rear panel of the car. A renowned emblem, of a white trident on a blue background, the emblem of the Maserati motor company. One thing was for certain, it didn't look the way it looked in any of the sales brochures now, twisted and with its front end crushed. It appeared to have hit something and then flipped onto its roof, landing with a great deal of force. Brody noted the scrape marks gouged into the road surface where the car had slid along on its roof. As he ran to it, he saw the puddle – fuel, he guessed – underneath the back end, a steady drip feeding into it.

Brody slowed to a walk, wary, his mind filtering everything through it, determining the greatest risk right now was that leaking fuel tank. He went along the side of the car, peering in the windows as he went, each with a spiderweb of cracks, but all intact. Through the driver's door window he could see the outline of the person sitting upside down behind the wheel. Brody stopped, swung round, not hesitating, bringing the heel of his boot backward, hitting the weakened glass, shattering it into a cascade of tiny pieces that fell downward rather than in, the way it was meant to.

He turned back to the Maserati. The man sitting upside down there appeared to be uninjured. Brody wasn't surprised. In his career he'd always found that drunks and gougers usually emerged unscathed from the most perilous of situations. No, it wasn't fair.

He leaned in, began fumbling about for the seat belt button, found it, pressed it, was relieved to hear the reassuring click as it unlocked. The belt recoiled automatically into its wall mount.

'Patrick O'Connor,' Brody said.

O'Connor nodded.

'Let's get you out of this car; that's the first thing.'

O'Connor raised his right hand.

'No. Wait,' he said.

Brody could smell petrol from inside the car, guessed by its angle some of the contents of the fuel tank was trickling down into the interior.

'We can't wait. I've got to get you out of the vehicle. Now!'

Brody reached in, was about to grab O'Connor by the shoulders, to hook his arms underneath his armpits and drag him out.

'Wait,' O'Connor said again, but louder this time.

No, Brody thought, *doesn't seem to be too much wrong with him at all.*

'Wait for what?'

'Just a sec,' O'Connor said, taking something from his trouser pocket with one hand. Brody strained to see what it was. Whatever it was was tiny, so not a weapon, too small. O'Connor began making a motion with his thumb against the index finger of the hand curled around whatever he'd taken from his pocket.

'What you at, O'Connor? What've you got there? Give it over. Come on. I said give it over.'

O'Connor turned his eyes up to him in his upside-down head, his forehead furrowing, looking like an odd, *Spitting Image* puppet character. His eyes didn't blink, not once, as they looked at Brody, like he was demanding his fullest attention, which he already had.

'I always wanted to go out with a bang,' O'Connor said, and gave a short, shrill laugh.

A blue spark ignited from the top of his clenched hand, around it a halo of white, smaller ones. Now Brody knew what he was holding there. A lighter. O'Connor flicked it again, and a long, slim flame sprang up. Then he lowered the lighter towards the floor.

Brody jumped back.

'And I got to drive this car,' O'Connor shouted, dropping the lighter, a ribbon of flame darting through the vehicle. It was almost pretty. 'But he never did.' And that shrill laugh came again.

Brody turned and ran just as the car blew.

56

The verdict at the coroner's inquest the following Wednesday was, in light of the new evidence uncovered by Detective Garda Steven Voyle, to refer the matter back to the Gardai for further investigation. The county coroner, Dr Ciara Bianconi, FRCPI, MFFLM, paid tribute to Voyle in her summing up.

Standing in his Louis Copeland suit, Voyle looked more like a movie star than he did a cop.

'Your dogged determination,' she said, 'to see this through is an example of the triumph of good over evil. You are an outstanding example of virtuous integrity, Detective Garda Voyle, and on behalf of this court and the citizens of this country, citizens whom we both serve, I commend you and thank you for your courage and tenacity in this matter.'

She looked over her half glasses at him, and Voyle, his expression suitably inscrutable and sombre, when in fact what he was thinking was how nice and twinkly sexy her eyes appeared. Considine was sitting on the witness bench and had not been called to give evidence: her witness statement had been noted; everything that was in hers was also in Voyle's.

They went for a coffee afterwards. It was the first time they'd done that, just the two of them, such a normal, run-of-the-mill activity. But not for these two. For them it was so much more.

Could it offer a new beginning, a cathartic new dawn in their relationship?

Ha!

Voyle did a lot of foot shuffling and hardly any talking, like he was keeping his mouth shut because he was afraid of what might come out of it. He flirted with the waitress, and Considine cringed. She sat back in her chair, holding her cup before her like it was a protective talisman. She didn't say much either. They drank their coffees.

When they were getting up to leave, Voyle shrugged.

'Sorry, Nic.'

'Me too.'

'You either like the music, or you don't.'

'What?'

'Bands, you know, you either like the music, or you don't. People are different, different tastes, you know.'

'Yeah, I know.'

'You do?'

'Course. So, what's it for you, the Stones, I'd say?'

'Doesn't everyone like the Stones... well, don't they?'

Considine rolled her eyes. 'Doesn't everyone like The Chieftains... well, don't they?'

Voyle laughed.

Considine laughed too.

'We're just different,' Voyle said, 'that's all. Opposites don't always have to attract.'

'Whoa, that's deep, Voyle.'

They were silent for a moment. Voyle got to his feet.

'Let's get back to the ranch, what you say?'
'Yes, that's a good idea.'

As Considine and Voyle were leaving the café, Brody was in the changing room at the Northside Boxing Club. He'd been training for an hour and had just showered and was tying the laces on his sneakers when his telephone rang. He picked it up from the bench beside him, glancing at the screen.

And froze.

The phone sounded again, and his stomach pitched. Still he didn't answer it. Not that he didn't want to. He did. It was just his finger wouldn't move. A young fella with *Junior Ace Team* printed on his T-shirt said, 'Mister, you going to answer that or what? It's doin' me head in.'

Brody smiled at the irony of a teenager complaining about the sound of a ringing telephone. He answered, brought the phone to his ear.

'Hello, Ashling.'

Silence. Brody waited.

'How are you, Jack?'

'I'm fine. And you?'

'Fine.'

'Good.'

Again, silence.

'Did I say something wrong,' Brody said, 'last time? I did, didn't I?'

'It's my stuff, Jack, that's all. It's fine now.'

It's fine now. What did that mean?

As if reading his thoughts, she said, 'There was a guy, okay. He dumped me. Plain and simple. Said I was too old. Gobshite. He was the same age as me. Yes, I know, better off without him and all that, and I am. It's just, when you mentioned, I mean, when you asked me what age I was, when we were lying in bed together, well... it stirred something up. I took it as a sign you were putting stipulations on it, on us.'

'I wasn't.'

'I know that, Jack. But we can't help our emotions... well, we can, but we first have to work them out. I did. My stuff. It fed into everything else, my expectations around the future, what I want from a relationship. I just needed to step back, that's all.'

'Are you still stepping back?'

'I rang you, didn't I?'

'Yes, you did.'

'No, Jack, I'm not stepping back. I'm stepping forward.'

'When can I see you?'

'How about right now?'

57

THREE MONTHS LATER

Donagh Hughes sometimes forgot that he no longer had a little finger on his right hand. Sometimes he would grab a pen and wonder why his grip was so loose, why the pen felt so awkward. Then he would remember, and for a moment he would be right back there, in that filthy hovel.

But that wasn't what was hardest to bear. No.

He shook his head, took a sip of coffee, and placed the dainty cup back onto its saucer, using his left hand only, and sat back into the leather armchair. He looked across the foyer, where he heard voices, loud voices, and saw a bunch of solicitor types as they filed into the restaurant. The hotel was close to Leinster House, the seat of the Irish parliament, popular with the movers and shakers of Dublin society and little changed in over a hundred years, all dark wood, deep carpets and discreet alcoves. Just like the alcove he was sitting in next to the staircase leading to the upper floors. You'd never find him sitting in here in the past, as if he was hiding from the world. He'd be like those loud solicitor types, cocky and out in the world and wanting the world to see him.

And what was hardest to bear was that *she* had put him through all this. The woman he'd married, had loved – once, that is – the mother of his children. Jesus, he'd known her for over thirty years. *She'd* done it to him. What's more, she'd shown no remorse either. Her last comment when she was being led down to the cells at the Circuit Court in Wicklow was, *I'm only sorry that he didn't die, the bastard.* And some thought what had happened wasn't her fault. Not really it wasn't. No. He was the one responsible, really, that somehow he had made her do it, drove her to it. Just like the big fella, the giant, whatever he was called, had been a victim too. You couldn't make it up.

The big fella. He'd known him too, as it turned out. Sean Dowding. Did a bit of welding, a bit of farming, a bit of this, a bit of that. And a bit of fucking his wife too on the side. Except it was more than that, more than a bit; they'd been at it for years. Still, he had to hand it to her, to Monica, that is, she was good, because he'd never had a clue.

Now he knew what it was like to have the shoe on the other foot. Cuckolded, what an ugly, degrading word.

Yet his only comfort was she hadn't actually killed anyone, hadn't been physically violent – not to him, or anyone else, far as he knew, that is.

No.

It was Sean Dowding who had. He'd done it all. Technically, that is. He was the pit bull.

And Donagh Hughes could – just about – live with that.

He saw the person he was waiting for come through the door, and got to his feet, waved discreetly across. The man smiled and came and stood next to him.

'Donagh, what're you hiding in there like a frightened rabbit for? God's sake, man?'

'I'm readjusting, that's all, getting my confidence back. It'll take a while.'

'Nonsense. It won't take a while. Look at me. Let's go have a drink. And I think there's some capital in this. I really do. A rebirth.' The man pointed to himself. 'Da dum. What you need is to work the public, get them back on your side. It's easy; you can come back from anything... well, almost. You could be a poster boy for something or other, male domestic violence maybe...'

'There wasn't any.'

'My man, you're missing a finger, remember. That's plenty to get you started. We can work it from there. I'll help you. Now, that drink?' He threw an arm around Donagh's shoulders, squeezed tight. 'You need to get back on the horse, get the horse back in the race, come on now.'

Gary Kennedy led Donagh Hughes across the foyer to the bar, like two long-lost friends. Except they were new friends. Both were surprised they'd never really connected before. They had so much in common, after all.

BRODY LEFT WORK EARLY. He drove out of the Phoenix Park gates beneath a clear, cold blue sky, the afternoon sun already pivoting towards the west. He wanted to make the evening special. When he got to the La Fontaine restaurant, he ordered a drink at the bar. He was ten minutes early. But you should always be early. It was not good to keep a lady waiting. He had just taken a sip of his vodka lime when he saw her appear at his shoulder in the mirror running along the wall behind the counter. He smiled. She was early too. He wondered what would have happened had he not been early? Would she have turned around and walked out? Was it some sort of test on her part?

He stood and kissed her softly on the lips. She wore a simple, short black dress with a plunging neckline, high heels. Christ, he'd never met anyone who could look the way she did in a dress like it. Yes, he knew this woman had so much more, but right now he couldn't think of what that might be; she radiated heat like a sweltering sun. He pulled a stool from the counter for her to sit, and she sat down. He felt himself blush as she crossed her legs, finding it difficult to steer his eyes away from wandering where he didn't want them to.

'You look a little...' she started, but her voice trailed off.

'A little?' he said, sitting next to her.

She gave a soft chuckle. 'Hm, distracted is the word I'm looking for.'

'I'm doing my damnedest not to be. You don't like distractions.'

'Oh...' She gave him a coy look. 'But if the distraction is me, then I'm fine with that.'

'It is you.'

She leaned forward and laughed. He realised he'd started sweating. And something else. That he was confused. That when it came to Ashling Nolan, he didn't know whether he was in lust or love, or both. But he was having fun finding out, they both were.

Brody caught the eye of the barman, ordered a couple of drinks, a chilled Chardonnay for Ashling, another vodka and lime for himself.

'Extra ice,' he told the barman.

EPILOGUE

GardaCommissionerOffice@garda.ie
       To: InternalOperations&Standards
       Cc: ChiefSuperTierney/Rafferty/Anderson-SuperMaloneNugentVillers

NOT TO BE DISCUSSED OUTSIDE THIS GROUP
Recent Events:

Recent events have caused concern on an operational level within the force. The investigation into the disappearance of Donagh Hughes and the unofficial revisiting of the 'suicide' of Robert Gilsenan have brought to stark light many deficiencies.

In the case of the first, the search for Donagh Hughes, operational best practices were set aside in favour of the vanity of the commanding officer, Superintendent Tony Harper. He also sought to subvert the work of the MCIU when this was always supposed to be a joint operation. The tacit support of Superintendent Fiona Ryan, newly appointed CO of the MCIU, allowed this situation to arise. She did not act in the best interests of the MCIU. She did not act in the best interests of the force. She should have. The MCIU has proven to be one of, if not the most effective unit within the force for combatting serious crime. I'd like to remind you, if reminding is needed, that it was serious crime who were responsible for finding Donagh Hughes. Yet the unit was relegated to playing a subordinate role in this investigation.

As regards the supposed suicide of Robert Gilsenan, we know now too this was not a suicide, but a case of cold-blooded murder. Again, it was the MCIU responsible for discovering this, through the dogged efforts of one of its members, Detective Garda Steven Voyle.

Gentlemen, the shenanigans displayed during these operations by the senior officers mentioned are nothing short of a disgrace. It cannot and will not be tolerated. Therefore, I intend to take action as follows: Superintendent Tony Harper will be offered the role of deputy commander of roads policing based at Dublin Castle. Either that or he takes early retirement. His choice. With regard to Superintendent Fiona Ryan, there is a mitigating factor. It is that it was she, despite everything mentioned – and available in more detail in the attached memo – who first detailed Detective Garda Voyle to look into the Robert Gilsenan affair. But I believe this was done for the wrong reasons, out of a combination of self-interest and vindictiveness. Nevertheless, an important result was achieved. This cannot be ignored or overlooked. Therefore, I recommend she remain in post as CO of MCIU – for now, that is, but subject to regular review.

In the meantime, discreet approaches will be made to Detective Sergeant Jack Brody to 'sound him out' about his considering a promotion to the rank of inspector with the objective of having him take over the running of the unit. I believe he is the person best suited to this role. Detective Sergeant Brody has, however, never put himself forward for any promotion since becoming sergeant. In my meetings with him, I came away with the understanding that he possesses an apathetic attitude towards senior officers. I'm sad to say, gentlemen, in light of all the above, that he may have a point.

Feel free to respond with your opinions on this matter, whatever they may be.

REGARDS, as always,
Commissioner Mervyn Mc Kay

ABOUT THE AUTHOR

I hail from Mayo in the west of Ireland, although I spent much of my life away, in the US, UK, Europe, Jersey in the Channel Islands and various parts of Ireland.

In my younger years I was incredibly restless. I left home and school at 16 and spread my wings. I've had over forty jobs, everything from barman, labourer, staff newspaper reporter, soldier in the Irish army, station foreman with London Underground, mason, and many more besides. I returned to education as a mature student in the early noughties and hold a BA in history and sociology from the National University of Ireland at Maynooth, and an M.Phil from Trinity College Dublin.

Since 2005 I've been a civilian employee of the Irish police, An Garda Síochána. However, I've been on extended sick leave since 2015 following a mystery illness which struck while travelling in Spain. It almost killed me. The doctors never got to the bottom of it and they call me the Mystery Man. But every cloud has a silver lining. It has given me the time to write. Although I've been writing all my life, most of my output languishes in the bottom of drawers.

Under my real name, Michael Scanlon, I was initially published for the first time in 2019 by Bookouture with the first of three crime novels. Working with Inkubator is another great opportunity for me. This time I'm using a pseudonym, as the style of J.M. O'Rourke books are so different, and also, I really like the name!

I hope readers like them.

ALSO BY J.M. O'ROURKE

The Detective Jack Brody Series

The Devil's House

Time of Death

A Deadly Affair

Printed in Great Britain
by Amazon